FLIGHT
OF COLOUR

FLIGHT OF COLOUR

To Ros,

Adrian Greaves
28. Feb. 94.

ADRIAN GREAVES

Penny Books

In Association with Debinair Publishing.

FLIGHT OF COLOUR

PENNY BOOKS

First published in Great Britain by Debinair Publishing, 98 High Street, TENTERDEN, Kent.

Copyright © Adrian Greaves 1993

The right of Adrian Greaves to be identified as the author of this work has been asserted by him in accordance with the Copyright Designs and Patents Act 1988.

ISBN 0 9520556 00

Printed by Whitstable Litho Printers, England.

FLIGHT OF COLOUR

Adrian Greaves was born in 1943. He was educated at Eastbourne and has a degree in psychology.

From the age of eighteen he saw commissioned service in the Welch Regiment which was followed by a successful career in the Police Service where he rapidly became a senior officer. A fascination for his former regiment's history and an investigator's inquisitive mind sent him to South Africa to research the disappearance of the Regimental Queen's Colour.

He became a full time writer in 1992.

He is married to Deborah to whom the book is dedicated.

ACKNOWLEDGEMENTS.

I tender my grateful thanks to the following without whom this book could not have been written.

UNITED KINGDOM.

Andrew.
My father, for his unstinting proof reading.
The Regimental Museum, South Wales Borderers, Brecon.
The Debling family.
David Heather.

SOUTH AFRICA.

Robin, for bravely flying me to makeshift veldt airstrips.
Helena, for her valuable help and assistance.
The Ladysmith Museum.

S. Carrington
1902

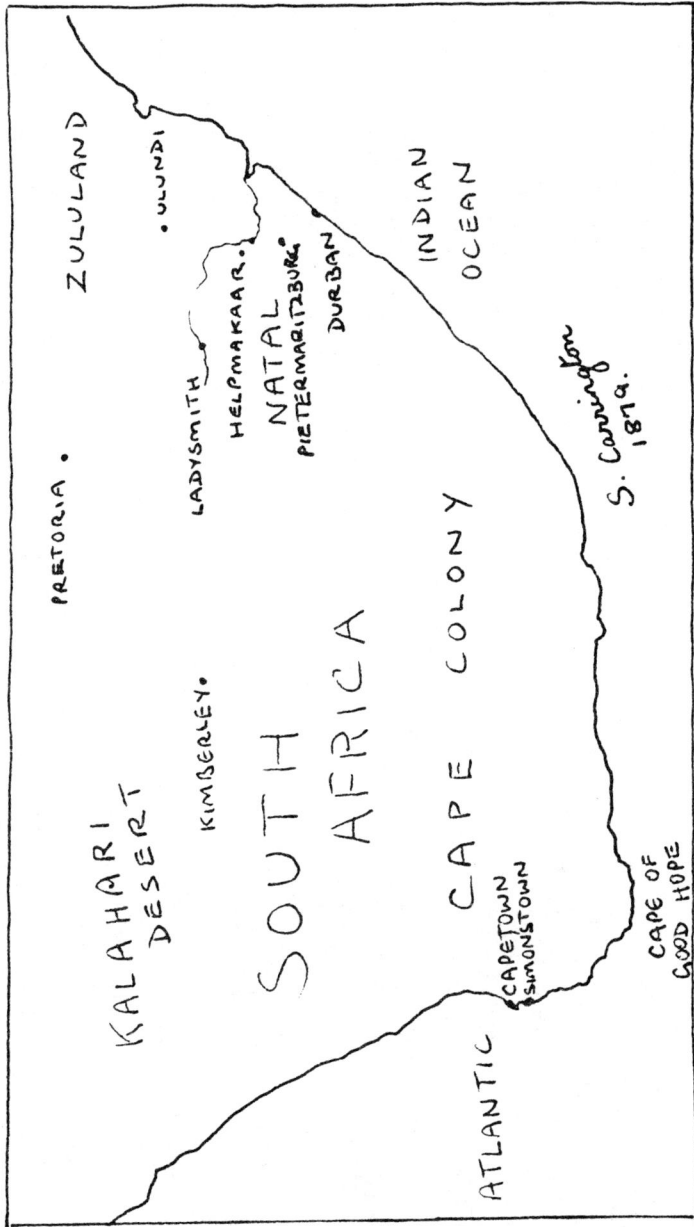

KALAHARI
DESERT

ZULULAND

• ULUNDI

PRETORIA •

LADYSMITH
HELPMAKAAR. •
NATAL
PIETERMARITZBURG •
DURBAN •

INDIAN
OCEAN

KIMBERLEY •

SOUTH
AFRICA

CAPE COLONY

S. Carrington
1879.

ATLANTIC

CAPETOWN
SIMONSTOWN

CAPE OF
GOOD HOPE

SOUTH AFRICA 1879

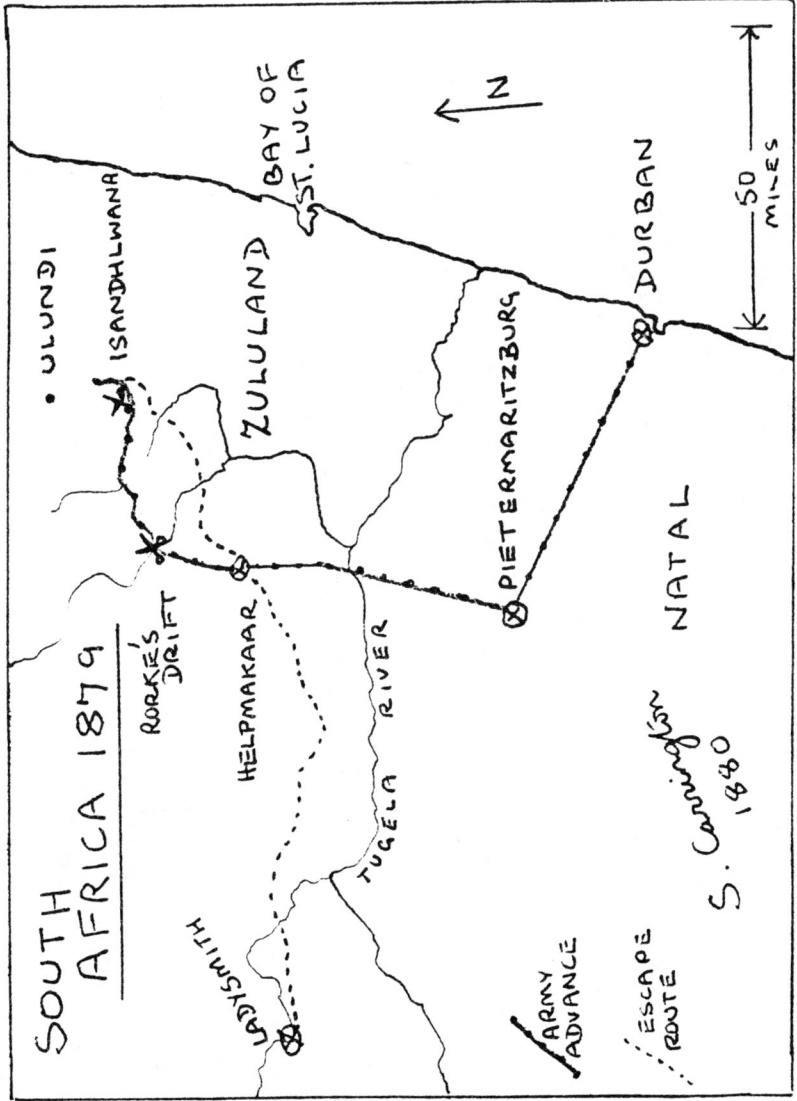

- OLUNDI
- ISANDHLWANA
- RORKE'S DRIFT
- HELPMAKAAR
- LADYSMITH
- ZULULAND
- BAY OF ST. LUCIA
- DURBAN
- PIETERMARITZBURG
- NATAL
- TUGELA RIVER

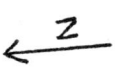

N

50 MILES

ARMY ADVANCE

ESCAPE ROUTE

S. Carrington 1880

PROLOGUE.

PRETORIA JUNE 1992.

Junior Minister Peter Sachs picked up the heavy red security file lying on his desk. It was now less than a week before he was due to present his overview of its contents to the Prime Minister and senior cabinet colleagues, and he was fully aware they were relying on him to formulate their new combined policy. The weight of the file in his hands indicated the severity of the task ahead and he involuntarily shivered. Inside the heavy leather cover was a collection of documents which previous Interior Ministers had wrestled with, and the solution to its most potent problem had eluded all of them. The problem was known throughout the world as Apartheid. Of the country's thirty million citizens, only five million were white and they were in total control of all the wealth, services and influence. White supremacy had long irked the rest of the world and while the situation continued, his country remained socially isolated. Trade, cultural and sporting ties with other countries were precarious although he was aware of the anomaly that other African countries openly ignored sanctions. The front line states were, moreover, very keen to use their generous foreign aid to buy South African luxury goods and produce.

At that moment he felt the physical onset of another panic attack begin to spread through his body. The attacks seemed to flare when he was under pressure or especially anxious. That strange overwhelming feeling of weakness coupled with the pounding heart and compelling desire to escape gripped him. He quickly took the small bottle of tablets from his briefcase. With a shaking hand he placed the small mauve lozenge in his mouth and chewed hard, he washed it down with a glass of iced water from the decanter on his desk. He knew he was increasingly relying on lorazepam tablets to maintain his self control; conversely without the panic-controlling drug, his condition would quickly become obvious to others. The effect of the medication was rapid, within moments his vision began to clear and his heart beat steadied. He took a deep breath

1

and turned his attention back to the file.

He remembered that day in June 1990 when he and a startled South African Parliament listened to Prime Minister De Klerk publicly state that the bastion of apartheid was to be progressively removed. The United Nations were generous in their praise and the future for the whole country began to look brighter. South Africa was at last going to seek respectability after 29 years of white rule and the transition to equal rights for all its citizens would result in a very different country.

Peter Sachs was also different; at forty two, he was the youngest junior cabinet minister in the South African government. His dark curly hair, general physique and handsome suntanned features - a physiognomy which suggested his Welsh ancestry, hid a sharp perceptive mind and a ruthless determination to succeed. He dealt with other budding parliamentarian rivals with the same indefatigable energy and perverse skill that had enabled him to successfully seduce a number of their wives. He was popular with his immediate colleagues but opponents thought long and hard before taking issue with him. Many a good opposition member had been humiliated by his piercing argument. To be appointed to the vital Interior Ministry was a great accolade, even more so for someone of his age. It was also the generous but well earned reward for many years' dedicated work as a member of parliament supporting the Prime Minister.

Secretly, cabinet ministers and many MPs were under no illusion that real progress towards equality would be fraught with the complexities of racial differences. If it were possible, Peter Sachs would be the man to prepare the groundwork. It would not only be a problem reconciling whites and blacks, the Prime Minister had told him; internal peace between the violently opposed black tribes and political groups had to be achieved. He picked up the file again and resigned himself to spending several hours reading through its complexities. He had already been extensively briefed by an expert team of civil servants and military advisers but even their considered views were not unanimous. It was important for him to understand and grasp the political manoeuvrings of recent years if he was to steer the country to peace. He had once been told at university that by looking at the past, one could often see the way into the future; at least it might spare him from making the same mistakes.

As he read through the thick file he made copious notes. After some three hours of uninterrupted work he assembled his thoughts and prepared a precis of events ready for Pamela, his highly efficient secretary, to type into a more readable form. He sat back and looked out of his window on to the beautifully laid out flowering gardens below. It could all be so straightforward; but avarice, distrust and hatred between the various factions would probably be insurmountable.

Another more serious question began troubling his mind. Regardless of the recent referendum for power sharing, would the white population ever really accept the blacks on equal terms? After all, the whites not only settled the country originally, they developed and owned the resources of the nation's wealth represented by the gold, diamond and other precious mineral mines. The country was supported by a loyal, dedicated and powerful police force even though ninety percent of the policemen and women were black. His thoughts turned to the armed forces. They possessed the only modern disciplined military force on the continent of Africa and the country was safe fom any attack being surrounded either by empty bush or desert for hundreds of miles.

'Why give it all away just to satisfy the rest of the world when South Africa was virtually self sufficient?' he asked himself.

The realisation that he wasn't at all convinced by the intended policy deepened within him. After all, no previous African country had ever prospered following independence. He knew they had all quickly succumbed to dictator rule with its unbelievable corruption, thuggery and looting by police and armed forces; followed rapidly by abject poverty for their populations. His deep seated, almost religious pride in white supremacy stemmed not only from his strictly religious Boer ancestry but also from the documented experiences of his country's neighbours, Angola, Zimbabwe and Mozambique . His task would not be easy.

Now, to a major extent, the future of his beloved country lay in his own hands. It was for Peter Sachs to influence his senior cabinet colleagues, to pull the opposing factions together and unite the country. South Africa had never possessed any unity of purpose; without the promise of unity, there could be no fresh start.

He turned to the text headed 'A.N.C .' He realised that the African National Congress were going to be his biggest problem. They were potentially the largest single group in the country and their influence was growing. Following the release of Nelson Mandela in 1990, membership of the previously banned A.N.C. had rapidly grown to form the largest single political party in southern Africa. The migrant workers' camps which serviced the cities and towns with abundant cheap labour also provided a rich source of recruitment for the political activists.

The encouragement to join the A.N.C. was overwhelming, the incentive was higher still. Waiverers received a severe beating while those who refused to join could simply expect a grisly and savage death. It was no real surprise that membership was almost total. There was no protection for those with independent thought. The local vigilante mobs who controlled the townships also meted out the appropriate punishments of appalling torture, rape, summary execution by the dreaded necklace treatment, or mutilation.

The dramatic growth of the A.N.C. had certainly impressed many foreign governments while causing alarm within the country's white community. Seen from abroad, the A.N.C. was an enthusiastic new black democratic party to counter the domineering whites. Nelson Mandela was feted across America and Europe to make amends for

4

decades of colonialism; and the ensuing lavish gifts of cash were immediately invested, for safety, in Switzerland. China and Libya were both quick to compete with each other for this new lucrative market for small arms. Weapon stores were secretly established along the far side of the border of South Africa within the front line states . Whilst championing the A.N.C., these neighbouring countries also needed South African imports to survive. Notwithstanding their economic dependence on South Africa, neighbouring governments had been easily intimidated into providing secret training camps for the 'Umkhonto We Sizwe', the militant wing of the A.N.C.

In the meantime, the rest of the world conveniently ignored the views of the largest tribe of Africa, the Zulus , who lived in comparative peace with the whites. The minister was philosophical as to why the pleas from the politicians of the Zulu Inkartha party for sanctions to be lifted went unheard, especially in Europe. All too often in modern politics, the voice of reason lacked an international audience, it simply lacked excitement. He listed his priorities. His prime task was the unification of the cabinet in support of the prime minister; that would not be easy. The concept of 'one man one vote' would not be popular with all the white voters, many of whom were already beginning to think of emigrating to the United Kingdom, Australia or New Zealand. Seeking an alliance with the Zulu leaders was just possible, but most difficult of all would be the task of persuading the A.N.C. that a prosperous and peaceful future for the country's black population depended on co-operation between the respective political groupings, especially with the Zulus.

He was not optimistic.

* * * * * * * * * * * *

5

CHAPTER 1.

ULUNDI MAY 1992

The potential heat of the early morning African sun was matched only by the steadily developing tension that could be felt throughout the country. Daybreak was just beginning to perform its miracles of light and colour, stirring the colourful and hungry bird life into noisy activity. Flight Lt. Robin Penny sat watching the display from the cockpit of his twin-engine Baron aircraft parked outside the departure lounge at Ulundi airfield. Robin's handsome suntanned features and brown curly hair gave him a youthful look which belied his character and flying skills. His tall frame relaxed comfortably in the pilot's seat but his senses were fully alert. His VIP passenger was due to return at any moment.

Ulundi has always been the capital of the Zulu nation and today it is home to half a million native souls. It is set in the centre of autonomous Zululand and is governed by its own tribal chiefs. The imposing and modern government building is situated on a small hillock in the town centre which enables it to dominate the surroundings. The majority of its subjects live in their finely woven huts made from the tough African grasses and cane. The more prosperous Zulus occupy the European styled bungalows which can be seen merging into neat estates near the parliament buildings. The kraals and their tilled plots of land spread haphazardly across the gently rolling plain which in turn, is dominated by encircling lush green hills in the near distance. There is nothing to attract the casual white visitor to the Zulu capital apart from the well tended memorial site of the final battle between the British and Zulu armies in 1879. Yet that same casual visitor would be met with courtesy, coupled with an endearingly unembarrassed curiosity.

To call it an airfield was being generous, it was a single tarmac airstrip with, unusually for Zululand, a small air-conditioned building boasting a staff of one smartly turned out customs offical, an elderly porter and a young policeman very keen to make a good impression. As is usual in Africa, all three employees were privileged members of a local politician's family; merit was a phenomenon as yet unrecognised by most Africans. Robin wondered how the staff managed to keep their uniforms so neatly pressed and clean as he pondered the limited facilities of the average African's kraal devoid of electricity and running water. The dogs, goats and cattle added to the mayhem, all living cheek by jowl with the human inhabitants in an atmosphere of smoke, dust and laughing children. He reasoned that they probably lived in one of the new European style homes.

Five years had elapsed since Robin left his job as a flying instructor at Shoreham Airport in Sussex. At the age of twenty five, life in England seemed to be getting him nowhere. Then a chance encounter with a South African girl took him to Durban on holiday. He was still here. Georgina had since married elsewhere but suntanned leggy beauties were a hall-mark of his new country. England with its cold rain, unsmiling faces and long depressing winters offered him no incentive even to contemplate going back. With his new luxurious life style and commercial pilot's licence, he enjoyed being in demand. His flat overlooking the beach at Umhlanga, just north of Durban, was an ideal home base especially as it was only a few minutes' drive from the airfield.

He shivered as the dawn threw off the remnants of the nightly chill. He had been at the airport for over an hour and the minister was late. It was already seven thirty in the morning and the growing golden orb of Africa's sun heralded another scorching day. He knew that the outside temperature would now rapidly rise to the high thirties and perhaps beyond. He could still see the end of the tarmac eight hundred yards away but already the heat haze was beginning to produce the distorting mirage effect of shimmering water on the runway. Such conditions would make his take-off difficult. Flying in Africa was always exciting ; taking off and landing frequently caused wild animals to dash across the runway, and hitting

7

anything larger than a dog could prove fatal. Taking off into a mirage meant that the runway would appear to be swaying and he wouldn't be able to see any straying animals.

Robin let his gaze drift towards the imposing government buildings on the other side of the valley where his passenger, Minister Sachs, was covertly meeting the young Zulu Chief Umbani for top level political discussions. They were attempting to hammer out an agreement between the White government of Pretoria and the rulers of the Zulu nation to ensure future co-operation. Following his lengthy security vetting, Robin had been appointed a temporary lieutenant in the South African Air Force and sworn to secrecy before he had been secretly engaged to fly Minister Peter Sachs to and from Pretoria and Zululand. This was their fifth visit in two weeks and he enjoyed being well paid to perform his beloved hobby, especially when it meant flying the popular and prominent Minister Sachs and staying at the best hotels when on duty. Having lived in South Africa for five years he was fully aware that the creation of a such a treaty between Pretoria and the Zulu nation would politically isolate the increasingly troublesome A.N.C. terrorists and their militant masters.

Any such agreement would inevitably incite the A.N.C. to further acts of violence against both the white community and the Zulus. Such aggression would in turn enable the extreme right wing politicians to urge Pretoria to unleash its mighty military machine against the A.N.C. "terrorists". Terrorism was a vicious threat poised to swallow South Africa together with all its wealth; yet Pretoria could easily crush the growing threat hidden within the townships and orchestrated from the capitals of Europe and America. But any military action would inherit the wrath of the world.

Robin knew that in spite of a near total relaxation of apartheid regulations, the white dominated government was growing steadily weaker as sanctions continued to take their toll. During the previous five years the price of gold and diamonds, South Africa's main exports, had fallen sharply thus damaging the country's balance of payments. All the while the A.N.C. progressively mustered foreign support and was using its supply of Soviet and Chinese instructors and weaponry to train a new generation of freedom fighters. These young men could easily slip across South Africa's nine hundred mile border and disappear into the townships until required.

Robin had learned that world opinion preferred to believe that the whole of Africa belonged to the black native, chose to forget that it was the white settlers from Holland and England who discovered the deserted Cape in 1650. Their following generations farmed the virgin soil and trekked north from the Cape in the search for fresh lands, only coming into direct contact with the black Bantu Africans of Zululand in the early nineteenth century. Even though the might of the British Army had eventually defeated the warlike will of the Zulus in the bloody battles of 1879, both groups had afterwards found it possible to live together in considerable harmony. A white man could still safely walk at will among these proud people, indeed their children would invariably happily flock around a visitor in the expectation of sweets or ten cent coins.

His mind wandered and he found himself trying to spot the minister's official Mercedes car and protective police escort in the distant car park of the Zulu parliament. Next time he must bring his binoculars, they would give him at least fifteen minutes' warning to complete his pre-flight checks before the minister returned to the airfield. The cars were still there and his attention was drawn to the cooking smoke rising lazily from nearby Zulu huts. He had given up trying to reconcile the contentment of the Zulu nation in its wattle and daub kraals with the luxurious trappings of state, the modern royal palace and government buildings financed by Pretoria. Flying to Ulundi gave Robin the illusion that he was able to fly back through time itself and land amidst an unspoiled age. Everywhere were laughing childen, gaily attired women busy at their work, contented cattle and dusty indolent menfolk in earnest conversation sitting in the shade and enjoying their pungent native tobacco.

9

Robin's attention was drawn to the distant flashing blue light of the escort vehicle as it swept out of the parliament car park and on to the road which would bring the minister back to the airfield. He stirred his relaxed body and mind back to reality. With the practiced eye of a professional flyer he systematically began his pre-fight checks; then hopped out on to the aircraft wing to make his visual check of the plane's exterior. Ever since he had learned to fly at Shoreham, he had never relaxed his attitude to safety; others might drop out of the sky but not Robin Penny. Standing on the wing the full force of the heat struck him; even five years had not fully acclimatised him to the heat of Africa and he noticed the first trickle of sweat run down his back. As the minister's car swept into the airport, the three airport staff together with the mobile escorting officers all performed exaggerated salutes as Minister Sachs left his air-conditioned Mercedes and climbed into the six seater aircraft. The minister smiled at Robin.

'OK Robin, let's get this show off the ground before we all melt in the heat.' Minutes later they were climbing into the cooler air towards an altitude of ten thousand feet before heading for Pretoria 300 miles away.

'I hope everything went well minister.' It was intended to be more of a statement than a question; being the minister's personal pilot, Robin was well aware that he was playing a small part in events which could bring eventual peace or catastrophic civil war to South Africa. The minister was thoughtful for a while .

'You know Robin, I think we are nearly there.' He now looked more relaxed. 'The biggest problem is convincing the Zulu leaders that we won't abandon them to the A.N.C. , they have suggested that if the whites give up minority rule...... or worse, they're forced to abandon South Africa .....the A.N.C. will attempt to annihilate the Zulu nation. They call it ethnic cleansing!' He paused ; 'and both sides know that this is exactly what will happen.' He went on, 'It would be civil war on a massive scale and make Shaka's reign of terror look like the proverbial tea party.'

10

Robin knew it was not for him to comment; this was something the respective cabinets would have to resolve.

They reached an altitude of ten thousand feet to clear the jagged Drakensburg mountains which always reminded Robin of the occasions when he had flown over the Swiss Alps. Far below, the lofty snow covered peaks looked so peaceful and beautiful as they stretched out to the south. He remembered his previous holiday last year at the Draken mountain safari lodge with Alison, his latest ex-girlfriend. She had since returned to the UK to finish her degree at Bath university. The memories of their safari, of the breathtaking scenery combined with the wild animals she adored, drifted back to him as the aircraft droned on over the arid and rocky countryside.

'We are having a "braai" on Sunday, the girls have ordered me to invite you,' the minister's voice crackled over the headphones. Robin didn't have to think twice, as the minister's al-fresco dinner parties were always extravagant affairs.
'I always obey orders minister, especially from your daughters.' They both laughed. The Sachs's barbeques were very popular.

'But isn't your brother due out here soon?' Robin had momentarily forgotten that his brother was arriving at Johannesburg from the UK on Saturday, although everything had been arranged months ago. Robin nodded and mouthed the word, "Saturday".

'That's OK, bring him along; what does he do, is he another pilot?'
'No,' he said. Robin smiled knowing his brother's inability to come to terms with aircraft, 'he's an historian, a writer, that sort of thing. He is coming out to visit Isandhlwana and Rorke's Drift. He used to serve in one of the Welsh Regiments, it was his regiment that was wiped out at Isandhlwana by the Zulus.'

The minister coughed in an attempt to clear that gradual

tightening feeling in his chest which had increasingly begun to bother him. He felt that same inescapable feeling of panic beginning to rise within him. That word "Isandhlwana" which evoked such strange and uncontrollable feelings in both his body and mind was beginning to work on him again.

He felt his heart rate begin to increase, the nausea was rising in his stomach and he noticed that strange buzzing sensation intensifying in his head. Again he began to experience the overwhelming urge to escape before the sensation engulfed him. His left hand involuntarily went towards the door lever and there was nothing he could do to control the movement. Robin detected the cough over the headphones and out of the corner of his eye he saw the hand reaching for the door lever. He looked in astonishment at the minister and saw the usually calm face was contorted into a mask of terror. The minister's eyes were bulging and his skin was a deathly white colour. Robin instantly presumed his passenger was in the throes of a heart attack; he leaned over and forcefully pulled the outstretched hand away from the door handle.

The minister was now gasping and desperately struggling to breathe. Robin instinctively put the aircraft into as steep a dive as he dared.

'Hold on Minister, I'll get you down!' shouted Robin over the intercom.

The aircraft screamed earthwards until the altimeter showed they had descended to five thousand feet; he began to level out to three thousand feet and simultaneously activated his radio transmitter. The ashen faced minister was now slumped in his seat. Using his military call-sign , Robin called Wonderboom airport.

'Pan Pan!' he called urgently, using the international emergency code. 'Charlie Zulu one zero I have a problem, my passenger appears to have suffered a heart attack, I am some fifteen minutes from you, he's still alive but I'll need an ambulance equipped for cardiac failure immediately on

12

landing.' The voice which replied was calm and to the point.

'Charlie Zulu one zero your message is understood.'

'Do you know who we are?' Robin asked as an afterthought, hoping the concern in his voice didn't show.

'Charlie Zulu one zero, yes we know who you are, everything will be ready.' Robin felt himself calming down. He glanced across at the minister who appeared to be recovering.

'Minister, are you feeling better?' There was a pause.

'Yes Robin, it must have been the altitude, I'm fine now, at least I'm beginning to feel better.'

Robin knew the minister's condition was nothing to do with the altitude, perhaps he had suffered a mild heart attack.

'I'm sorry minister, but I thought you were seriously ill; I've arranged for an ambulance to meet us.'

'No problem Robin, you did the right thing. It's probably just as well that they give me a check over.' The minister closed his eyes and began to relax as those dreaded feelings of panic began to subside within him.

The next few minutes were routine; the radio beacon at Wonderboom Airport guided the small aircraft towards the end of the runway but Robin was already positioned to land. A quick call to the control tower dispensed with routine landing procedures and the aircraft gently touched down. Wonderboom Airport was situated just to the west of Johannesburg and was used by the S.A. Airforce, freight airlines and private flyers. Formalities were minimal compared with the main Johannesburg passenger airport but Robin had always been impressed by the friendliness and professional efficiency of its operations. He noticed the ambulance with its flashing lights making towards them with a police escort racing along behind. As soon as the aircraft came to a halt off the main runway, the ambulance was alongside. A smartly suited man in his mid forties, complete with medical bag, jumped from the passenger side of the vehicle and climbed up onto the wing. Robin leaned

13

over and opened the minister's door.

'Just stay where you are minister until I've checked you over,' said the doctor with calm authority. Minister Sachs nodded.
'I think I'm over the worst of it. I couldn't breathe during the flight but everything's beginning to get back to normal.'

The doctor swiftly completed his examination while behind him the ambulance crew had prepared a stretcher and were agitating to get involved with this mysterious but obviously important patient. After a few moments had passed, the doctor put his stethoscope back in his bag and waved the ambulance crew away.

'I don't think you are in any danger minister but I would like to run some proper checks back at the hospital. Just stay where you are for a few moments and I'll get your car here then we can both go there in comfort.' The doctor turned to Robin and smiled,
'Well done young man, but I don't think there's too much to worry about.'

Robin beamed back at him; he had immediately taken to the minister from the first time they had met. He was genuinely relieved that the drama was at an end and his worst fears had not been realised. Within a few moments the minister had been gently assisted into the back of his ministerial car by the attentive ambulance crew and with a wave to Robin he was gone.

'Well that was different,' Robin mused, and set about the task of refuelling.

A few hours later Peter Sachs returned to his luxury home set on the side of one of the low hills which enabled its privileged residents to enjoy the full panorama of Pretoria basking below them. His anxious wife Helena and two teenage daughters were already waiting and came to the door as his chauffeur driven car swept into the drive. Elegant and tall Elizabeth was twenty and in her second year studying law at the International University in

Pretoria. Annie, aged fourteen and a smaller replica of her sister, greeted him as though he was returning home from one of his diplomatic trips in one of the globe's far flung corners. He was pleased to see that even a minor health scare bound the family even closer together.

'Are you really OK daddy?' asked Annie as family spokesman , her big eyes pleading for a positive answer.

'Yes my love, it was only a minor scare, it could have happened to anyone,' he put his arm round her and paused, realizing his answer was unsatisfactory. 'Look , it was nothing, we went a little too high and I nearly blacked out, it won't happen again.'

'I hope they allocate you a more reliable pilot next time,' muttered Helena. Both girls looked at each other, for they had both taken a liking to Robin for their own reasons. Peter shook his head.

'I really don't think it was anything to do with Robin, I'll just have to get him to fly a little lower next time.' They all laughed, hugged each other and proceeded to enjoy their evening.

Later that night, Peter Sachs checked that his household were all fast asleep and quietly went into his study; he gently closed the door and silently turned the key in the lock. He went to the large battered metal travelling trunk which he used for safely storing family documents and interesting but valuable personal memorabilia.

The trunk had once belonged to his great grandfather and nobody was permitted to open it without his being present on account of the secrets it contained. As the rest of his family were women, it was highly unlikely that they would pry. Even so, he kept the only key in his official safe which had been set in the concrete floor and lay hidden under a full size imposing lion skin rug. Taking the key, he opened the trunk.

He lifted the lid and quietly released the metal cover inside the lid. It formed a secret compartment about four feet long, nearly two feet across and four inches deep. Inside lay his great-grandfather's battered leather-bound diary and a soft looking package which completely filled the remainder of the secret space. He put the diary on one side, gently lifted the package out and laid it on the floor. It was wrapped in an aged, once white cotton sheet and was buttoned down one side like a pillow case. That strange feeling was beginning to manifest itself again and he looked down curiously at his hands. They were very slightly shaking, this hadn't happened before, perhaps his condition was, as he had feared, getting worse.

'Pull yourself together,' he urged himself and slowly unbuttoned the retaining flap of the sheet.

He gently lifted the sheet away from the contents to reveal a heavily woven green cloth with proudly embossed lettering in gold and black thread on its slightly faded background. As he gently unfolded the heavy silk material, the shape of the Union Jack began to emerge on the top left hand corner and the meticulously sewn-in lettering formed the names of unusual places from countries all over the world. It was slightly torn in the top right hand corner, there were remains of earth stains along the right hand edge.

The material weighed nearly ten pounds, ten pounds of a beautifully crafted woven masterpiece measuring five by three feet. The top of the flag portrayed a magnificent royal crown over deep blue lettering displaying the legend,

"II WARWICKSHIRE"
XXIV

Peter Sachs was holding in his hands the long lost but well preserved Queen's Colour of one of the famous British infantry regiments which had formed the backbone of Lord Chelmsford's 1879 army of invasion into Zululand. This army totalled over three thousand five hundred well equipped and trained troops whose orders from London were to conquer the Impi regiments of the Zulu King

Cetshweyo. At the time, Cetshweyo was thought to be in command of more than fifty thousand warriors poised to invade white Natal. The invading British force entered Zululand from Natal on the 1st of January 1879 with the intention of gaining permanent peace by destroying and subjugating the native army of the Zulu King.

On the afternoon of the 15th January 1879, a Zulu force of over twenty five thousand warriors surprised, attacked and then annihilated more than two thousand British soldiers and native levies. The troops had been guarding Chelmsford's base camp positioned at the foot of the stark rock outcrop known as Isandhlwana, or "clenched fist" in Zulu.

The site had been chosen by Lord Chelmsford because of its dominating position over the far reaching grassy plain before it. The casualties of the three hour battle included "G" Company of the 2nd Battalion and the whole 1st Battalion The 24th Regiment of Foot, each unit recruited from the valleys of South Wales. At the time, Lord Chelmsford had divided his invasion force between the main camp defenders and an attacking column, and was steadily advancing into Zululand with the column searching for the Zulu army. They reached a point about fifteen miles ahead of the base camp when distant gunfire was heard behind them.

The advancing column was ponderously turned round but the Zulus had already systematically destroyed the base and slaughtered its brave defenders. A shaken Lord Chelmsford and the remainder of his demoralized army immediately withdrew to the relative safety of Natal without even stopping to bury their dead colleagues strewn round the battlefield or to look for the battalion's Colours.

Each regiment's Colour flag had historically been the pride of the regiment, the woven place-names recorded the regiment's battle honours since the unit's foundation. It served two purposes, it was both the unit's most treasured possession as well as signalling the rallying point for all the regiment's soldiers in battle. The Colour of the 2nd

Battalion had last been seen in the Regimental Officer's Mess tent at Isandhlwana by one Lieutenant Chard of the Royal Engineers. About five hours before the Zulus attacked he had peacefully breakfasted in the mess tent at Isandhlwana before returning to his own command at Rorke's Drift about ten miles away. A small detachment of some thirty soldiers of the 2nd Battalion under Chard's command had been left to guard the Buffalo River crossing point on the border of Natal with Zululand. This fording point was known to the soldiers as Rorke's Drift after the Englishman who had earlier established a small trading post on the river bank.

Peter Sachs gently refolded the Colour flag and placed it back in the secret cavity of the trunk. As he replaced the inner lid, he noticed that his hands were still shaking but his breathing was becoming steadier.

'What trouble have you got me into, Samuel?' he said, as if it were possible to speak to the memory of his great grandfather. He shook his head wearily as he locked the trunk, replaced the key then silently made his way up the grand staircase to his bedroom. He realized that two moments of truth were approaching; one for himself, the other for his beloved country.

CHAPTER 2.

SENNYBRIDGE, WALES.

Peter Sachs's great grandfather, Samuel Carrington, was the eldest son of Joshua and Martha Carrington. Samuel was born at Gaer Farm, Sennybridge, in the middle of a tremendous thunderstorm on the 25th September 1855. The baby boy was named after Joshua's own father who had coincidentally been killed by lightning several years earlier. Joshua was a successful hill farmer with some of the best grazing land around the small village of Sennybridge which lay approximately ten miles to the west of Brecon in Wales. He had taken good care to see that all three of his childen received a sound education and Samuel had set a good example by being diligent. By the time Samuel left the small village school, he could read and write and possessed a satisfactory knowledge of the distant lands beyond his native Wales. He was a popular and likable lad, polite to everyone and always ready to help anyone in distress.

By his eighteenth birthday, Samuel had already worked with his father for nearly four years. It had always been a foregone conclusion that he would become a farmer ; after all, there was little else that a strong young man could do in rural Wales. Being bright, he was aware that the family estate would eventually pass to him but nothing had ever been formally discussed within the family. Life and events surrounding Samuel's life were dictated by the seasons ; month followed month as he steadily took on more responsibility from his gently ageing parents. He had grown into a reserved but tall and good looking young man. His bearing and appearance, especially his shock of shoulder length black curly hair, invariably turned the ladies' heads when he visited Brecon market for the monthly sale. Samuel was becoming well aware of his ability to draw admiring glances and took some care with his grooming, especially when away from the farm.

It was on one of his visits to Brecon market during the

annual summer fair that he met Bethan Royal. He vaguely remembered her when she attended the previous Farmers' Association Christmas social, but no girl had previously mattered to him, at that time all girls looked much the same to Samuel. Living on a farm in a small rural community, he lacked the opportunity to meet young ladies, and in any event they didn't feature strongly in his life of outdoor interests and pursuits. But fate intervened with far reaching consequences as is so often the case.

Bethan unwittingly attracted Samuel's attention this market day as the crowd began to disperse homewards along Free Street towards the town centre. Her pony reared and became unmanageable as some small boys passed noisily nearby. She was struggling to regain control from the seat of her two wheeled trap, to the noisy amusement of a group of merry farmers leaving the Tavern Hotel next to the market. Samuel was facing a long lonely ride back to the farm when he saw and seized the opportunity of a more comfortable ride home. He handed the reins of his horse to an onlooker and quietly stepped up to the shying pony from one side and grasped the bit in its mouth. Using all his considerable strength, he held the animal's head kindly but firmly while calming it with soothing words. He looked up into Bethan's anxious eyes and smiled at her.

'If it's all right with you miss, I'll hop up with you and see you on your way.' Bethan nodded her assent and Samuel climbed on to the carriage seat beside her and took the reins.

The frightened horse set off along the road but shied at the junction and set off once more, but this time down the hill in the opposite direction. Samuel pulled hard on the reins and after several hundred yards, the horse began to respond. Samuel turned the horse and trap round using the entrance to the barracks, then with control regained, let the animal trot back up the hill. He turned them into Free Street and brought the carriage to a halt next to the tavern. Samuel collected his horse from the patient bystander, tied his reins to the back of the trap and resumed his seat beside Bethan. He winked cheekily at her.

'Are you all right now?' he asked kindly.

'Yes thank you, that was very kind of you to help,' she replied softly.

'I live your way, I'll come with you until you feel happy to continue on your own.'

Bethan had already resolved that this was unlikely to happen; it was not every day she would have the opportunity to be on her own with this handsome young man. In less than a minute they had trotted out of Brecon to the begrudging envy of those who had previously been amused by Bethan's plight. During the journey he could not help but notice the dark curls beneath her bonnet and her deep brown eyes which unashamedly looked him straight in the eye when they spoke. Her slender interlocked hands implied a degree of helplessness which warmed Samuel.

The combination of events, the lingering warmth of the late afternoon sun together with Bethan's closeness gradually enveloped Samuel in a dreamlike aura which encompassed his whole being. He was pleased as the town fell behind them and the pony slowed to a more leisurely walk; this journey would give him at least two hours to acquaint himself with the girl. Their track home lay along the valley of the River Usk which followed the meandering waters through the peaceful hills. By the time they reached Sennybridge, the bond of friendship had been formed and over the next few months the young couple met whenever they could. They walked, talked, fished in the river and rode happily together along the lanes and over the high hills of the Brecon Beacons.

Bethan was the only daughter of the local parson and at the age of eighteen, was very aware of the lack of suitable young men with whom a young lady could become acquainted. Her father's connections with the gentry of the county were well established. That summer, Bethan was found employment as governess to the two young but

21

precocious Priestly children at the nearby Trecastle Grange. Before taking up her position, Bethan's father had dutifully inspected the Grange and was introduced by Mrs. Priestly to the six resident staff . Over afternoon tea in the sitting room, the parson had discussed his daughter's future and agreed her conditions of service with the polite but smiling Mrs. Priestly. Bethan's father was more than satisfied that his daughter would be in good hands. Arrangements were made then and there for Bethan to take her meals with the family in accordance with her new status, and a small bedroom at the rear of the building was prepared for her private use. It was agreed that her main duty would be to take full responsibility for the children's education until they reached the age of ten when they would be sent away to boarding school.

Mr. Priestly had inherited his father's trading company together with its four sailing ships which plyed the routes to the colonies from Cardiff. His considerable fortune increased as trade prospered. Little Timothy Priestly was five years old and immediately adored Bethan , Emily at eight years of age could already read and recite numerous nursery rhymes. The children were well cared for by their mother who was assisted by an elderly but kindly nanny. Bethan would normally be free to spend each weekend with her own family which enabled her friendship with Samuel to blossom.

A year went by. Bethan grew more beautiful, Samuel matured and was now effectively running his father's farm. Both young people were aware of their special bond and neither had the time for any others of their own age group. Their relationship was still platonic although Samuel was fully aware that the closeness of Bethan was beginning to stir both his body and his emotions. Bethan had been well indoctrinated by her father that sin would result in her eternal life being spent in the fires of hell. She realized that her growing feelings would have to wait; after all, Samuel was not putting her under any pressure and his intentions were obviously honourable even though the matter had not yet been discussed.

When they were apart, both were fully occupied with their own work until they could meet again. Sundays were especially treasured. After chapel, they would have lunch at the Carrington farm or with Bethan's parents and then set off into the hills or fish the nearby river and brooks. It was the togetherness which mattered, not the activity.

Bethan became well known locally and respected as the Grange governess. When Mr.Priestly was at home he would occasionally observe her lessons with the children but he never made comment. She would be aware of his steely blue eyes watching her but this caused her no distress or concern; unlike her own father, he was a handsome man and she naturally respected this paternal interest in his children's progress.

Mrs. Priestly was a pale, sickly lady in her early thirties. Her husband was some ten years older than his wife, though they appeared to Bethan and the whole community to be happily married. Autumn came and one dank grey October morning Bethan went down to breakfast to find Mrs. Priestly being hurriedly carried across the hall by the kitchen staff and out to the waiting family carriage. Bethan rapidly established that her mistress had collapsed during the early hours and had then quickly lapsed into a coma. The nearest medical assistance was at Brecon and Bethan joined the remaining anxious staff gathered round the carriage. In spite of the pouring rain, Mr. Priestly calmly supervised the preparations for the journey. As soon as his wife was made comfortable on the narrow carriage seats, Mr. Priestly gave urgent orders to the coachman then leaped in beside his wife. The coach moved off splashing through the puddles and driving rain towards Brecon and medical assistance.

Mrs. Priestly died during the latter part of the journey and the whole community attended her funeral in the village cemetery beside Sennybridge chapel. Bethan's father conducted the service under a magnificent canopy of black storm clouds ; Mr. Priestly stood at the graveside without any display of emotion, he appeared to Bethan to be almost oblivious of the proceedings. Bethan stood between the two children, all three held hands while the service moved from prayer to hymn and then to the finality of life when the coffin was slowly lowered into the grave. A light rain began to fall hastening the departure of the many mourners. Bethan returned with Mr. Priestly and the children to the Grange, Samuel accompanied his family back to the farm. Neither had been able to speak during the service but when their eyes met, their united gaze said everything.

Time passed and by the second week before Christmas, staff at the Grange had already prepared the house for the forthcoming family celebrations.   Bethan was joyously anticipating her first Christmas with Samuel and their combined families. Her pleasure was not to last. Mr Priestly took her by surprise that morning when he entered the classroom where she was conducting a geography lesson. She stood up out of courtesy as he entered the room.

'Bethan, please come into my study for one moment,' he said sternly.

 The children looked at her expectantly. She gave each child a book to read then obediently followed Mr. Priestly along the oak panelled passage lined with foreboding paintings of the family ancestors. Bethan always felt uneasy under the gaze of these staring eyes; she had the distinct impression they were watching her wherever she stood in the hallway. In the well appointed study Mr. Priestly indicated that she should sit down on the sofa opposite his desk, then looked directly at her.

'I know you have made arrangements for the forthcoming holiday, but I am asking you to reside at the Grange over Christmas in order to be with the children.' Before she had time to think she heard herself replying,
'Certainly Sir , I would be pleased to help.' He smiled as he commented,
'Bethan , I'm grateful to you and I know the children will enjoy having you here over the holiday.'

As she left the study she could feel the disappointment beginning to rise within her. How could she be so stupid, how was she going to see Samuel over the holiday? She felt total despair as the tears trickled down her cheeks. Samuel was due to collect her that evening and for the first time in her life she felt the heavy feeling of dread which began to foreshadow his coming, she knew his disappointment would match hers. How was she to make him understand?

At six o'clock that evening, Samuel dismounted from his gelding and tied the reins to a convenient branch of the old oak tree which dominated the front of the grange. He knocked at the heavy wooden door and was admitted by the housekeeper. Bethan came down the staircase from the classroom   and held out her hand to Samuel. When the housekeeper had gone, Bethan led him to a sofa in the anteroom and related the morning's events, she watched his face tighten as he listened. Samuel fumed as his anger grew.

'He has no right to keep you here over Christmas, this is our time, what about our own families and our own arrangements?'   He knew he was powerless to intervene and Bethan watched him helplessly. He turned his back on her more by way of a gesture of despair than of rejection and she put her arms around him.

'Samuel, please, please understand, I'm only doing this for the children.' she said. Samuel made no reply, there were no words to express his feelings, he felt all the joyous anticipation of Christmas drain away from his body and soul   only to be replaced by the heaviness of sudden, unexpected, disappointment .

Mr. Priestly came into the hall and paused as he saw Samuel turn to face him, he had already decided to have no part in any discussion about the matter. He condescended a polite but firm,

'Good afternoon Samuel,' and almost without a pause he

went on, 'Bethan, would you please attend to your duties
with the children,' and without as much as a glance at
either of them, he returned to his study. As Samuel turned
his back on Bethan and purposefully walked towards the
main door, Bethan whispered loud enough for him to
hear,
 'Come at midday tomorrow , we can talk then.'

Samuel strode from the Grange leaving the heavy door
wide open to the wind and unhitched his horse. Leaping
into the saddle, he deliberately drove the animal at
speed across the lawns in order to make his feelings
known, then straight through the carefully laid out flower
beds before turning down the gravel drive to the main
gate.

That evening at the Grange , little of consequence was
said over supper, Mr. Priestly talked lightheartedly of the
visitors due to attend the Grange for the forthcoming
festivities but Bethan lacked the appetite for conversation
or her food. She retired to her room early with the
intention of going to bed. She snuffed out the candle,
climbed into her cold bed and attemped to find solace in
sleep. The day's events had caused her quite enough grief.

Bethan had not been asleep very long when she was
awakened by the sound of her door being quietly opened.
She never locked the door although she had been provided
with a key which hung unused on the back of the door. At
first Bethan thought she had left the door ajar, that the
draught which always blew around the house was opening
the door. She lay still and warm in bed unsure what to do.
Part of her wanted to drift back to sleep but an alarm was
beginning to activate itself deep within her mind. She held
her breath and listened. At first, all she could hear was the
sound of her own heart pounding loudly; then she heard
movement near the door and saw a glimmer of light from
the hallway. Bethan sat upright in bed instinctively pulling
the bedclothes up around her neck.

 'Who is there , is anyone there?' She could hear the fear
in her own voice.

'It's all right Bethan, it's only me, I just want to talk to you,' whispered Mr. Priestly. Bethan felt relieved that the intruder was her employer and thought perhaps one of the children had become ill.

'Is it one of the children?' she asked with concern in her voice.

'Let me light your candle then we can talk.' He went back into the hallway and collected the night lantern which illuminated the long wooden panelled passage outside hers and the children's rooms. He came back into her room, put the light down on Bethan's dressing table and sat on the edge of her bed. Bethan was quite astonished and held her breath.

'Bethan, let me be honest with you,' he paused as if to collect his thoughts. His husky voice wafted the smell of brandy on his breath. 'Since my wife died I feel a great need to talk to you; I need you, the children need you.' Bethan began to feel concerned, but on realizing the children were just down the corridor she felt her confidence slowly returning . He went on, 'Bethan, I am by any standards a very wealthy man and I can offer you a very comfortable position,' he paused for effect, 'as my wife.'

Bethan gasped for breath as he sat on her bed and put his hand on her arm.

'No - that's not possible!' she protested as she tried to resist him by pulling her arm away, but he was too strong. She began to scream but he put his free hand over her mouth and pushed her down on to her bed. Bethan's scream was stifled and she flailed frantically with her legs in the attempt to free herself but to no avail, the bed covers were too tight.

Her struggles coupled with the warmth of her body aroused his feelings and she felt his body pressing against her - his open mouth brushed her naked neck as he began to kiss her; she desperately stretched her free arm towards the empty stone water jug on her bedside table. She grasped the handle and raised the jug above his head, then

27

with all her might, swung the heavy object downwards against the side of his unprotected head.

The impact stunned him and his eyes grotesquely rolled in their sockets then half closed. He slowly slid from the side of her bed onto the floor. There was a deep gash on the side of his head which began to bleed profusely and for a moment she watched in horror as the dark stain of his blood spread slowly across the floor. She threw off her bedclothes and ran downstairs to the kitchen for fresh water and a bandage. On returning to her room, she found him sitting on her chair nursing his bloodstained head in his hands. She determinedly went over to him and examined her handiwork.

'Let me clean the wound.' Her voice now contained some authority and he nodded. Bethan was relieved that she had been able to seize control of the situation and went on, 'I'm sorry to have hurt you but you have invaded my privacy in a most alarming manner.' Bethan gently washed the blood from his face then firmly placed the bandage against the gash. Mr. Priestly looked at her, his eyes almost pleading for forgiveness,
'Bethan, my offer is still open to you, I insist that we talk about it again in the morning.'

He rose from the chair and, still holding the bandage to his head, left her room.

Bethan tidied the disarray of her normally ordered room then washed her hands in the water bowl. The cool water had a soothing effect on her and, with a deep breath, she went over to the bedroom door and firmly locked it. To her surprise Bethan began to feel sorry for her employer. As she once more lay warmly in her bed her earlier fear and anger began to melt into a new and strange sensation of excitement.

For the remainder of the night her sleep was interrupted by repeated moments of sensual awareness alternating with dreams of her father standing over her. He was holding his bible and preaching at her not to sin, he talked of eternal hell and the disgrace that her actions had brought upon her family. She awoke at daybreak and felt strangely confused by the nature of her dreams with their tantalising bodily sensations. As Bethan dressed, she mulled over the events of the previous night. By the time Bethan joined the children for breakfast, the housekeeper had already informed them that their father had fallen in his study and struck his head on the side of the desk. As Bethan was finishing her meal, a bandaged Mr. Priestly entered the room. He looked sternly at Bethan.

'I must away to Brecon this morning, I intend coming home during the evening. When I return I would like us to continue our conversation.' Bethan looked at him in uncertainty but merely nodded so as not to give the children cause for concern.

Samuel arrived at midday as he was bid. Bethan had sent the children to their playroom and took Samuel by the hand into the privacy of the dining room. He looked very serious and Bethan wondered how he would react to her tale. They sat at the table. He listened without interruption as she related the night's sequence of events. As Bethan finished, she looked at him and saw from his face that he was upset although his demeanour was calm. He looked at her and took her hands in his.

'We must leave here at once and you must tell your father everything; we don't ever need to return to this accursed place.' Bethan suddenly felt torn between her responsibilities to the children and her wish to be with Samuel. She felt the tears forming and attempted to control herself.

'I can't leave the children, and if I did, where could I go? It's his word against mine; would father believe me?'

Both sat silently looking at their entwined hands while Samuel thought hard. What Bethan had said made sense, her postion was indeed precarious. If she left the Grange, her prospects of further employment in the locality would be non existent.

At that moment, they both heard the sound of a carriage as it drew up outside the main door. Mr. Priestly strode into the hallway and gave his cloak and hat to the housekeeper who had scurried from the kitchen in mischievous anticipation of trouble.

'Where is Mistress Bethan ?' he enquired.
'In the dining room Sir, Mr. Samuel is with her,' replied the housekeeper obsequiously. Mr. Priestly took a deep breath then purposefully entered the dining room and Bethan rose up to face him. She saw that his wound had been stitched with three neat knots of fine thread. The side of his face was still red and the wound looked painful and swollen. He addressed Samuel coolly.

'Good day Samuel, what are you doing here?' He immediately went on. 'And was it not only yesterday that I asked you not to interfere with my staff... and as soon as my back is turned you are back!' said Mr. Priestly agitatedly.

Samuel had remained seated but now slowly rose to his full height. He looked coldly at Mr. Priestly and took a deep breath to calm himself.

'And when my back was turned you threatened Bethan , you entered her room when she was asleep. What you did was not the action of an honourable gentleman.' To Samuel's mild surprise Mr. Priestly advanced towards him until their faces were only inches apart. Mr. Priestly fumed with rage.

'Leave my house this instant you young pup, it's about time the likes of you were kept in your proper place. Get yourself back to your farmyard!' His face had gone florid with rage and Bethan thought the wound would pop open like a ripe plum. He went on, 'Leave now, farmhand, and under no circumstances will you return.'

With that he pushed Samuel hard in the chest as if to propel him towards the door. Samuel stood his ground, he was too tall and well built to be easily pushed around; with the speed that accompanies fury, he grasped his assailant's hand and as easily as he could flick a stook of corn, twisted Mr. Priestly's arm behind his back and threw him towards the floor. Samuel had not noticed the chair in the way and the startled Mr. Priestly crashed headfirst into the chair catching his wounded face on the wooden arm. The chair collapsed under the sudden impact. The forcible contact of face and chair was more than enough to undo the attention of the surgeon that morning and the stitches burst open.

Mr. Priestly lay there for a moment with fresh blood pouring onto the dining room carpet.

'Mrs. Evans!' he shouted loudly and the housekeeper came running. Mrs. Evans, her hands covered in flour, nearly fainted when she saw her master lying on the floor in a pool of blood, parts of the broken chair were still underneath him.

'Look what has happened to me, HE did this,' said Mr. Priestly pointing at Samuel. 'This is an offence for the Assize, you'll regret this day.' He painfully picked himself up as Samuel grabbed Bethan by the arm and led her towards the door.

Bethan resisted him.

'Samuel , please, I cannot go with you - I cannot leave the children.' Samuel looked at her in sheer disbelief .
'If you don't come with me now, you will not see me again .'
'Samuel I am truly sorry, I cannot leave,' she pleaded.

Samuel stormed out of the Grange for the second time in two days but this time he felt utterly dejected. He truly wished the world would come to an end as he slowly rode home. It was all beyond his powers of reason, he could find no explanation for the astonishing events. Later that day he began to suspect Bethan.

The following afternoon two constables from the Magistrates' Office in Brecon rode out to the farm and arrested Samuel. In handcuffs he was escorted back to Brecon and lodged in the Assize court cells. Samuel was bewildered, events had happened so fast that he was totally confused. In the days that followed, he began to believe that he was the victim of a plot between Bethan and Mr. Priestly; there appeared to be no other valid explanation for the recent events. His father visited him on the third day and Samuel was distressed to see how he had aged. Mr.Carrington related how the story of Samuel's actions had spread around the community, nothing like this had occurred in living memory and the tale improved with the telling as it was passed on by word of mouth. After the incident, Mr. Priestly had summoned the surgeon to repair his face again; and the following morning he travelled to Brecon and laid a complaint of assault against Samuel.

His father comforted him as best he could but Samuel could see the bewildered look on his weatherbeaten face. In the days that followed Samuel was not permitted to see anyone, indeed, there was no one who wanted to see Samuel. There was no word from Bethan. He had disgraced himself, his family and his village by striking the respected owner of the Grange.

He languished in the Assize cells with only straw to sleep on, two thieves for company and sparse rations. It was ten days following his arrest when a warder informed him he would be arraigned before the court the following day to be dealt with by the visiting circuit judge. Samuel's heart sank when he learned that he would have to answer the serious charge of battery; he knew that men had been deported for less. He was very well aware that Mr. Priestly was a respected member of the gentry and that the Judge would belong to the same class. His future began to look perilous.

On the 22nd December 1876, Samuel, feeling wretched, was brought up from the cells into the dock in handcuffs. His escorting warder had advised him to say little for fear of provoking the judge who was suffering from gout. Samuel looked around the near empty courtroom. His father sat looking dejected but managed a weak smile of encouragement. Apart from three casual visitors sheltering from the rain and the constables who had arrested him, only Mr. Priestly, his housekeeper and the surgeon were present. Bethan was absent. As Samuel stood in the dock , the Judge limped into the courtroom. He remembered the warder's advice about the judge's gout. Judge Stevenson was a portly gentleman and the heavy wig and gowns gave him an awesome appearance.

The clerk rose to his feet.

'Samuel Carrington, you are arraigned before this court to answer the charge of unlawful serious battery against one Edward Priestly of Trecastle Grange on the 11th of December Eighteen Seventy Six; how do you plead, guilty or not guilty?' The clerk of the court looked expectantly at Samuel.

'Guilty sir,' he replied with as strong a voice as he could manage .
'Sit down,' ordered the clerk.

Mr. Priestly was called to take the oath, then briefly related the facts surrounding the assault. Being tall and handsome, he looked imposing in his best clothes, and the wound on his face had begun to heal leaving a bright red scar between his right ear and eye. He did not embellish the tale, he did not need to. Bethan's absence from the trial completed Samuel's dejection; he felt tired , disinterested and lonely as the hearing proceeded.

His mind was still in turmoil when he heard the clerk order him to his feet. The judge looked sternly at him.

'For this wicked and unprovoked attack, you will go to prison for five years,' said the Judge. Samuel looked at him in sheer disbelief. The judge continued. 'Or you may enlist in the army for ten years, the choice is yours to be made within the hour.'

The clerk turned to the warder,
'Take him down,' he said with bored disdain in his voice.

Samuel's world collapsed ; his despair was complete.

CHAPTER THREE

Samuel was led back down the well worn steps to the cramped Court cells where other unfortunates were held awaiting their trials. The heavy handcuffs were beginning to chafe his wrists and the thought of spending the next five years in prison was totally beyond his comprehension. There were no washing facilities at the Assize cells and the toilet bucket was only emptied once each day. Samuel's clothes were becoming quite revolting with his own body odour and accumulated grime from the cells. He had previously known nothing about prisons except that they were unpleasant places housing thieves and other ruffians, and the overall experience since his arrest was proving to be rather a shock. In his own eyes he was totally innocent; he had merely tried to protect himself but, of course, the judge was as intent as Mr. Priestly on Samuel's punishment. He sat on the wooden bench with his head held in his hands .

'Someone to see you lad,' said a bailiff. Samuel looked up and saw his father at the cell door. He held his hands out to the stooping figure.

'Father, please forgive me,' it was as much as he could do to hold back his tears.

The old man smiled weakly as he was shown into the cell and sat down beside his son. Samuel saw how he had aged and he knew this whole business must have seriously distressed both his parents. His father looked at him sadly.

'What will you do Samuel?' This was the very question that Samuel was wrestling with; after all, he knew nothing about either enlisting, or the army.

'Father, if I go to prison I will be shamed for life, no one will ever want to know of me again, I've lost everything.' His father put his arm round Samuel's shoulders and gave him what comfort he could .

'Scuse me Sir,' the ever present bailiff was looking at Samuel's father, 'I reckon as knowing about this, he ought to go in the army, that ways he gets fed and paid, sees the

world and if he survives he gets out a free man ...and that's
my advice.'

'And very good advice it is too, thank you.' replied the
old man slowly. He drew out a florin from his pocket and
handed it to the grateful bailiff. 'Well Samuel, it seems you
have no choice in the matter.' Samuel looked at his father
and again tried to smile.

'And who would have thought of me as a soldier,' he
paused,' I suppose that is what I must do .... and what of
Bethan, what will she think ....has she contacted you, have
you seen her?' His father slowly shook his greying head.
'No lad, nothing at all; she hasn't been seen since that
dreadful day.'

An unctuous court clerk came to the cell door and
smirkingly called Samuel's name. Samuel stood up with a
look of resignation on his face.

'What's it to be lad, prison or army?' asked the clerk.
'Army sir.'
'Right, wait here and they'll collect you later.'

The official departed and Samuel smiled to himself, he
couldn't do anything other than wait with his wrists still
manacled and the door bolted. Gradually he began to feel
better. For the first time in two weeks Samuel could detect
a glimmer of hope. If only he had heard from Bethan ; but
nothing, not even a note had been sent. His father was then
asked to leave by the same condescending bailiff and with
a final hug for his son, departed with Samuel's messages
for the family and Bethan. Later that afternoon a large and
resplendent recruiting sergeant arrived at the Assize Court
to collect Samuel. The handcuffs were removed and after
rubbing his wrists, Samuel signed the enlistment form
which was to save him from prison.

Samuel was marched down the hill from the Courthouse
to the Regimental Headquarters of the 2nd Battalion the
24th (2nd Warwickshire) Regiment which was situated

less than a quarter of a mile from the Assize Court along the Watton Road. As he approached the barracks, he blinked in the unfamiliar sunlight and desperately looked around for any sign of Bethan. Apart from some sympathetic looks from passing locals, there were no recognisable faces. Samuel and escort swept into the barracks at the double and halted outside the guard room. Samuel was led through the guard room and placed in the detention cells where he would have to wait until the following Monday when the next training cadre commenced. He was, to his great relief, required to bathe and then provided with clean but rough clothes prior to the issue of uniform. His two cellmates consisted of one deserter who was anticipating a flogging and another similar unfortunate, Owen Thomas, who had also chosen enlistment rather than jail for sheep stealing. To the prisoners' collective surprise, army food was most wholesome and very satisfactory. During the following Monday morning, Samuel and Owen, by now good friends, were taken from their cell to join their fellow new recruits .

Life in the army suited Samuel with all the constant activity. He was pleased that the rigours of farming the harsh countryside had toughened him for what lay ahead. Over the next few weeks he became proficient at drill and his musketry skills were outstandingly good for someone who had never previously handled any weapon . During the fourth week of his training he was unexpectedly marched at the double from the parade ground to the Adjutant's office in the regimental headquarters block overlooking the main Watton road. He had a visitor, and visitors for soldiers in barracks were very unusual. Samuel was excited and very curious . When he saw Bethan's father he was delighted. He realised that the parson could easily obtain access to the barracks in order to minister to one of his flock.

But the parson looked sternly at Samuel and proffered him a seat on a low wooden bench at the back of the room. The escorting sergeant stood rigidly to attention by the door. The austere military office was as clean as a new pin and frugally furnished apart from two framed scrolls and a ceremonial sword hanging on the wall behind the adjutant's desk. The adjutant, who Samuel thought was hardly older than himself, was standing at the large window overlooking the parade ground as if wishing to dissociate himself from the ensuing conversation. Samuel took his seat and sat to attention. He had learnt that the army did everything to attention, except sleep. The parson broke the silence .

' Samuel, it's about Bethan, I thought it right, for the sake of the past, to come and see you lest you heard from another,' he paused. Samuel looked at him expectantly .
'Bethan is to be married to Mr.Priestly; here is a letter from her.'

The parson placed the letter in the bewildered recruit's hands. Before Samuel could react to the shock of those words, the adjutant turned as if his action was prearranged and spoke firmly to the stunned recruit.

' Right lad... that's it , back to your duties.' The sergeant who marched Samuel to the office barked out the necessary orders and Samuel was gone .
'A most distasteful business,' said the parson, 'he was such a promising young man, but I'll wager he'll make a fine soldier.' The adjutant nodded. He had already received favourable reports that this particular recruit was very capable and willing to learn.

'Left right, left right,' barked the sergeant as Samuel's mind slowly went numb with disbelief.

As he was marched at speed round the drill square to rejoin his squad, tears began streaming down his face and his breath came in great uncontrollable sobs. The energy drained out of him as he slowed to an uncertain halt, his shoulders drooped and he began to slump forwards, it was only due to the quick thinking NCO that he didn't collapse. The NCO looked around to make sure no one was looking and supportively put his arm round Samuel's shoulder.

'It's all right lad, it's happened to lots of us - you know what women are like - you'll soon get over it,' he said with real compassion in his voice.

'But we were engaged ,' Samuel protested.

'And I knows lots of women who leaves their menfolk even when they're married,' added the NCO knowingly, trying to console his most promising recruit.

'You can take it from me,' the NCO continued, 'it's all for the best - in a years time you'll have someone much better.' Samuel took a deep breath and blew his nose.

'You're right I suppose - but it was a hell of a shock, and - thank you.'

'That's all right lad, now brace up straight and let's get going again before someone thinks I've gone soft in the head.' Samuel braced himself .

'Left Right- Left Right- Left Right,' barked the NCO.

Samuel refrained from opening the letter until he was on his own. He walked to a corner of the barracks and read the letter. It was final.

"My Dear Samuel,
What has happened has divided us forever. I must now think of the children and my decision has pleased them greatly. Without you, there can be no love in my life. May God go with you.
                Bethan."

* * * * * * * * * * *

Samuel completed his military training on the 2nd June 1877 and along with his new recruit friends was transferred to Cardiff Barracks for normal regimental duties. The rumour was already circulating around the barracks that the new recruits were to be posted to South Africa's Cape colony where the 1st Battalion was fighting a minor skirmish with the natives. Towards the end of the year, confirmation was at last received and the announcement was promulgated on the notice board outside the guardroom. Samuel read out the details for those who couldn't read. All were elated to have two week's Christmas leave prior to travelling to London for embarkation to Africa as part of the 2nd Battalion.

Samuel decided to take his leave on the the farm. He reserved a seat on the morning carriage to Brecon and sat in silence for the duration of the long journey home. At Brecon he hired a horse for the two weeks from the market farriers then set out for the farm. He kept well away from the main Sennybridge track lest he encountered anyone who would recognise him. During the whole leave period, Samuel didn't venture into the village; there was no one he wanted to see anymore. All the available time was spent instructing his two brothers in the ways of the farm. Both had matured and grown alarmingly tall, after all, it was nearly one whole year since he last saw them. Samuel knew he was now going to be away for several years and was saddened by the dawning reality that he may not see his parents again. Over supper one evening, Samuel's father revealed the contents of his will relating to the farm. As Samuel had anticipated, the farm and remaining capital had all been bequeathed to the three sons in equal proportions, along with requests that their mother be well cared for during her lifetime.

On the 1st February 1878, the sixty recruits from Cardiff travelled by train to join their main parent unit, the 2nd Battalion, who were arriving at London Docks from their previous garrison at Chatham. During the afternoon the troops boarded HM Troopship 'Himalaya' for passage to South Africa. In the middle of a torrential downpour, and with the ubiquitous military band playing on the quayside, they sailed for Capetown and were soon lost in the evening mist.

Following the inevitable sea sickness which always accompanies troopships traversing the English Channel and the Bay of Biscay, the passage quickly settled down into organised rounds of sunbathing, weapon training and deck sports. On the 28th February, the decks were lined three deep as the cheering soldiers experienced their first view of land after those many weeks at sea. In the far distance the spectacular Table Mountain with its billowing white clouds began to rise from the spray of the rolling waves. The distant mountain appeared to the excited soldiers like a huge lump of flattened granite set against its perpetual backdrop of deep blue sky. As the ship neared the harbour of Capetown, the soldiers could easily make out the shimmering clusters of white buildings with their red roofs. Already the ship was having to adopt a more cautious approach due to the bustle of unusual small ships around the harbour entrance.

Slowly the 'Himalaya' eased past Capetown and into the neighbouring refuelling station at Simon's Bay to replenish the vessel's exhausted coal stocks; from there, it immediately proceeded on the short two day journey to the military port at Durban.

By early evening on the 3rd March, disembarkation had been completed and the milling soldiers were all allocated to holding areas on the quayside by their supervising NCOs. Great amusement was had by all at the plight of unfortunate individuals of all ranks trying to regain their land legs after so long at sea. Discipline was quickly re-established; the battalion of nearly seven hundred men formed up in their columns and the two mile march began to Smith Barracks on the north side of Durban. Without the accustomed cooling sea breeze, the heat of the evening struck them all and within minutes their bright red jackets were soaked in sweat. Their packs and recently issued white pith helmets were not unusually heavy but the sticky humidity exaggerated both their efforts to march and the weight of their loads. The whole local population of several hundred souls had turned out at the dock gates to wave and cheer; after all, the Army was here to protect them from the savage black hordes rumoured to be massing along the border to the north.

'Welcome to the land of beetles, bugs and fleas,' joked a

resident.

'Don't forget the ticks and mosquitoes,' added another laughingly.

Children of all ages and colours ran beside the soldiers cheering and waving until the column reached the edge of the settlement; there the excited youngsters were ordered back by a ferocious looking sergeant.

The rough roadway of hard sun baked sand quickly created a heavy cloud of fine choking dust which settled on the column of marching soldiers winding its way out of the town. The streaming sweat on their faces gradually mixed with the swirling dust turning the troops' faces into muddy masks. After another unbearable hours march they reached Smith Barracks with its row upon row of white army five-man bell tents. The camp was manned by a reserve company while the 1st Battalion was engaging the rebels several hundred miles to the north. The new 2nd Battalion arrivals washed themselves down in a nearby stream and then made themselves comfortable in the spacious tents which were to be home for the foreseeable future.

Life thereafter was organised into a regular routine of drill, battle training, ceremonial duties at the Governor's residence, musketry practice and, to Samuel's delight, learning to ride.

As the days went by, all ranks of the newly arrived 2nd Battalion readily associated with the reserve garrison from the battle hardened 1st Battalion. They listened in awe to stories of the exploits of their comrades still engaged in the 9th Kaffir war on the northern boundary of the province. It was more of an uprising than a war and casualties to the regiment had been very light. Once the new arrivals became acclimatised to the heat of the country, they were speedily instructed in the fighting tactics used by the natives in the recent uprisings .

Surprisingly, British army strategy had changed little since the Napoleonic wars. When facing an enemy, any enemy, soldiers were trained to form lines, columns or squares according to the strength of the foe. Samuel learned that rifle fire was delivered either by volleys under strict control or, exceptionally, by independent fire but only when a unit came under serious pressure .

'There is no room for independent thought or action in the British army,' said one sergeant knowingly, 'soldiers are trained to fight, and if necessary, to die together.' Everyone laughed.

Most of the soldiers were relieved that all decisions on the forthcoming campaign would be made for them; that was one of the attractions of the army, it provided for every need. They spent many weeks perfecting their skills, and always in full uniform of buttoned red tunic and blue serge trousers, regardless of the heat.

Samuel felt very much at home. His colleagues were all from the valleys of South Wales and spoke with that beautiful song-like Welsh accent. Every company boasted a choir, including the Headquarters Company to which Samuel had been temporarily attached on the grounds that he could both read and write. Each evening as the golden sun melted onto the horizon, the sounds of their beloved hymns could be heard far across the plain. Thoughts of Bethan played less and less on his mind as time went by.

The camp site was situated on a vast grassy plain with scattered outcrops of rock dotting the veldt. In the far distance stood a line of low green hills. During each day the temperature climbed until it was almost unbearable, and even the British Army was obliged to cease its activities between noon and mid afternoon until the faint cooling breeze arrived from the coast. It was mid-summer at home and Samuel was surprised to learn that the height of the African summer would not occur until Christmas. During his limited free time, Samuel would often venture out on to the plain where he could watch the big herds of kudu, zebra and springbok grazing. It was a beautiful unspoilt country and he was beginning to feel a great affinity with Africa's vastness. He was very surprised when he saw his first giraffe, he was quietly sitting in some long grass idly watching a soaring vulture when a tall male giraffe came into view about five hundred yards away. He involuntarily stood to gain a better view and the animal immediately took fright, moving off at a slow lolloping run, but it was yet another lesson learned.

When writing his monthly letter home to his father, Samuel took great care in describing the animals. He knew his father would not appreciate military matters, but animals were something he really understood.

On the 4th July 1878, the recruits were all paraded and kitted out with full battle order. From now on, through day and night, they would always have their rifle and ammunition by their sides. Under the command of the recently arrived 2nd Lieutenant David Black, the HQ Company set out ahead of the 2nd Battalion on the three week march to join the main invasion force assembling at Pietermaritzburg. Their progress was slow but steady due to the cumbersome ox led waggons laden with their equipment, ammunition and stores they were escorting. The countryside through which they passed was hot, dry and barren with only the occasional river to ford.

These waterways were always welcome. Once the water containers had been refilled, the soldiers were permitted to wash their clothes and then swim while their clothing dried on the rocks. When crossing the frequently rocky terrain, Samuel noticed that the rocks had been scorched dark brown by the incessant and unremitting heat. The column progressed north and the arid landscape gave way to scrub grass as they climbed into the low hills. The troops noticed passing signs of habitation with friendly native kraals scattered on the hillsides and the following Sunday, the party arrived on the outskirts of Pietermaritzburg at the temporary fortification of the assembling invasion force.

A few days later, Samuel managed to get himself involved in one minor skirmish while on a reconnaissance patrol consisting of six mounted infantrymen. Their task was to patrol and secure the proposed route to Helpmakaar near the Zulu border; they were to observe a nearby kraal whose warriors had persistently harried the British supply lines for food. As they approached the offending kraal, a small group of armed natives appeared on the brow of a nearby hill less than one mile away. The troopers spurred their mounts into the gallop and gave immediate chase which prompted the warriors to retreat into a nearby rocky ravine. To the surprise of the troopers, they came under sporadic but badly aimed rifle fire; clearly those armed with captured weapons had no real idea how to aim or use the rifle sights. Under the leadership of Corporal Jones, the patrol dismounted and using the cover of the boulder strewn slopes, returned fire at the enemy who made little effort to use any cover. Samuel fired at a tall native standing on a rock and was astonished to see the man bodily lifted into the air by the impact of the shot before falling into some scrub. After some ten minutes there was no further sign of the enemy. The nervous soldiers cautiously advanced on foot and found four bodies, one shot by Samuel; the remainder had fled after taking the rifles from their dead. By comparison with the soldiers, the native bodies looked half starved and Samuel felt sorry for them.

'No wonder they had been raiding the supply lines,' he said to one of his fellow troopers. It was Army policy to leave enemy bodies where they fell. They would either be recovered by the natives or eaten by the many predators resident in the surrounding rocky hills.

The latter part of 1878 found the two Welsh Battalions at Pietermaritzburg quietly but seriously preparing for war.

The recent peace was too fragile to last. The land hungry Boers, who had previously supported recent British campaigns, had completed their trek east and were already settling along the borders of the Blood River in Zululand. Being a proud nation, the Zulu King objected to the Boers' encroachment on to his fertile lands as well as fearing the Boers' custom, although illegal, of taking slaves. King Cetshwayo regally demanded their immediate withdrawal. The Zulus had hitherto been relatively peaceful and the King had enjoyed friendly diplomatic relations with the British administration in Natal. The Zulu kingdom was autonomous; and although peaceful, the King still had an army of over fifty thousand well trained warriors at his disposal. Their regiments, or impis as they were known, were ruthlessly controlled by the King's indunas who would order summary execution for any misdemeanour.

To resolve the matter the British administration appointed a boundary commission which decided that the Boers should withdraw from Zululand. This decision greatly alarmed the recently arrived Governor to South Africa, Sir Bartle Frere. Since the neighbouring Boer Transvaal had been annexed by the British, the Boer trekkers were now legally British subjects and could be ordered to withdraw from the disputed areas. Frere realised that such an order would probably provoke the Boers into an uprising, and if they remained where they were, the Zulus would certainly attack the Boers in considerable strength. Such a massive Zulu force would then be in a position to threaten British Natal. The British Military Commander in South Africa, Lieutenant General Sir Frederick Thesiger, well aware that the British forces in South Africa were hopelessly under strength, was instructed by his political masters to prepare plans to subjugate the Zulus either politically or by annexation. The alternative was to risk an unpopular war against the Boers. The Governor appealed to the British Government for reinforcements to fight the Zulus but this was refused on the grounds that there were already sufficient resources locally. The British Commander, now Lord Chelmsford following the death of his father, decided to recruit local white volunteers and enlist some seven thousand native levies to support the British Force.

In the meantime, life for Samuel was exciting and hectic. The whole regiment had long been anticipating total war against the Zulus. Training had been conducted at near fever pitch for many weeks and huge supplies of stores were being assembled in specially established camps around Pietermaritzburg. The two battalions of the 24th Regiment were now joined by numerous other units assembled for the invasion and the whole area surrounding the town had become one extensive military garrison. Horses and waggons were being requisitioned in bulk and large numbers of near naked native levies were being trained to shoot and march, to the hilarity and mirth of the regular troops. The civilian population had taken on an air of expectancy and pride as morale soared. Being amassed was a huge military force to control once and for all the warlike Zulus. The forthcoming war was also excellent for business; prices had escalated as shortages occurred and many a businessman saw a whole years trade in less than one month. With large numbers of troops moving 'up country', opportunities for further trade were most promising.

On the 15th of December 1878 the newly formed British Column, spearheaded by the 1st and 2nd Welsh Battalions, began the long march across Natal to the settlement of Helpmakaar near the Zululand border. The route from Pietermaritzburg lay across the pleasantly rolling plains of Natal, and most days the toiling column managed to travel an average of fifteen miles. Samuel and his friends felt very much at home marching across countryside which reminded them so much of home, apart from the burning heat of the day and utter dryness of the soil.

Because of the heat, they marched lightly. Each soldier's individual valise containing his military equipment was carried on the accompanying waggons which were pulled by either oxen or horses. Every soldier carried his own breech loading Martini-Henry rifle weighing nearly ten pounds, two ammunition pouches each containing twenty rounds, a barrel shaped two-pint water bottle and a 21 inch bayonet suspended from his belt. The white helmets had long since been camouflaged by rubbing them in the dark soil or stained with strong tea to make them less conspicuous to an enemy. The officers were mounted and wore similar uniforms but of a better quality. They were differentiated from the troops by their white belts or Sam

Browne belts which had become popular with officers serving in the Indian Army. All except the bare footed native levies wore excellent leather boots which could be resoled in a matter of minutes by the quartermaster's staff.

Two days before Christmas, the column arrived at Helpmakaar on an unusually hot afternoon, and within hours, the regimental lines had been neatly established. Precise neat rows of white bell tents took on the form of an established village and homely smells of fresh bread and army stew soon wafted across the camp creating an air of normality for the troops. Although everyone knew war was coming, the soldiers were excited and in remarkably high spirits. After all, the British Army was the best in the world and the Zulu army were armed only with shields and assegai stabbing spears. Nothing was going to spoil the troops' celebration of Christmas, not even the scorching mid-day temperatures blown in from the endless surrounding veldt. Samuel and his small group of friends spent the day idling the time away talking or swimming in the nearby stream. The main event of the day was a church service in the evening which was to precede the regiment's Christmas dinner.

For a few fleeting moments during the service, Samuel's mind drifted back to his home and family; but he had steeled himself to block such thoughts from his mind and sang with added gusto.

Zulu ministers had meanwhile been duly summoned to a meeting with Governor Frere which took place on the banks of the Tugela River on the 11th December 1878. The Zulu emissaries were informed that the Boers would leave the disputed land once the Zulus had compensated them for their losses, an impractical proposition for natives. They were also instructed to end the Zulu practice of indiscriminate executions by the King for his pleasure. The Zulu army was ordered to be disbanded and all Zulus were to be free to marry. Hitherto, Zulu warriors were only permitted to marry when they had defeated an enemy and 'washed' their spears in blood, a situation which resulted in a huge army hungry for war, any war. In addition , heavy fines in terms of hundreds of prime Zulu cattle which were their sole form of currency, were to be surrendered to the British for alleged minor transgressions. Lesser requirements were made including the appointment of a British Resident official to oversee the transition.

The terrified Zulu emissaries dawdled back to the king in fear of their lives at having to deliver news of the ultimatum. The news actually reached King Cetshweyo ahead of them from a white trader, John Dunn, living near Ulundi. The ultimatum was barely considered by the Zulu King as its terms were so outrageous.

The Zulus were given three weeks to comply with the British demands which Lord Chelmsford knew was impossible. In anticipation of King Cetshwayo's rejection, the assembled force was ordered to invade Zululand via Rorke's Drift.

The scene was set for war, a war which would rock the British Empire.

CHAPTER FOUR

The days following Christmas saw an ever increasing number of troops, ox waggons laden with supplies and field guns lumbering into the hitherto isolated mission station of Rorke's Drift, a short distance from Helpmakaar. Before the invasion, the site was only identified by the ramshackle cluster of wooden buildings which consisted of the Rev. de Witts' house, store room and church. Visitors to the riverside outpost were few and far between and there were no comforts to be obtained on arrival at the mission other than spiritual .

The advance camp of the Centre Column now contained over five thousand troops and covered an area roughly one square mile. The tents and covered waggons had all turned a light brown colour from the incessant clouds of dust kicked up by the struggling oxen and marching troops. The ground was sandy and strewn with boulders from the Oskarburg crag which formed the backdrop to the drift. Being slightly elevated, the guards and lookouts had a good view for some fifteen miles over to the grassy hills of Zululand. The whole scene across the Buffalo river looked inviting and peaceful. Any hint of a threat was absent.

Shortly after arriving at the drift , Samuel and his friend , Owen Thomas, were both posted from the Battalion Headquarters' Company to "G" Company which found itself desperately short of capable mounted troopers for reconnaissance duties. The two had become firm friends since those distant days of their compulsory enlistment at Brecon; they respected each other's company.

Both soldiers were known to be excellent riders with a keen eye for spotting trouble on patrols. During one of the many grooming sessions in the headquarters horse compound, Samuel had entertained the off-duty soldiers and casual on-lookers to an amusing display of bareback riding, other soldiers quickly gathered round to watch the entertainment. Encouraged by their applause, he rapidly progressed to some wilder stunts but the horse he had chosen was smarter than Samuel. While balancing on one leg on the trotting horse's back, the animal decided enough was enough and bucked hard. Samuel suddenly found himself unceremoniously hurled to the ground in a cloud of dust.

For a moment or two he was uncertain what had happened. His shoulder ached and the wind had been knocked out of him. He lay still for a moment and through the dust he could see the feet and legs of the onlookers. He took a painful deep breath and rolled over onto his hands and knees.

He rose to his feet brushing the dust from his uniform to find himself looking into the sternly monocled eye of Lieutenant Pope, Commanding Officer of "G" Company.

'You're just what I'm looking for soldier,' the officer paused thoughtfully. 'Someone performing that trick might just confuse the Zulus should they ever decide to attack us.' This sounded promising to Samuel .
'Private Thomas is even better Sir, could he come too?' he asked in a cheerful tone in the hope that he wouldn't be separated from his friend.
'We'll see what the adjutant says,' replied Lt. Pope as he set off to acquire the two possible scouts.

Samuel and Owen grinned at each other in anticipation of some real excitement. Samuel had proved to be the better rider but Owen had a canny knack of being able to interpret the tracks of both animals and men, and he could spot any trouble before it was too late. That evening they were both called to see the Regimental Orderly Officer who brusquely instructed them to collect all their belongings and equipment and report to Lt. Pope at "G" Company. Their duties were to include scouting for the Company and to act as messengers in the event of a battle.

The two friends were delighted; this was going to be much more interesting than being required to perform mundane administrative tasks whilst attached to the Battalion Headquarters. In addition, Lt. Pope was a very popular officer with a reputation for caring for his command as well as being generally held in high regard for his military competence.

"G" Company of the 2nd Battalion had been thoughtfully bivouacked next to the Buffalo river and to the north side of the main British camp well upwind of the noise, smells and effluent created by some five thousand soldiers and their accompanying oxen, horses and mules. The British troops were well trained in matters of camp hygiene with designated wash areas and properly constructed latrines. Their animal compounds were always well away from the troops' tented area. However, the supporting native regiments saw little point in such niceties and all attempts to educate them had failed. Their camp sites were accordingly appalling by any standards and their white officers despaired.

The two friends picked their way through the never ending lines of tents and cumbersome general service waggons laden with three month's supplies and equipment. Most of the soldiers were sitting in groups talking and smoking. Others were writing letters home either for themselves or for their colleagues who couldn't write. There was a gentle murmur of conversation and activity in the air which blended unobtrusively with the smells and rising smoke from the cooking areas.

They reached their destination outside the main "G" Company HQ tent and waited nervously. The camp site was stretched out across an obvious flood plain of sand with good defensive views across the river and grassy plains to the rear. It was unlikely that such a strong force would be attacked but Samuel noticed the precautions that were in force. Guard vedettes were posted about six hundred yards out from the company lines and coloured marker posts had been hammered in at intervals of one hundred yards to assist the soldiers to set their rifle sights accurately - should the enemy approach.

Lt. Pope was writing a report at his field desk as the two prospective scouts waited in expectation at the entrance to his tent, he looked up as Samuel coughed to attract attention. The officer nodded to them to enter the tent and both remained standing to attention as he explained that his Company was short of experienced scouts and messengers, he then outlined their new role for the advance into Zululand.

They were to report to Lt. Pope on a daily basis to be briefed as to their duties. During the advance into Zululand they were to be the forward eyes of their new commander and the two hundred men of the company, and any relevant information was to be relayed directly back to him. In their tent that night, both young men excitedly whispered well into the early hours before falling asleep just after midnight .

The next few days were occupied with the continuous preparations for war. 'G' company was divided into four platoons and these units of troops repeatedly rehearsed tactics and formations until they became second nature. Supplies were checked and re-checked by the Quartermaster's staff, nothing was left to chance. The officers went regularly to and from the Headquarters briefings and the near fever of anticipation grew to the level that an observer could almost feel it. Samuel and Owen spent most of their time exercising their horses by scouting the surrounding area and re-cleaning their equipment until it gleamed. They regularly visited the drift where a detachment of Royal Engineers had prepared huge wooden rafts to ferry the waggons and troops across the river. It occurred to Samuel that it would take several days to ferry the whole column across the river. Word of all this activity must have reached the Zulu King, and Samuel hoped that the far bank had been cleared of Zulus as any sudden retreat would involve a long swim back across the rock strewn river.

Whilst riding these vast and deserted plains, Samuel once again felt relaxed and at peace with his new world. He was aware of the same long-forgotten sensations he enjoyed as a child when riding his first horse over the hills at home. He had named this horse 'Pagan' to the chagrin of his parents. Now he was a mature man of twenty three years. He even felt proud of himself for turning the disaster of his relationship with Bethan into the future he could now enjoy. In his wildest childhood dreams, he never expected such drama and excitement as were now generally anticipated. He even found himself looking forward to the inevitable battle. But like all soldiers facing conflict, he nevertheless felt some apprehension. The growing infectious excitement which develops from the confidence of superiority was, however, the dominant element of his emotions.

And as a mounted scout, he would no longer have to endure the dust-choking marches within the slowly advancing column. The inevitable blistered feet from marching then standing around under the constant cajoling of the pitiless NCOs was especially frustrating when the column could only move at the pace of the slowest waggon. He felt reborn with enthusiasm and determined to enjoy this new opportunity of freedom. Sitting in his saddle with the warm dry breeze from the vastness of the veldt in his black curling hair left him in awe of the excitement Africa appeared to be promising. From then on, he would relish every opportunity to sit and stare at the distant hills wondering what adventures and opportunities lay beyond them.

The ordered routine of the advance camp was suddenly broken as the news rapidly spread like a ripple on a pond that the advance, and the awaited war, would commence the following day. No-one slept much that night.

At just after 2am on the 11th January 1879 the bugles sounded reveille. During the night a thick mist had formed and gently falling rain now reducing the visibility to twenty yards. Samuel and Owen quickly got dressed, collapsed their tent and packed it into a neat bundle ready for collection by the quartermaster's storemen who were responsible for siting and erecting each campsite. Every soldier now slept with his rifle by his side in the event of an attack and the accompanying ammunition pouch formed a convenient if hard headrest.

The soldiers were already assembling at the cookhouse for breakfast which consisted, as usual, of oatmeal cakes and rough rye bread washed down with water or weak coffee. Rations were considered by the soldiers to be very satisfactory. Each man was entitled to a daily ration of local groceries or one ounce of unsweetened lime juice, one pound each of fresh bread, biscuits and fresh or preserved meat. The long standing tradition of one half gill of medicinal rum each day was still permitted although only the regular white regiments enjoyed this facility. The native regiments were difficult enough to control at the best of times, without the added complication of drunkeness.

The next task for Samuel and Owen was to get their horses ready and by 4 am the whole Company was paraded for inspection by Lt. Pope in readiness to join the Regiment. They joined the unwieldy procession to the drift reaching it by 4.30 am.

To Samuel's surprise, the native troops were not permitted to use the ferry. The waiting regular soldiers watched and cheered as hundreds of natives at a time linked arms in one huge mass and charged at the seventy yard wide flowing river. The impetus of the warriors at the rear pushed those at the front steadily across the river; the momentum was then maintained from the far bank with those on dry land then pulling the remainder across. It was nevertheless noted by many that there were quite a number of drowned natives floating downstream.

By midday the Zulu riverbank was secure and the column gradually reassembled itself during the rest of the day ready for the onward march towards the Zulu capital of Ulundi. The mist had lifted and the hot sun rapidly dried the rain sodden army, spirits rose again. Some seventy miles of uncharted country now lay between the troops and Ulundi. Menacingly ahead, but as yet unseen, waited the largest and best prepared warrior army Africa had ever witnessed.

Moving such massive numbers of troops and equipment

forward was a tedious task with only two or so miles being travelled each day. The weather had turned hot again but during the first day the waggons repeatedly bogged down in the surface mud from the previous night's rain. The sandy ground was pitted with rocks to jam the wheels and numerous streams criss-crossed the route.The tracks made by the leading waggons rapidly eroded under the weight of their loads and the incessant pounding of countless hooves .

Roving ahead on his horse, Samuel felt sorry for his foot slogging fellows. The marching troops were clearly frustrated at the laborious stop-go pace. Their tension , and not a little fear, was intensified by the growing need to be on constant alert. Now that they were in enemy territory, the reality of an attack at any time had dramatically heightened everyone's awareness of their vulnerability. The whole trundling column extended over one mile and crawled along desperately slowly during the first few days of the invasion.

It soon became obvious to every man in the column that several weeks would elapse before the Zulu capital at Ulundi could be reached. It also became apparent to a number of senior officers that if the Zulu Army could be encouraged to attack the column en route and thereby destroyed, the King and even Ulundi itself could easily be taken by a token detachment of mounted troops. The suggestion was diplomatically passed to Lord Chelmsford who was also greatly concerned with the slow rate of progress.

Lord Chelmsford accordingly gave orders that the column would re-group itself on the high plateau below the rocky peak known as Isandhlwana, meaning "clenched fist" in Zulu. This would give the Column a strong, easily defendable base just ten miles into Zululand. The peak was just visible from Rorke's Drift and communications could easily be maintained by signal heliograph. Small streams babbled from the prominent rockface to provide an adequate supply of fresh water and the area immediately to the west was lightly wooded which ensured a sufficient supply of firewood for cooking.

A new plan was formulated.

Lord Chelmsford announced to his assembled commanders,
'The advance towards Ulundi will be achieved by leapfrogging a series of prepared and heavily defended staging camps. From each new camp, small mounted units will deploy and search for the Zulu impis. Once found, their role is to sting them into attacking the heavily defended main British positions.' His subordinates were impressed and fresh orders were issued down the line.

The British Commanders were fully aware that the Zulus would relish the opportunity of attacking the British column while it was encamped. The Zulu chiefs' favoured set piece attack would enable them to use their famous 'buffalo horns' tactics. In a typical attack, the main Zulu force would closely approach an enemy position and halt, the left and right flanks would then encircle the enemy. Once surrounded, the men would be systematically slaughtered and the surviving women and children absorbed into the Zulu nation. This simple tactic had proved so successful that it had enabled the Zulus to crush all their neighbouring tribes over a vast area. In less than fifty years they achieved the total domination of a huge tract of Southern Africa .

Due to the size and strength of the British camp at Isandhlwana, Lord Chelmsford did not consider that this tactic could possibly be implemented. Furthermore, Africa had never seen firepower on the scale possessed by the invasion force. The Martini-Henry rifle was accurate at a range of over four hundred yards, and accompanying the column was 'N' Battery Royal Artillery who were equipped with six seven-pounder guns and two rocket barrels; they also carried more than sufficient ammunition for a whole series of engagements.

The proposed camp site took its name from the prominent, almost sphinx like, rock outcrop which dominated the surrounding barren plains of scrub grass. Its south wall rose steeply to a height of four hundred feet above the plain and extended for nearly half a mile in the direction of the Nquto plateau to the east. At its base lay a flat grassy plain which spread for over five miles in the direction of Ulundi and the enemy .

The camp site occupied a naturally elevated position overlooking the well worn native track to Ulundi. The location would be easy to defend and the site offered an excellent field of fire. Any attack by the Zulus would be clearly visible during their long advance across the plain. The British would enjoy the benefit of having their backs to the rockface which also denied the Zulu the opportunity of surrounding the camp. In any event, the Zulus were only armed with spears and sticks and the troops did not anticipate any attacker getting through the volleys of rifle and artillery fire, and certainly not close enough to be within spear throwing range.

The marching soldiers felt more cheerful as they toiled up the rocky slope to the campsite, one of the officers had pointed out the similarity between the strange shape of Isandhlwana and the sphinx dog collars worn by the soldiers on their lapels. It was a good omen and spirits were rising.

By mid afternoon on the 20th January 1879, the new position was well established. About five hundred yards to the south of Isandlhwana was a small rocky hill manned by lookouts and the adjoining plateau was already occupied by the 1st Battalion. Like Samuel's 2nd Battalion, the 1st were also recruited exclusively from the valleys of South Wales, and it was not uncommon for many Welsh families to have sons and nephews serving in both units. The 2nd Battalion were sited half way along the rockface and two hundred yards forward onto the plain. Between the two sister Welsh regiments were 'N' Battery, Royal Artillery, and a squadron of Imperial Mounted Infantry. To the left and north of the 2nd Battalion were two battalions of the 3rd Regiment Natal Native Contingent consisting of locally recruited natives sympathetic to the British cause.

The Column Headquarters and Lord Chelmsford's tent were situated immediately behind the 2nd Battalion next to the rockface and the soldiers were able to observe all the comings and goings of senior officers during the evening. The total fighting strength of the column amounted to over five thousand soldiers of whom nearly two thousand were highly trained Europeans. The ammunition carts containing five hundred thousand rifle rounds were strategically sited to the rear of each unit under the jealous guard of their respective Company Quartermaster Sergeant and their staffs. No army had previously reached such a state of well prepared readiness.

'G' Company were in the midst of erecting their tents when Quartermaster Bloomfield called for Owen and Samuel. Both ran to him in anticipation of their orders.

'Right my lucky lads,' he bellowed, 'out you go and patrol up to and around that conical hill out there.' He pointed to the small round hill set on its own in the centre of the plain, 'If you see Zulus, ride like hell and report, you'll be relieved at midnight.'

The two friends sped off to the Company horse lines and prepared their mounts ready for the first exploration of the plain. They rode out through their own company lines to their comrades' good natured shouts of,
'Keep you eyes peeled!' and,
'Don't get lost!'

Then they set off. They rode together but kept some twenty yards apart in case they came across Zulu scouts hiding in the grass. During the intense heat of the afternoon both riders found it difficult to concentrate, there was no shade to offer horse or rider any respite from the baking rocks and shale over which they rode or from the sun beating down directly overhead. Visibility beyond one mile was poor due to mirages from the shimmering heat and on several occasions they were nearly convinced by their imaginations that the optical tricks of the heat were Zulus creeping through the grass towards them .

59

The plain was crossed by several small streams or dongas which had eroded their way through the soft soil creating gullies up to ten feet deep. Both riders quickly realised that these gullies could easily hide many hundreds of Zulus and both became acutely aware of their vulnerability so far from the main camp. By the time they were relieved, neither had actually seen a Zulu but many of the wild animal calls after dark had sent numerous shivers of undiluted fear down their spines. By the time they crawled into their bedrolls they were truly exhausted.

The following day saw constant activity with additional store waggons arriving from Rorke's Drift and troop positions being strengthened. After a quiet morning grooming their horses, Samuel and Owen were sent forward on another reconnaissance. It was just before lunchtime and both had been supplied with cold salt beef and bread to tide them over during the day. This time they were less fearful of what they might find. The overwhelming confidence of the column was almost total and the outcome of the battle, if it ever came, was now a foregone conclusion in every soldier's mind. The air of superiority was so great that standard precautions against attack were not enforced, no rock breastworks had been built and the broken glass normally scattered in front of a position to deter bare native feet was missing. The normally obligatory range marker posts in front of the expected field of fire were still packed on the waggons.

About three miles out from the main camp, the two scouts sat down by the side of a stream for their lunch meal of bread and cold meat. Afterwards, as they were cleaning their knives in the sand, they observed a large detachment of troops leaving the campsite heading out along the track towards Ulundi.

Samuel left Owen to maintain the lookout and rode towards one of the outriders to ascertain the purpose of such a large patrol. He learned from an accompanying forward scout that it was a large advance party under the command of Major Dartnell. It consisted of one company

of mounted troops together with sixteen companies of the
3rd Natal Native Contingent, their role was to locate and
provoke the elusive Zulu impi. About one hour later the
troops had disappeared into the far hills and the
remainder of the afternoon was uneventful.

At about 5 pm Samuel and Owen were alerted by the
sound of gunfire in the direction of the departed troops.
Neither had any idea what was happening so Owen
immediately galloped back to report to Lt. Pope while
Samuel continued to strain his eyes searching the distance
for signs of activity. The firing lasted nearly an hour but
nothing untoward could be seen .

Being alert to the possibility of an attack, Samuel
quickly spotted the lone rider far out on the horizon
heading back towards the main camp. He decided to
investigate and rode off further out across the plain to
head him off. The dusty figure approaching was a scout
from the Natal Mounted Police and the pair fell in beside
each other .

'What's happening?' asked Samuel excitedly.
'Zulus, they're everywhere!' panted the nearly exhausted
scout.

He quickly related that the Zulu impi had been
discovered and engaged, and that there were 'many
thousand' Zulus. He reassured Samuel that the initial
engagement had been successful although inconclusive.
The scout was returning to Lord Chelmsford with an
urgent request for reinforcements before the Zulus
reassembled, after a brief chat with Samuel, the scout rode
off in a cloud of dust .

Samuel noticed that the rider's horse was nearly
exhausted but he was certain that it could manage the last
two miles to camp. Samuel trotted his horse back to the
previous vantage point just as Owen arrived back to
confirm that the column HQ officers had also heard the
distant battle and were awaiting developments. The
remainder of their patrol was uneventful but on returning

to camp at midnight, they discovered that 'G' Company had been placed on forward picquet duty some two thousand yards out from the main position. They then spent the next half hour searching through the darkness for their colleagues somewhere out on the plain.

Picquet duty involved half 'G' Company being 'on alert' for two hours with the remainder sleeping under the stars. The nights were always bitterly cold and with only one blanket per man for protection and only one hot meal at midday, the duty was not generally highly regarded. As Samuel and Owen had been on patrol for most of the day they were excused further guard duty and both enjoyed an undisturbed night's sleep. The soldiers were still excited by the earlier distant action and those on guard duty peered into the darkness with added enthusiasm. Each soldier had seventy rounds of ammunition and one unopened ammunition crate was located in readiness on the Company waggon adjacent to Lt. Pope's tent.

During the night Maj. Dartnell had again urgently requested further assistance from the main column. Lord Chelmsford feared that a full Zulu attack on Dartnell's comparatively small force could compel Dartnell to withdraw and the opportunity of engaging the Zulus was too attractive to miss. Chelmsford decided to reinforce Dartnell's advancing column at dawn and meet the Zulus in greater strength.

'G' Company were stood to at dawn which broke just after 4 am. There had been no sightings of the Zulus during the night. There was, however, considerable activity back in the main camp area and shortly after 5am the lookouts could see their parent 2nd Battalion, reinforced by mounted infantry and native troops, forming up ready to march out. Lt. Pope rode back to ascertain the nature of events. He returned half an hour later with the information that Lord Chelmsford was riding out with half the main column strength to support Major Darnell's harassment of the Zulu impis.

Left to defend the main camp were the bulk of the 1st

Battalion supported by other British units, an estimated 822 well armed European troops, together with a similar number of the Natal Native Contingency. Over one hundred waggons, their animals and all the tents were left behind to give the impression to any distant Zulu scouts that the camp was still fully manned. Lt. Pope was greatly irritated that his 'G' Company were to be left behind while the remainder of their 2nd Battalion were to march with Lord Chelmsford to confront the Zulus. 'G' Company watched in indignant silence as the reinforcements marched by and an hour later they disappeared into the hills to the East. 'G' Company then settled down to lie in the warming sun and wait for breakfast. Lt. Pope decided that two days of mainly cold rations entitled his men to a hot breakfast, it would also offset their disappointment at being left behind and the fires were accordingly lit in the cooking area .

Just as they were settling down to breakfast a native scout approached from the main camp to report that a large force of Zulus were approaching the main camp from the North. Lt. Pope was puzzled by this curious information. Lord Chelmsford and Dartnell were looking for the Zulus to the East. He felt the first flicker of apprehension and immediately ordered his men to rapidly finish their breakfasts and immediately prepare for a return back to the main camp. In the midst of their preparations they heard the bugle call of 'Stand To' being played to alert the remaining companies along the base of Isandhlwana. There was still no sign of a single Zulu .

'G' Company marched steadily back to take up their allocated defensive position some four hundred yards in front of their absent parent Battalion line. In the event of an attack, 'G' Company would open fire first and gauge the strength and will of the Zulus. The remaining troops of the column were already extended fifty yards out from the camp and standing almost shoulder to shoulder. The thin defensive line extended right across the 900 yards of the camp length and when nothing further happened the soldiers again began to relax . The veldt remained barren for as far as the eye could see.

'The officers are getting jumpy,' shouted one of the soldiers. Those within hearing distance laughed. Rifles were carefully laid down, helmets removed and soldiers were soon to be seen sitting around and smoking their pipes. Lunchtime approached and each platoon of 'G' Company was recalled in turn to the Company kitchen for a hot meal. Rumours in the main camp were rife;

'Lord Chelmsford and his reinforcements were all dead.'
'The Zulus had surrendered without further fight.'
'The Zulu army is approaching.'

Still the camp maintained the air of total confidence.

While 'G' Company were being fed, several hundred Zulus were observed from the main Headquarters to be moving eastwards along the Nquto Plateau about four miles away. A large chasing party consisting of a company of mounted troopers led by Lt. Col Durnford was rapidly assembled to attack this force. Within a few minutes the Zulus disappeared and Durnford set off in hot pursuit. Samuel and Owen were called for by Lt. Pope and instructed to ride for one mile out onto the plain to watch and report any developments.

The two friends galloped back across the veldt to their previous vantage point and settled down to wait events. Owen led the horses to the stream to drink while Samuel lay down on a rock to scan the horizon with his telescope. There was nothing new to be seen.

Samuel lay in the hot sun and felt very inclined to doze after all the excitement of the last few days. The sound of the babbling stream wending its way through the rocks was very soporific and he could hear the horses contentedly drinking. He mustn't sleep, he knew that sleeping on guard duty was a flogging offence and stirred himself. Owen had taken off his boots and was sitting on a nearby rock with his feet immersed in the cool water. 'Boys will be boys,' thought Samuel and considered joining his friend.

'What will you do when this is all over?' asked Owen. Samuel thought for a moment.

'Perhaps I'll make my fortune picking up diamonds or prospecting for gold,' he said thoughtfully. 'Then I'll go home and take over the farm; do you want to come and work for me?'

'No thanks!' replied Owen, 'I'll get my own place, get married and have children.'

'Anyone in mind?' asked Samuel idly.

'Several; depends on who is left when we get back,' laughed Owen.

Samuel picked up the telescope and again scanned the plain ahead, there was still nothing new to see apart from the miles of dry yellow grass gently moving in the afternoon breeze. He idly moved the telescope to his left and towards the plateau. Through the eyepiece, Samuel noticed what appeared to be a huge nest of ants erupting somewhere in front of him. He lowered the telescope and looked at the ground immediately in front of where he lay. African ants had a ferocious bite especially when they managed to get into one's clothing. But there were no ants and he could see nothing unusual. He curiously picked up the telescope again to investigate and immediately saw the creeping mass of black dots. Samuel was stunned by what he saw. He was watching the entire Zulu army descending from the plateau some four miles distant. He felt his body go very cold as a shiver of fear spread down his back.

The whole far horizon had become a mass of swarming Zulus steadily approaching Isandhlwana from the north.

'Bloody Hell!' he muttered. He urgently shouted out to Owen and pointed to the plateau.

'What is it?' Owen called back.

'Zulus,' shouted Samuel, 'bloody thousands of them and they're all coming this way!'

Owen leapt to his feet and picked up his boots, he struggled to get into his boots while unhitching the two horses from the knot of grass where they were tied.

'Don't lose them now for Christ's sake!' urged Samuel. Owen carefully led the horses up to where Samuel was standing. Samuel calmly pointed to the plateau and handed Owen the telescope.

'Jesus wept!' was all Owen could say. With the naked eye little could be seen other than the very dark shadow spreading down from the distant hills. The approaching Zulu army then began to fan out across the veldt directly in front of them.

'You know what's happened?' Samuel said quietly, 'they've hidden up and waited until our force divided,' he paused and thought rapidly. 'Is it going to be us or Lord Chelmsford ?' he asked earnestly.
'Perhaps they've already done for Lord Chelmsford,' replied Owen, 'and now they're coming after the main column.'
'It will take them at least an hour to get here. Let's get back,' retorted Samuel.

They spurred their horses into action and rode furiously back to 'G' Company. They arrived back in a cloud of dust and urgently sought out Lt. Pope. He came out of his tent and listened attentively before immediately dispatching Owen back to the main camp with the warning that the Zulus were approaching in considerable strength. Within a matter of minutes the urgent 'Stand To' bugle calls could be heard echoing back from the rockface and shortly afterwards the whole garrison began to take up defensive positions. The sound of steady distant gunfire could now be heard as the outposts on the edge of the plateau to the North began firing at the approaching hoards until they were forced to retreat back to the camp.

The Zulus were now spread out and approaching at a fast run to the left as well as swinging round to form up directly in front of the camp. Their front ranks extended over one mile wide and their depth could not be accurately assessed, but still they poured over the edge of the hills. Lt. Pope was standing up in the stirrups of his horse watching with growing consternation as the Zulus approached, his monocle had dropped from his eye and he looked round for his second-in-command, Lt. Richard Smith. He shouted to him.

'Zulus, they're coming straight for the camp, assemble the company and retreat back at the double!' Lt. Pope had never seen such a multitude and it was readily apparent that even his Company was powerless to stop these numbers. It would, he thought, take the combined firepower of the main camp to stop them. Nearly one thousand rifles firing carefully aimed volleys would easily stop them. Nevertheless, he urged his officers and Sergeants to make haste.

The soldiers needed no encouraging as the distant Zulu masses could now be clearly seen by everyone. The Zulu commanders had assembled an attacking force of over twenty five thousand warriors and, by using the ravines which cut across the distant high plateau, they had been able to hide from the eyes of the roving British scouts. Shortly after midday, an unsuspecting mounted trooper received the shock of his life when he peered over the lip of a mile long ravine to see the whole Zulu army sitting silently. He fired some warning shots into the massed warriors before riding for his life. The Zulus stirred like an angry hornets' nest and the orders rapidly went to the Induna Chiefs to attack.

On the plain, the air had gone still in the afternoon heat and a faint humming noise could be heard from the direction of the attack. As 'G' Company retreated back towards the camp they again heard the 'General Alarm' being sounded, the officers came running and riding to the Headquarters tent with considerable urgency. Having delivered his warning, Owen returned to 'G' Company just as Sergeant Williams of the Headquarter's staff rode in at speed calling for a messenger to alert Lord Chelmsford. Sgt. Williams was an overweight, red faced little man who had never been known to do anything very fast. Today was the exception and Lt. Pope thought the sergeant was going to burst with the effort of the short ride. Lt. Pope handed the envelope to Owen.

'Get this immediately to Lord Chelmsford, the main impi is approaching, don't get stopped by anything as it's life or death to us.'

Owen nodded and stuffed the dispatch into his saddle pouch, he was now grimly aware of his colleague's plight. He drove his horse towards the track to Ulundi taken earlier by Lord Chelmsford. Half a mile from the camp he slowed his horse to a canter, he wasn't sure how far he might have to go and there was no point exhausting his horse yet. As he rode further from the camp he could clearly see the massed ranks of Zulus to his left sweeping across the plain towards Isandhlwana. He attempted to assess their strength but gave up, they kept coming down off the high plateau in block formation and Owen felt distinctly uneasy out on the plain away from the safety of his friends. To Owen's astonishment he saw Col. Durnford's returning patrol now retreating rapidly before the advancing Zulus.

It appeared that Durnford was about to be engulfed by a sweeping detachment of the encirlcing Zulus. Owen reigned in and stopped on a small rise half a mile from Durnford. He watched intently as the soldiers fired volley after volley into the Zulus at a range of about three hundred yards. Wave upon wave of Zulus fell, their places swiftly taken by others and the whole black mass swept on relentlessly in their attempt to complete the encirclement. After about ten volleys the attack faltered and stopped. Durnford was skillfully controlling the withdrawal back to the main column but he was clearly in great danger of being surrounded. So, suddenly, was Owen.

He saw that he had been observed and some twenty Zulus were sprinting through the knee high grass towards him. Their black and white leather shields were held high and the sun glinted on their razor sharp assegai blades. Their impressive feather head-dresses had the effect of making each Zulu appear to be over seven feet tall. Owen goaded his mount into action away from danger and easily rode around the group and on in the general direction of the original track. He was now out of sight of Durnford but the sound of renewed volley fire could still clearly be heard behind him.

The sound of the battle grew more distant as he swung into the hills. At about 2 pm Owen saw a small detachment of horsemen and he galloped towards them. They were patrolling Mounted Infantry from the command of Lt. Col. Russell, a senior member of Lord Chelmsford's staff. Owen took directions and ten minutes later he personally handed the message to Lt. Col. Russell himself. The officer grimaced when he read the contents and put the document down on his field desk.

'Get me a messenger for Lord Chelmsford,' he called to his adjutant who passed the order on. Owen stood by the side of the desk and let his eyes fall on the report. It stated simply.

> 'HEAVY FIRING TO LEFT OF THE CAMP.
> CANNOT MOVE AT PRESENT.'

There was no mention of the imminent attack on the main camp. This surprised Owen, on the other hand, it was not for him to give advice.

'What shall I do now Sir?' asked Owen. The officer looked at Owen's dog collars.
'You're 2nd Battalion aren't you? Follow the track and join your unit there; we'll be making back when we get our orders.'

Owen saluted him, remounted and followed the track round the low hill to his battalion who were still formed up as a marching column. He reported to the adjutant who listened in near disbelief as Owen related the sequence of events over the last few hours. At that point the sound of distant cannon fire could be heard from the direction of Isandhlwana .

'Join the Headquarters Company boyo,' said the adjutant, 'and hold on to your horse , you might need it if things get bad.' Owen wasn't sure how serious that comment was, but for several hours there were no fresh orders.

* * * * * * * * * *

Back at the main camp everyone was waiting for the gathering Zulus to attack. The drummer boys were chatting excitedly, this was real adventure. Regular firing could still be heard on the far left flank and it was getting steadily closer. By now the garrison had formed itself into a semi-circle around the camp with the two ends formed up against the base of the cliff face, this would prevent the enemy getting behind the line.

The firing was coming from the outlying scouts who were rapidly retreating back to camp. Samuel and 'G' Company were still positioned four hundred yards out in front of the main defences directly ahead of the Headquarters area. The Zulus were now massed approximately two miles from the main camp and doubts about the British tactics began to occur to Col. Pulleine and his officers. Perhaps the defending line might be stretched too thinly and too far out to be able to withstand a sustained attack from such a multitude.

While the officers earnestly talked and pondered over the problem, the Zulus surged forward and everyone instinctively crouched down as the Royal Artillery battery behind their vantage point opened fire. Still the Zulus came on and at a range of half a mile Lt. Pope, monocle now firmly in place, gave the order to prepare the first volley. Samuel was still holding his horse which he quickly but loosely tied to the ammunition waggon, then urgently joined the front line .

'What are you doing here?' asked one of his platoon jokingly.
'Safest place with you lot about to fire!' he replied

teasingly.

The chanting of the Zulus could now clearly be heard. Their head feather plumes swayed in unison and their warpaint made them appear terrifyingly ferocious. The European soldiers were now looking at their adversary with considerable respect; the massed ranks of Zulus were not intimidated by the artillery fire and continued their advance. Intermittently but in unison they crashed their assegai spears against their stiffened leather shields and let out a fearful roar which was accompanied by stamping feet. The sound reminded those whose homes were near the coalmines of the hissing, pounding steam engines at the pit heads. The effect of the stamping was to create a shock wave through the ground, every soldier felt personally intimidated as the ground beneath his feet vibrated. The first ripples of fear began to be apparent; two of the company drummer boys began to cry. These boys were the orphaned sons of soldiers and in battle their task was to issue ammunition as required. Most of them were aged from ten years and none had ever seen a battle before. Ordinarily they would be thus employed until the age of sixteen when they would join the regular army.

Lt. Pope gave the long awaited order to the platoon officers and almost in unison the orders came .

'Range six hundred yards, aim, FIRE!'

The impact on the front rank of Zulus was as effective as taking a freshly sharpened scythe to standing corn. But as the front rank fell those warriors behind ran over the fallen to take their place. Terrifyingly they came on. Volley after volley was fired but to no avail.

Lt. Pope could see Durnford's column to his right falling back on the main camp but they were still over half a mile away. He could see that they were in very great danger of being overwhelmed if their retreat slowed. During the next two minutes 'G' Company fired some ten further well aimed volleys and this seemed to slow the advancing black wall. Lt. Pope could see that his own company was also in growing danger of being encircled and gave the order to continue the withdrawal back towards the safety of the main camp.

The Zulus on their South flank turned their attention from 'G' Company to Durnford's struggling troop. It appeared to Lt. Pope that Durnford's volleys were becoming ragged and the terrible realization came to him that they might be running out of ammunition. 'G' Company still had over 30 rounds per man and without further delay he ordered the company to advance towards Durnford's position firing a volley every fifty yards. Once again the Zulus surged forward and Lt. Pope realised the folly of his action and re-ordered the retreat. The Company held together and, so far, no casualties had been suffered.

As 'G' Company continued to withdraw, Quartermaster Bloomfield was frustrated with having to reload the waggon with the heavy ammunition case he had just unloaded. He stood on the back of the waggon to supervise the loading. While straightening up to ease his back, the top of his head blew off as he was struck dead by a stray bullet from a Zulu rifle. He slumped in a heap over the side of the waggon and only merited a casual glance from those nearby. The frightening pressure from the Zulus was now mounting, they appeared to be rapidly closing around the whole camp nothwithstanding the steady volley fire from nearly one thousand rifles.

Suddenly the Zulus changed tactics. To a man they lay down in the grass and virtually disappeared .

'Christ, where the hell are they?' shouted a soldier lowering his rifle.
'Wait for it!' ordered a sergeant, 'they're creeping up on us!'

The mass of Zulus rose once more. Again, there was a mighty roar and a thunderous crash of assegai spears on shields. Each time they performed this action they re-emerged some fifty yards closer to the soldiers. Each time the order 'FIRE!' was shouted and hundreds of warriors fell. Still they came on .

It was now evident to the camp commander, Lt. Col. Pulleine, that his total defence was in peril of being overwhelmed. He gave the order for the bugles to sound the 'Retire' call. By now the regular volleys of the defenders had given way to uncoordinated fire. The platoons urgently formed themselves into defensive squares for the final withdrawal into the camp itself. By now the Zulus were less than two hundred yards from the retreating British line urgently reforming itself in front of the tented area of the main camp. The whole front line had now reduced to three hundred yards in length and the soldiers took comfort from their colleagues who were now standing shoulder to shoulder and two deep. Casualties were still remarkably light. Lt. Pope shouted for Samuel who was now part of the defending line.

Samuel crouchingly ran over to his officer. Lt. Pope had the look of despair written on his face.

'I think we might be done for Laddie; get your horse to the Battalion tent,' Lt. Pope paused for breath, 'and if we are dead men - then save the Colours.'

'Yes Sir!' replied Samuel firmly . Turning, he ran back to the retreating waggon for his horse while keeping his head well down. Samuel heard an order from his sergeant.

'Rapid Fire At Will!' and saw with dismay that the leading Zulus were less than fifty yards away. He leapt into the saddle and keeping as low as he could, galloped his horse back into the camp area and on to the Battalion Headquarter's tent housing the Colours.

Behind him the disaster was almost complete. On the very spot where Samuel had last stood, the terrifying front wave of warriors crashed against the defenders in savage hand to hand fighting. There was a brief blur as red jackets rapidly sank under the onslaught of shining black bodies until 'G' Company were totally engulfed by the stabbing

73

mass of warriors.

Not one member of "G" Company survived.

The Zulus rushed on to the main camp defenders, propelled by the sheer weight of the warriors behind. With their assegais stabbing and slashing they engaged the main line of troops in ferocious hand to hand fighting. For a few minutes the bloody bayonets held the Zulus at bay until a hail of spears from within the Zulu ranks punctured the British line. The leading warriors broke through the gap turning left and right behind the troops so that the Zulus were now able to slash at the soldiers from behind. They fell in clusters.

The only steady rifle fire was now coming from the area being defended to the south of the line by the five companies of the 1st Battalion left behind that morning by Lord Chelmsford. Samuel saw that their defending line was also in disarray, and Zulus were breaking through and charging into the tented area behind their line to attack the surviving soldiers from the rear. Samuel jumped down from his horse and entered the empty tent. At the far end he saw both Colours cased and standing on a wooden plinth. He picked one up and realised for the first time that it was heavy and ungainly. Saving both Colours was an impossibility for one man so he selected the Colour on the right. He remounted his horse holding the Colour staff like a lance so that, if necessary, he could use it as a battering ram to force his way out.

The Zulus were steadily overwhelming the defenders. The noise of the terrible battle rang in his ears; the crash of gunfire was mixed with men screaming. Both sides were shouting, and the whole battlefield appeared to Samuel like a scene from hell. For the dying soldiers , it was hell itself. As he galloped along the lines of tents to make good his escape, Samuel could see the Zulus slaughtering the remaining troops. It was clear that the battle was irrevocably lost.

He galloped past the remaining survivors of the 1st

Battalion and saw that they too were now surrounded. Their firing had virtually ceased and the remaining soldiers still standing were desperately fighting back to back. Samuel sped over the plateau beside Isandlhwana and headed down the track back towards Rorke's Drift. The bodies of soldiers who had attempted to escape lay in clumps at irregular intervals and it was soon apparent to Samuel that the Zulus had also sealed off the only escape route. It occurred to him that a considerable force of Zulus were probably just ahead of him on the way to attack the Rorke's Drift garrison. He shuddered as he rode past the bodies of soldiers whose jackets had been removed or torn open. The soldiers' bellies were slit wide open according to the Zulu custom of releasing the living spirit from the dead.

Samuel became accutely aware of his own predicament when a small group of four Zulus rushed at him from the cover of some nearby rocks. He instinctively fired his rifle at the first Zulu and the bullet went straight through the charging warrior instantly killing him and one immediately behind . The next Zulu fell under his horse's hooves as Samuel spurred the frightened animal into action. One Zulu remained and defiantly stood his ground directly in the path of the charging horse. Samuel lowered the Colour staff like a medieval knight in a jousting tournament and the brass lion finial on the top of the Colour pole caught the Zulu squarely on the chest collapsing his rib cage and knocking him heavily to the ground. The warrior's outstretched spear struck the horse but was knocked away by the animal's flying hooves.

Two hundred yards further along the track Samuel reined in and paused to listen. He had to think calmly and logically if he was going to survive.

Ahead and towards the gorge he could hear the occasional shot , a muffled scream and then the sound of hundreds of spears being thudded against shields. His view was obscured beyond about one hundred yards due to the slope dropping away and the tall yellow grass. There were also clumps of thorn trees which could easily conceal the enemy. His immediate thought was to take cover until nightfall, although it was still only mid-afternoon and anyway, Rorke's Drift still lay at least ten miles away. Perhaps he could hide, but what of his horse? If Rorke's Drift was taken, then he would need the horse to reach the safety of Natal. If he stayed near the horse it would attract the Zulus who would undoubtedly be on the lookout for survivors .

He rode over to a clump of waist high grass and dismounted. He noticed his horse was wheezing and then saw the steady flow of frothy blood about its mouth. One of the ambushing Zulus had managed to stab the horse and the blade must have penetrated its lung. Samuel's decision was made for him, he pulled his rifle from its scabbard and, as an afterthought, took the hunk of lunchtime bread from the saddlebag .

'I can't shoot you - the Zulus will hear,' he mumbled to the horse. He slapped the beast on its rump and pushed it away; the animal paused, then cantered off back up the hill towards the carnage. 'Stupid animal,' he thought but then realized that it would naturally return to the main camp horse compound .

It dawned on Samuel that his red jacket made him highly visible and he removed it quickly. His white undershirt was nearly as obvious so he pulled it off and rubbed it in the red earth to dull its brightness. He pulled it back on then stuffed the neck of his shirt with long grass to camouflage his face and settled down to consider matters. He protectively lay down on the Colour and peered through the grass. Within minutes, several long columns of Zulus trotted past his hiding place and headed down the track from the battlefield; all were looking intently towards the Drift but none came his way. Half a mile back up the track in the direction of Isandhlwana there was an unreal silence punctuated by the occasional shot. A plume of black smoke was slowly rising from the camp area; with some luck this smoke might alert the small garrison at Rorke's Drift.

The time passed slowly and Samuel nibbled his bread; he hadn't realised how hungry he was. Hiding in the grass, he could not escape the terrible memories of the battle. His friends were all dead and he shuddered as the vision of the ghastly slaughter played on his mind. How could such a well armed force be annihilated so quickly? Samuel could only think that the soldiers had aimed too high at the Zulus' head plumes; either that or there must be many thousands of dead Zulus around Isandhlwana .

Eventually it began to get dark. Samuel slowly rose to his feet and cautiously looked around. He could see nothing to indicate any danger. He still possessed the Colour and in its present form it constituted too great a burden. He gently untied the leather throngs and pulled off the case. He then released the lacing securing the Colour to the staff and neatly folded the flag. It then occurred to him that, being predominately dark green, the Colour wrapped round his body would further camouflage him until darkness fell, as well as keeping him warm at night.

It would make an excellent cape.

CHAPTER FIVE.

During the late afternoon, sporadic rifle fire could be heard coming from about a mile ahead of Samuel's intended route to safety. At one stage several hurried volleys echoed around the hills which indicated that at least one group of escaping soldiers had remained intact until they reached the Buffalo River gorge. He feared for his comrades' survival if the Zulus had succeeded in cutting off their escape. Samuel slowly stood up, stretched the stiffness out of his limbs and looked around.The sight of some twenty or so bloodied soldiers' bodies not fifty yards from his hiding place made him shudder. The ritual mutilation of their corpses brought home to Samuel the chilling reality of his predicament. There was obviously a large force of Zulus between himself and Rorke's Drift. Behind him the victorious Zulu army was probably still plundering the main camp stores and arming itself with British rifles.

And what of Lord Chelmsford? Samuel reasoned that the Column Commander and the two Welsh Battalions had, in all probability, also been defeated. If not, why had the Zulus attacked the main camp? The whole situation was a complete mystery to him and if he didn't escape he might never know. Samuel also pondered the possibility that he might be the only survivor who had witnessed the whole battle.

Using all his field skills and with his senses straining to detect the slightest hint of danger, he began to move quietly away from his hiding place in the long grass. He felt horribly vulnerable. The fly covered bodies of escaping fugitives from the battle lay at intervals along the track and in the nearby grass. All had been mutilated and stripped of their weapons and ammunition. It was now evident that a large force of Zulus had swept around the back of Isandhlwana to cut off the escape route to Rorke's Drift; they had clearly been very effective, and Samuel grudgingly admired the Zulus bravery and military tactics.

There was no detectable movement anywhere, there were no animal noises or birds singing , only the sound of the flies on the corpses reminded Samuel that he was awake. The pervasive presence of death hung in the air and in spite of the suffocating heat, Samuel shivered.

He cautiously moved on.   The downward slope became more wooded and waterlogged from the myriad of small streams trickling towards the river below. It then   fell steeply away dropping into a rocky gorge through which the Buffalo River flowed. The river was about five hundred yards ahead and several hundred feet below his position but he could already hear the roar of water as it cascaded through the gorge. Samuel saw that he would have to leave the security of the long grass for some two hundred yards to reach the trees nearer the water. Once there, he would have some cover to enable him to   reach the boulder strewn river. He set off cautiously   in the crouching position   with the Colour held tightly under his left arm and after about half an hour he reached the marshy ground next to the torrent .

The sound of water cascading through the rocky gorge would cover any noise he might make clambering over the rocks. It was still light enough for him to be observed   by any passing Zulu scouts and the rocks afforded him a better hiding place until darkness fell. He remembered previously crossing the river with the invasion force about a mile upstream   so Rorke's Drift could only be another five miles or so away.

Samuel was exhausted, the demands and shocks of the day had begun to take their toll. He again felt a gripping feeling of terror well up inside his body and it took a few moments   to calm down. His arms and legs were going stiff   and his chest ached from the day's exertion. Perhaps he could rest for a moment hidden as he was by the boulders. He placed the precious Colour next to where he sat. Apart from himself, the Colour might be all that survived from his once glorious battalion.

He sat staring at the cascading water then involuntarily froze as a weak human cry came from behind the next big boulder. Samuel thought fast; if it was a Zulu he dared not use his rifle for fear of attracting others. If he stayed where he was he risked detection as the Zulus would investigate any sounds and anyway, they would certainly use the boulders to cross this stretch of the river.

Samuel fixed his bayonet and, holding his rifle at the ready, he moved forward to investigate. If it was a Zulu it might be possible to bayonet him; even two or three shouldn't be too much of a problem as long as there weren't others in the immediate vicinity. Samuel crept slowly round the rocks in the direction of the cry; his heart was pounding in anticipation as he prepared to use the bayonet or the rifle butt as a club.

Instead, to his utter relief, he found a badly wounded European NCO of the Natal Native Contingent. The man had been repeatedly speared through his shoulder and chest and was delirious. Samuel shuddered as he then saw the man's gaping stomach wound. He had been given up as dead by the Zulus after being subjected to a half hearted disembowelling. The man was huddled against a small rock moaning and clutching at his deeply lacerated stomach. Samuel knelt down beside the man who was incoherently muttering about going to church. There was nothing Samuel could do, there was nothing even a surgeon could do. It was obvious that he must put the agonized man out of his misery. His hand went to the bayonet still on his rifle but not even Samuel could face that prospect. He lay the man down on the shale and gently rested his head onto a flat stone. Picking up a large rock, Samuel held it high above his head and then let it fall onto the wounded man's forehead. The man's legs jerked convulsively but to Samuel's horror, he was still alive and moaned loudly. He felt sick as he picked up the rock again but this time all his strength went into the blow. As the rock stuck, the skull visibly distorted. Samuel knelt down and felt for the man's pulse; this time he was dead.

Samuel felt physically sick but his mind cleared

miraculously as he became aware of the threatening presence of someone else behind him. He turned round slowly and found himself looking up into the barrel of a Martini-Henry rifle held by another white NNC corporal. Behind him stood yet another NCO. Above the blanketing roar of the water, the two NCOs had been able to get within ten feet of Samuel. Both stood staring at him with astonishment and unadulterated hatred in their eyes.

'Robbing the wounded is one thing, murdering them is a gallow's job!' shouted the one with the rifle to his friend. The other man nodded. Samuel was stunned by the accusation. He began to stutter out a reply but the corporal approached him and painfully jammed the rifle point into his chest.

'We were going to get him back and now you've murdered him!' he shouted. The corporal paused for thought before going on. 'We'll take you back instead.' He turned to his companion who had just noticed the Colour flag on the rock .

'What's this?' exclaimed the second NCO as he went over to the rock. 'Look Corp , he's got away with one of the Colours, we've got ourselves a real one here!' The enormity of their capture began to dawn on the corporal; there would be praise enough here for such a capture, there might even be a promotion. The junior NCO awaited his superior's orders.

'Go and warn the others!' shouted the corporal, indicating up the far bank, 'and get some help to bring in Jones's body, I'll stay here until you get back and don't be long!' The corporal was fully aware that the Zulus could come back at any time. The NCO scrambled off across the rocks and Samuel noticed that the Colour was still in a heap on the ground. Samuel sat down utterly dejected by the twist that events were taking. Coupled with his own exhaustion he began not to care.

The corporal sat himself down on the top of a high boulder and watched the progress of his colleague as he scrambled off the rocks and disappeared into the trees on the far bank. All the time he kept the loaded rifle pointing directly at Samuel. The minutes went by and gradually it got darker. Samuel began to think of a way to escape, he might be able to scramble round the boulders then dive into the swift flowing torrent but he would first need to distract the corporal for a few moments. Above the steady roar of the water, there was the single, almost inaudible sound of a soft thud and Samuel wearily looked up. The corporal was sitting bolt upright and his eyes were nearly popping out of his head. There was an assegai shaft sticking out of his back and he slowly began to fall forward. Samuel moved swiftly, his tiredness instantly forgotten. He gathered up the Colour and, keeping below the line of the boulders, darted away from the scene. He paused about twenty yards away. He heard the babble of shouting voices from where the corporal now lay writhing on the boulder and saw two Zulus scramble up to where the wounded corporal lay. One turned him over and pulled his spear out of the terrified man. Both then roughly stripped him of his red jacket. He feebly tried to ward them off with his hands as they gored and slashed at his stomach with their assegais.

Samuel was transfixed by the bloody scene. Then the corporal lay still. One of the Zulus then noticed the body of the other dead soldier. He saw that the man's head was crushed and that his spirit had already been released and accordingly ignored him. He did pick up Samuel's rifle and after examining it, put it over his shoulder. Both Zulus then sat down on the same boulder previously occupied by the corporal as though waiting for something else to happen.

Hardly daring to breathe, Samuel seized the unexpected opportunity to make good his escape. He slowly crawled away from the two Zulus until he reached the river bank and was relieved that the noise of the torrent masked any sounds he made. He furtively looked for a place to climb the steep bank. There was nowhere to hand, he had to move further downstream with the chilling water up to his chest until he found the roots of an overhanging tree to haul himself out.

Beneath the tree stump was a cavity where part of the bank had collapsed. Samuel explored its depth and found that it was big enough for him to hide in. He climbed into the hole and pushed the soft sandy earth back up to partially block off the entrance. He was soaked and suddenly he felt very cold.

His predicament was now even worse. The surviving NCO would have related the story of Samual's deed to his colleagues and it would only be a matter of time before he was branded a thief and a murderer. As if it wasn't bad enough being trapped some five miles inside Zululand, he almost certainly had to now contend with being branded a very wanted criminal.

Samuel tried to reason his case in his tired mind but there was no solution or excuse. The events themselves would be enough to hang him. The army would not believe him even though he knew he was not a deserter. He decided to get some sleep and wait to see what dawn would bring. Exhaustion and shock took their inevitable hold and wrapped in the Colour to conserve his warmth, he slept soundly in the burrow.

* * * * * * * * * * *

Later that night, he didn't even hear the artillery shells exploding back in the main camp as Lord Chelmsford and the accompanying two regiments marched back in to Isandhlwana. As their marching column approached the disaster site, every officer and soldier was well aware of the catastrophe that had befallen their colleagues. As a precaution, they fired several artillery rounds into the camp in case a Zulu force was waiting for them. Nothing moved. The camp was manned only by the one thousand six hundred bodies of the defenders. The Zulus had removed most of their own dead and the toll of their dead and wounded was incalculable. Following their heroic deeds, many thousands of warriors would not be returning to their villages.

The British survivors were devastated by the ease with which their camp had apparently been annihilated. Lord Chelmsford could not comprehend how he had been duped into dividing his force, and where had the Zulus come from? His various commanders had explicit orders to ensure that the whole area was overlapped with sufficient patrols and all had reported the vicinity clear. He was mystified and worried. His personal reputation was now in jeopardy and he dreaded the effect that this major defeat would have on the whole of Southern Africa .

With his carefully assembled and well trained force now decimated, there was nothing to stop the Zulus invading Natal. His thoughts depressed him still further. He refused to allow anyone to enter the wrecked campsite and his column camped for the night on the small plateau previously occupied by the 1st Battalion. During the night, reports reached Lord Chelmsford that the staging post at Rorke's Drift was both under attack and on fire. By dawn nothing could be seen except for a pall of smoke hanging over the drift some ten miles away.

As soon as daylight broke, the column formed up to move out and all were startled to observe a huge column of Zulus slowly approaching from the direction of Rorke's Drift. Several thousand Zulus held in reserve for the previous main battle had taken it upon themselves to attack the Drift. They had feared being left out of the battle and of missing the opportunity of washing their spears in their victim's blood.

They had achieved nothing. Rorke's Drift had not fallen and the Zulus, commanded by Chief Dabulamanzi , had suffered the loss of nearly one thousand warriors killed or seriously injured. As the Zulu masses approached the retreating British, they skirted around the column. The Zulus were exhausted and had not eaten for two days. The British possessed insufficient ammunition for another major engagement and the two columns cautiously passed each other with only four hundred yards between them. One of the Zulu speaking British officers warily rode towards them and called out to the warriors. The reply was quickly relayed back to Lord Chelmsford. Rorke's Drift had not been taken.

Samuel awoke to the immediate realisation that he was a fugitive. For the second time in his existence, fate had conspired to place him in the wrong. He pondered the fairness of life but it didn't help matters. He decided that he must now avoid both the Zulus and the British. His thoughts ranged no futher than the present dawning day but firstly he must escape from Zululand.

He peered from his hiding place and saw nothing moving. All along both river banks he could see the bodies of slaughtered soldiers and horses cut down while attempting to escape across the river. Just as he was about to move he heard a distant murmuring sound and anxiously watched as several thousand Zulus came through the trees from the direction of Rorke's Drift and began crossing the river. These must have been the Zulus that gave chase to the escapers, mused Samuel. At least his route back to Natal would be clear once they had crossed the river. Many were injured and they all paused to drink from the fast flowing water. It took about fifteen minutes for the Zulus to reassemble on the far bank. They totally ignored the bodies of the British soldiers scattered about and then set off as one unit towards Isandhlwana.

Samuel allowed a few more minutes to elapse and then he eased himself out of his hiding place. There were no further sounds coming from the trees and he stretched his aching limbs. He noticed that one of the nearby bodies was lying on a rifle. He nervously went to the dead soldier and moved his body away from the rifle. He tried to avoid looking at the man but as he moved the body he couldn't help but notice the frozen look of terror on the dead soldier's face. The rifle was in perfect working order and Samuel slipped the ammunition pouch off the body. To his relief it contained over twenty rifle rounds.

With the Colour still wrapped round his body, he realised that he would look very conspicuous dressed in the flag but, having saved the Colour thus so far, he wasn't now inclined to discard it. He looked at the nearby dead horses and saw that one had a leather dispatch pouch attached to the saddle pommel. He pulled the pouch from the saddle and went on to investigate some nearby dead soldiers. Samuel relieved one of his leather trouser belt and threaded the belt through the flap of the pouch. He folded the Colour neatly into as tight a bundle as possible and packed it carefully into the pouch. In any event, Lt. Pope might just have survived and he would vouch that Samuel had obeyed his order. With the belt now over his shoulder he could comfortable carry the Colour without it being obvious.

Samuel was aware that the NCO who had seen him the previous evening might not recognise him if he wore a jacket to cover his white shirt. The Colour was now safely secreted in the pouch, all he needed was a jacket. He looked again at the bodies and saw one clad in the dark blue uniform of the Royal Engineers. There was no alternative. Samuel took a deep breath and attempted to remove the soldier's jacket. Rigor mortis had long since set in and getting the sleeves off the man's stiff arms was a struggle. With a final heave the jacket came away. Samuel felt guilty at robbing the man's body but there was no alternative; the jacket more or less fitted.

He decided not to make straight for Rorke's Drift, it would be too dangerous. The NCO would have alerted his colleagues and they would undoubtedly be on the lookout for isolated soldiers. If he was ever found with the Colour he would certainly be identified as responsible for the death of the wounded soldier and arrested. Samuel didn't relish facing the disgrace of a Court Martial, even less the thought of a firing squad. Accordingly, he kept away from the track and cautiously moved off through the trees towards Natal. He was not sure what to do, it was even doubtful if he could reach safety, but at least he was still alive. He knew it would be a long and hazardous walk and the steadily climbing temperature would not assist him.

CHAPTER SIX.

However hard he tried, Samuel could not cleanse the horrors of the previous two days from his thoughts. Each time a fresh gruesome cameo flashed through his mind he felt nauseated . As if the grisly memories of the battle weren't enough to haunt him, the reality of the devilish sequence of events which made him a fugitive began to concentrate his thinking. Samuel set off; he began climbing the steep side of the gorge towards the high ridge which overlooked the river. As he toiled up through the trees and vicious thorn bushes scattering the slope, he pondered the plight of other fugitives. If, indeed, there were any British survivors from the battle, they would probably be in the area ahead, perhaps somewhere between Rorke's Drift and Natal. It would be better to avoid the Drift itself as this would be the first place the NCO would organise a search for him. It would be safer to strike off across wild country and report to a different unit whilst the general confusion following the disaster still reigned. He guessed it would take several weeks before any semblance of military order could be regained.

He paused for breath near the top of the steeply angled slope and looked around. Rorke's Drift was now clearly visible some three or four miles distant and there were definite signs of human activity within the camp. A thin trail of cooking smoke was rising and he could see figures moving around the Mission area. The heat of the sun was now sufficient to create the usual shimmering distortion across the plain; the camp was too far off for him to decipher their activities or whether the figures were soldiers or Zulus. Having seen the lengthy column of Zulus returning from Rorke's Drift less than an hour earlier, he anticipated that the few soldiers left to defend the Drift were long since dead; presumably the figures were those of looting Zulus.

Samuel looked back towards Isandhlwana. The rocky peak stood proudly defiant against the far horizon but its shape now looked distinctly menacing. It would stand forever as a monument to the fallen Welsh soldiers and the bravery of the Zulu nation.

He wiped his brow; was it really only three days ago that a proud modern army passed this point on its way to defeat a native rabble? Now the young men of the Welsh valleys and English countryside lay abandoned and scattered on the plain, bloating in the intense heat and vulnerable to the scavengers that would soon pick them clean. Samuel thought of the thousands of modern rifles together with the four waggons loaded with ammunition, all now in Zulu hands. He frowned at his own mental image of native warriors attempting to understand the artillery pieces, nevertheless the Zulu army was now a force to be taken even more seriously.

Samuel did not relish being sent back to fight the Zulus again and he involuntarily writhed at the prospect of having his spirit liberated by a razor sharp assegai .

As he stared at the distant horizon towards Isandhlwana, he noticed a thin grey haze materialising above the distant plateau. He stared hard at this phenomenon before realising what it was. The haze was fine dust being stirred up by the tramp of marching feet. It had to be Lord Chelmsford's column approaching from Isandhlwana. He stared across the middle distance and imperceptibly the ghostly mirage moved in his direction.

Gradually it dawned on Samuel that the Zulus had probably seized the tactical initiative after Lord Chelmsford divided his force. They had cunningly attacked the weakest element, the main camp. He then remembered the bedraggled Zulu force that had marched by less than an hour ago; would they attack Lord Chelmsford on his retreat back to Natal? The Zulus had either taken evasive action or were lying in ambush; there was no sign of them anywhere on the horizon. Samuel reasoned they would avoid another fight so soon after yesterday's battle. He felt the flood of relief sweep over him. Within a few hours the British force would reach his position and he would be safe. Samuel sat down to await their arrival reasonably confident that the immediate area was free of Zulus.

But one thought nagged him. He had temporarily forgotten the surviving NCO who would forever blame Samuel for the loss of his two friends. Although his conscience was clear, there would be no acceptable or legal defence to the charge of murder at a court martial other than the claim of putting the mortally injured soldier out of his misery. And what of the death of the Corporal speared to death whilst guarding him? That additional suspicious death could easily be attributed to Samuel. He reluctantly reasoned that it would be safer for him to press on ahead of the returning column rather than remain in the vicinity of the one person who could identify him. He decided to head for the staging post at Helpmakaar which was about ten miles back into Natal. Setting off, he realised that he was very hungry as he hadn't eaten properly for two days. It was unlikely that he would find anything to eat on the way and he had never bothered to learn which berries and strange fruits were edible or poisonous. Now was not the time to experiment unless things became desperate. Keeping a wary eye for trouble, he pressed on in the general direction of Rorke's Drift but intended keeping about one mile south of the camp to avoid detection.

At his nearest point to the camp he could clearly see that it was manned by British soldiers. The Drift had held!

The urge to head straight for the soldiers and their camp comforts was intense; they would have food, water and he craved their camaraderie almost as much. Then a vision of the accusing NCO brought him back to his senses; there was no alternative, he must go on. By midday he had skirted the camp and at one of the meandering loops of the Buffalo River, drank his fill from the clear cold water and refilled his water bottle. Refreshed, he scanned the plain in front of him and then set off.

An hour later he found himself at a point known as Noustroppas near the original route between the drift and Helpmekaar. The going underfoot was slow and tedious due to the soft sand. Samuel knew he was getting weaker with exhaustion and there was now the distinct possibility that he might not have the strength to walk all the way to Helpmakaar.

The unceasing heat from the sun was blazing down upon him and his resolve gradually began to deteriorate. Samuel drank the last of his water. He was so tired and thirsty that his imagination began to play subtle tricks on his mind .

Then something in front of him appeared to move , he peered hard to clear his vision and began make out the shape of a horse , or was it a rock? Whatever it was, it looked just like 'Pagan' the first horse he owned as a child. But when he weakly shouted, 'Pagan!' the animal didn't respond to him. Peering through the stinging sweat in his eyes and trying desperately to focus on the visionary objects ahead, he could also just make out the shimmering shape of an army waggon on the side of the track. Samuel knew that if he approached the iridescent objects they would teasingly fade away; he was tempted to try as his distant memories reminded him of the fun that children enjoyed when chasing shadows. He struggled on through the soft sand and the outline of the horse gradually became sharper. And now the waggon appeared to be real.

When Samuel was about two hundred yards from the horse it trotted cautiously towards him and stopped some twenty feet away.

'Just like a horse,' he muttered.

The two looked at each other. The horse was too stocky to have come from the British Army; perhaps it was from one of the Boer volunteers or the Natal Horse Regiment. It was saddled but its tack was unfamiliar. Samuel took a step towards the horse ; it took one step back. The process was repeated several times and Samuel resigned himself to the horse's stupidity and turned his attention to the waggon.

He looked for signs of human activity. There was no one in sight and the rough sandy track was clear as far as he could see in each direction. He wearily pushed himself over the the soft sand for the final hundred yards towards the waggon; it had obviously been abandoned in a hurry, one wheel was deeply sunk into the sand up to its front axle shaft. The waggon was facing away from the Drift and Samuel saw that the traces had been cut through. Something untoward had happened for the driver to abandon his load but he had had the presence of mind to take the horses, perhaps to make good his escape from a Zulu scouting party.

He leant his rifle against the waggon and hung the pouch containing the Colour over the rifle barrel. Slowly he pulled himself up onto the waggon intent on discovering something to eat or drink. There were ten identical wooden cases stacked neatly on the back of the waggon, all still strapped to the floor. Each case was stamped with the insignia of the Army and gave no indication of its content. He removed his bayonet from its scabbard and pondered how to open the cases. Each was bonded with wire and secured with heavy brass screws.

'Surely there must be something here to eat,' he realised he was talking to himself and smiled inwardly, 'things are getting bad,' he said loudly. The horse , which had come up to the waggon to investigate, snorted in reply .

Samuel decided to ignore the horse; the stupid animal might just succumb to its own curiosity and allow itself to be caught. Each wooden case bore the same identification number so he presumed he only had to open one to discover their collective contents. With his bare hands he prised the holding wire from the nearest case and examined the retaining screws holding the lid. There was no alternative, he had to chisel away at the lid with his bayonet.

Eventually one plank gave way under the force of Samuel's exertions. He tore at the lid in a frenzy of effort until the wooden planks were all torn away. He gingerly

91

pulled away the inner sacking covering to reveal a neatly packed officer's camp bed. He despaired and pondered the merit of opening the other identical cases. He sat down on the front of the waggon and put his head in his hands. He could feel the gravelly courseness of dried sweat on his forehead and in his hair. His thoughts slowly turned to the horse. He reminded himself to ignore the animal and instead he retrieved his bayonet. With an exaggerated gesture he returned it to the scabbard on his belt.

Samuel's mind began to hallucinate as he slowly collapsed across the driver's bench. He could feel the gentle pull of sleep beginning to take its effect. In his imagination he could smell fresh bread - this was going to be a wonderful dream. He breathed in deeply and the aroma grew stronger. This time he breathed in more sharply and there was just the faintest aroma of roast meat. He sat up with a start,

'Of course - what a fool!' he cried out feebly.

He leapt to his feet and lifted the driver's seat to reveal two packs of army rations. The drivers must have forgotten their ration packs in their haste to escape .

Samuel gently opened the first muslin pack in full anticipation of the contents and let his eyes gaze at the bread and meats in the bag. He hungrily attacked one of the loaves of bread but found eating difficult as his mouth was so dry; he pulled a piece of cooked beef from a small joint and greedily gnawed at it.

'If there is food there must be water,' he croaked.

Staring him in the face was a two gallon water container, and it was full. Samuel couldn't believe his luck. The horse watched intently and then impatiently snorted at the sound of water sloshing in the container as Samuel drank his fill then tore off a chunk of bread .

He indirectly looked at the horse. It was standing patiently next to the waggon looking up at him. 'Why not?' he thought. He climbed down from the waggon and went to the tailboard. As he anticipated, fastened to the back of the waggon was a folded leather bucket for just such a purpose. He poured about half the remaining water into the bucket and held it out towards the horse.

The sweet smell of fresh water was too good to resist and the animal gave in. Samuel gently took hold of the reins and looped them round the waggon footrest. He began to feel stronger. Looking back towards Rorke's Drift there was still no sign of movement on the track and it was time to move on. Picking up the rest of the food, he bundled it into the jacket and secured the package to the saddle pommel. The horse was still licking at the bucket when it noticed the piece of bread being held out. Without any reservation it took the bread from Samuel's hand and then licked his fingers .

'I don't know where you've come from but we're both in this together,' he said as he stroked the animal's nose, 'and for a start you can have a new name.' He put his face close to the animal and whispered 'Pagan' into its nostrils. Pagan nuzzled his arm and Samuel knew the bond had been formed. He checked over the horse for injuries and it appeared healthy. He adjusted the stirrups to his own leg length and, after putting the Colour pouch over his shoulder, carefully climbed into the saddle. Relieved to be mounted again, and without another glance at the waggon, he pointed Pagan away from the track . Riding back into the harsh scrubland for about half a mile, they were soon behind a thin veil of thorn trees, they then turned East towards Helpmekaar. He could now reach the outpost by late afternoon, with luck.

When about two miles from Helpmakaar he brought Pagan back on to the original track. Rehearsing his story again in his mind he approached the outpost defences, noticing that his arrival was creating considerable interest. There were numerous guards all around the position which had previously been a small trading post before being converted into a military staging camp of several hundred soldiers. He rode up to the camp as though he belonged there.

'Where are you from?' hailed a voice from the first
vedette.
'Isandhlwana,' replied Samuel.
'Come on in,' answered the guard.

Samuel reined in beside the soldier as others gathered
round.

'Is it true ?' asked several almost at once.
'Is the column destroyed? ' asked a young soldier.
'Are the Zulus coming?' asked another.

Samuel leaned forward in his saddle.

'The main camp has been massacred and every man
there is dead. Lord Chelmsford and one Regiment have
possibly escaped.' he said. The soldiers' faces showed
their horror. They had already seen some survivors reach
Helpmakaar but their officers had kept them away from the
enlisted ranks for fear of causing undue concern.
'Where do I go?' asked Samuel.
'Over to the Orderly Room,' answered a guard, 'that's
where the other survivors went.'

Samuel eased Pagan past the curious soldiers and
headed for the Orderly Room. He wearily tied Pagan to a
tent post and entered the storeroom which now served as
the local Headquarters.

Two young infantry officers were busy writing reports
and both looked up at Samuel with looks of astonishment
at his ragged appearance.

'Isandhlwana?' asked one of them.
'Yes Sir.'
'Which unit?' asked the other.
'Royal Engineers Sir,' answered Samuel.
'Are there any others with you?'
'No Sir, I'm the only one.' He paused for the effect to sink
in.   'I was spotting for the guns and saw everything -

when the camp was overwhelmed I headed South and came round across country. The Zulus killed everyone.'

'Is it true that Lord Chelmsford has survived?' asked the other young officer. His eyes were wide open and he appeared enthralled at having a survivor to question.

'I don't know Sir, all the 1st Battalion are done for; Lord Chelmsford and nearly all of the 2nd Battalion had left the camp a few hours before the Zulus attacked. I'm sorry - I don't know what happened to them.'

As distinctive footsteps approached, both officers leapt to attention. Major Fitzgerald, the camp commander, had heard of the new survivor and decided to come to hear of the events for himself.

Samuel was brought a bowl of hot stew and a pot of steaming coffee. He ate steadily as he talked and his story was recorded by one of the junior officers. About an hour later he finished answering their questions and was directed to the camp quartermaster for a clean uniform. He went outside the tent and untied Pagan. One of the officers came outside the tent and lit his pipe.

'Well done lad. The orderly will show you where to sleep; get some rest now and we'll arrange for you to return to one of the Royal Engineer units tomorrow,' said the officer. As an afterthought he asked innocently, 'By the way, did you see anything of an infantryman with an assegai in your travels?'

Samuel looked vaguely at him. 'Only dead ones Sir,' he replied nonchalantly.

'It's just that we've had a report of a demented soldier who has killed some of his comrades, apparently armed with an assegai.'

'I'm sorry Sir, I 've seen no one like that.'

'Come back in the morning lad and we'll sort you out,' replied the officer as he went back into the tent.

That evening Samuel watched the spectacle of sunset with mixed emotions. He was relieved to have survived the battle but anxious for his future. The Army would certainly press home the search for the demented soldier and it would only be a matter of time before all the survivors were questioned, regardless of where they were. In any event he had irrevocably committed himself to an untrue explanation and the truth would immediately come to light under questioning. He knew little enough about the Royal Engineers and his tale would not stand up to any investigation. He had at the most one day to make good his escape. And what of the Colour?

As an ordinary soldier he would soon be challenged about the pack at present secreted in his bed roll. But first he needed to sleep. He already felt his strength returning, having washed and eaten well. Pagan was safe and cared for in the horse lines. Tomorrow they would begin their new life. He went into his allocated tent and within minutes fell asleep.

When reveille sounded at 4 am , he pulled on his new uniform and joined the other soldiers around the perimeter. The first yellow rays of sunlight began to stretch across the grasslands as the 'Stand Down' bugle call sounded. At one of the breakfast tables a few minutes later, Samuel was soon the centre of attention; a number of soldiers at the post had friends and relatives with the main column and they were hungry for news. He kept to his story but gave whatever information he could . Shortly after breakfast he presented himself back at the Orderly Room.

'You're a keen one,' remarked the administrative NCO who had been present the previous evening . 'Come back at noon but I can't see you going anywhere yet, no-one knows what's happening.'

Samuel thanked him and, as planned, made his way to the Quartermaster's tent. He picked out the same individual who had re-kitted him and smiled disarmingly.
'I'm being returned to my unit,' said Samuel in a matter of fact way. 'Can I please have a riding cape?' Such an item

would keep him dry in the event of rain and double as a small tent at night.

The Quartermaster Sergeant remembered Samuel as the survivor from the previous afternoon and readily accepted the logical request. Signing the receipt with a false signature and with the new cape under his arm, he stepped back into the warming sunshine. 'Now for some supplies,' he thought and set off for the cooking tents. He again selected one of the staff with whom he had previously chatted and requested a ration pack for two days. Anything more would arouse suspicions as there was nowhere more than two days' ride away.

'Help yourself,' was the friendly reply .

Samuel dusted down an empty flour bag and selected two large freshly baked loaves. He then helped himself to a single joint of cooked meat, resisting the temptation to be greedy. He chatted inanely to the cook and then made his farewell.

Without hurrying, he casually headed for the horse lines. As soon as he arrived Pagan came over to him; the horse looked well and Samuel placed his pile of rations and the cape on the ground. One of the guards idly enquired what he wanted.

Samuel gave him the same answer and added,
'Look after these things while I get the rest,' and trusting the soldier, he returned to the tent for his rifle and bed roll containing the Colour pouch. Back at the horse lines he added the bedroll to his pile and went to the adjacent saddle tent. There were some sixty saddles all carefully laid out on several sailcloths. He hoped the guard would presume that everything was above board. He selected a well polished saddle and picked it up.

'Which way you going then?' asked the guard who was pleased to have someone to talk to.
'Back towards Durban,' he replied. 'But I expect we'll all be back here soon.' They both laughed. Everyone now

knew the war was not over yet.

About ten minutes later Pagan was saddled and Samuel fastened his belongings across the back of the horse. With a wave of thanks to the guard he set off at a casual pace behind a party of mounted scouts heading for the Durban road; this group conveniently made his own departure less obvious. If the authorities did think of searching for him later, the first place they would look would be along the road to Durban. Within the hour he would have doubled back and begun shadowing the track in the opposite direction, inland to Ladysmith.

Samuel had deliberately not shaved and now sported three full day's growth of beard. He pulled his riding cap down over his eyes; and once away from the camp, headed back across country towards the Ladysmith track. He would not be missed for the best part of the day then no-one would find him.

For the time being there were a number of clear priorities in his life. Getting away from the sphere of military operations was most important if he was to avoid capture. The best route lay inland as no-one would expect him to take that route leading away from civilisation.

During their time in Africa, all the soldiers had heard astonishing tales of diamonds being discovered on the edge of the Kalahari Desert at a place called Kimberley. He could surely find work there. If not, then the gold fields of Johannesburg might be the answer. There was, though, another problem. He didn't know where Kimberley was and a map had to be found. Ladysmith was some forty miles further inland and he had sufficient rations to get there comfortably in two days. Someone there would know the way to Kimberley.

Before then he must find some civilian clothes.

CHAPTER SEVEN.

The track to Ladysmith climbed gently towards the west over the rough undulating countryside. At times it was difficult to see exactly where the route lay as native cattle paths and streams criss-crossed the route. On more than one occasion Samuel ended up hopelessly lost or, having accidentally followed cattle tracks, in a native kraal. Apart from the knee high rocks strewn about the base of the hills and the ubiquitous dry brown grass, the countryside closely resembled the low hills of mid Wales. Using the overhead sun as his guide, Samuel kept heading due west in the hope that sooner or later some evidence of civilisation would show.

Two days later there was still no sign of habitation so Samuel headed up the side of a long flat topped hill. Like most travellers to this area, he was intrigued by the shape of the bigger hills, which all appeared to have been neatly squared off on top as though a giant fist had flattened each one. On reaching the highest point, he was very surprised to find himself on a relatively level but elevated plateau. There was some fresh grass growing to one side and Pagan needed feeding. Samuel dismounted and left the horse grazing while he set off to walk round the lip of the plateau which was about one mile all the way round. He reckoned that he was about five hundred feet above the surrounding countryside.

As far as the eye could see, there was no sign of life.

He looked around and to the South East the far off peaks of the Drakensburg Mountains rose up above the clouds. Continuing his walk while peering down into the valleys he saw, with considerable satisfaction, the outline of Ladysmith some ten miles further away to the west. There was no hurry so he sauntered back to where Pagan was grazing.

The high plateau was not the best place to bivouac as the wind was now gusting strongly. It would get bitterly cold up here at night and there was no sign of any water. He remounted Pagan and they retraced their route off the plateau. When nearly back down both heard the sound of running water. A small spring was gushing from the hillside and wended its way along a shallow gully. The position was sheltered and would be more than adequate to protect them through the night. Some branches from one of the nearby thorn trees would provide both fuel for a fire and the support for a lean-to shelter. Later, watching the flames crackle as sparks rose into the dark night, Samuel realised his resolve to survive was hardening, he was even beginning to enjoy himself. He thought about the Colour for a while; he might even keep it out of revenge for the savage blows inflicted on him by fate. Although Samuel was in no way a vindictive person, the wild justice of keeping the Colour began to appeal to him.

Just before midday he came across a substantial waggon track which was obviously the main route between Ladysmith and Durban. His route had been more southerly than anticipated, and to a casual Ladysmith observer it appeared that the lone rider was approaching from Durban. Although Ladysmith was a garrison town, its isolation from the theatre of war precluded any active involvement in the Zulu war.

The military camp itself was situated on the outskirts of the small township of timbered shacks, houses and stores. Apart from the main street, there wasn't very much activity in Ladysmith , so named after a former Cape Governor's wife. Several hundred people eked out a meagre living by general farming or in the employ of the military.

A ring of nearby hills formed a low barrier around the area. The Klip River, a minor tributary of the Tugela River, flowed by the north side of town. Were it not for the military presence, hardly anyone except the residents would know of the town's isolated existence.

The following morning Samuel rode on towards the town. As he approached a small hillock he left the track and rode into a rocky area well out of sight from the track. After making sure his presence was not being observed, he dismounted and placed his rifle, bayonet and the pouch containing the Colour under a large rock. Any one of these items would undoubtedly lead to questions that were best left unasked. Having made sure that everything was totally hidden, Samuel brushed over his tracks from the cache and headed back for the main track.

Obviously his appearance had changed, his dark beard was now a reasonable length and although he was still clearly a military character with his jacket and braided trousers, no-one could guess which unit he came from. Riding into town just before noon, the main street was totally devoid of life. Being accustomed to the heat, he had forgotten that townspeople would avoid any normal activity until the stifling temperature abated later in the afternoon. The main store was open and he directed Pagan towards the horse rail outside the store. Having dismounted slowly, Samuel hung the reins over the horse rail then limped up the steps into the store. The name over the establishment proclaimed that it was owned by one Harvey Greenacre.

The balding proprietor was bending down behind the counter and looked up at Samuel. The store appeared to be well appointed and in importance was probably second only to the church as the centre for the community.

'Yes lad, what do you want?' said Mr. Greenacre. Samuel had never quite got used to the direct approach of the white community in South Africa. They were a hardy people, but perhaps they reflected the harshness of the country.

'Well then, what's it to be?' Mr. Greenacre repeated.

'Some information please Sir,' Samuel looked directly into Mr. Greenacre's eyes so as not to lose the initiative. 'I've been with the Natal Horse until my discharge; I'm on my way to Kimberley but I need some work in order to eat.' He shuffled his feet to heighten Mr.Greenacre's awareness of his disability.

'Hurt yourself then?' the proprietor enquired, his voice sounding a little more considerate.

'Yes Sir, a riding accident, I broke my leg falling off a rogue horse - it's mending now but I'm no use to the army any more.' The man looked sympathetically at him.

'What sort of work do you want, and for how long?'

'Any work Sir, perhaps for a couple of months, just enough to enable me to buy some supplies to get me to Kimberley.'

Mr. Greenacre looked thoughtfully at Samuel.

'Sit down,' he said pointing at Samuel's leg. 'Would a glass of water be in order?' Samuel nodded. Mr. Greenacre went into the backroom and the sound of voices drifted through to the main storeroom. After a few minutes he returned with a glass of water, accompanied by his comely wife. She appeared to be a friendly soul and after surveying him from top to toe, smiled at him. Samuel took the water and nodded his thanks.

'There's a place out on the Acton road, about twelve miles from here near the Spion Kop stream called Chaldon Farm. They need some help.' His wife interrupted the conversation.

'It's run by Mr Dives and his young daughter,' she said, 'since Mrs. Dives died they have run into all sorts of difficulties.' She paused still looking intently at him. 'A young man like you might just get a job there for a while.'

The Dives, it seemed, were long standing friends of the Greenacres, they were casually acquainted since meeting on the same boat out from the UK and met again by chance in Ladysmith when the Greenacres took over the store. The Dives had purchased some land and over the six years since their arrival, worked hard at making it productive. The Dives' beef cattle were well known for their quality and the army was always keen to buy as many head as the canny farmer would sell. When Mrs. Dives died, the Greenacres had made the effort to visit the farm for her funeral.

Samuel thanked them both and rose to his feet,

remembering in the nick of time to emphasize his injured leg.

Mrs. Greenacre suddenly remembered something important.

'I think I've got some supplies for the Dives which have just come in, if I get them ready, would you take them?' and she added, 'It will save them a long journey to town to collect them.' She went into the backroom and soon re-emerged with a pack of medicines and some skeins of gaily coloured cottons which she wrapped in a piece of muslin.

'There you are,' she said with a broad smile, 'they'll be pleased with that.'

Mr. Greenacre escorted Samuel from the shop to the sidewalk and went over the directions again. The two shook hands and with a cheery wave to Mrs. Greenacre, Samuel set off for Chaldon Farm.

Nearly two hours later he came to the neighbouring Trichardt's Farm where a black worker gave him fresh directions. He continued along the roadway and turned left down a track between two small hills. About three miles further south he could clearly see the distant dominating high ground of Spion Kop hill. A hand carved sign on a post indicated that he was nearly at Chaldon Farm. Ahead, he saw a neat timber farmhouse with two low outbuildings. The newly fenced pasture contained several hundred cattle and the fields were irrigated from a stream which flowed just beyond the farmhouse. Walking Pagan slowly up to the farmhouse, he dismounted just short of the verandah and called out.

'Is there anyone here?' There was no reply from the house although he thought he caught a glimpse of a face at one of the windows.

'Over here!' came a reply from the side of one of the barns.

103

Samuel limped towards the man who looked about forty years of age and appeared to be too thin for a veldt farmer. His pleasant looking face and arms were suntanned to a golden nutbrown colour. He was wearing strong hessian trousers and a smock; cheap hard wearing clothes which were typical of the farmers in this locality. He looked Samuel directly in the eye and took his offered hand.

'It's Mr. Dives I presume?' enquired Samuel. The man said nothing, apparently wondering how this dusty soldier would know his name and, more to the point, what he wanted.

'I called into the store in Ladysmith and asked for some work; they said you might be able to use someone. Anyway, I've brought you some goods from Mrs. Greenacre... to save you the journey.' The mention of Mrs. Greenacre's name made the man feel more at ease. He looked at Samuel's leg.

'What about your leg?' he asked.

Samuel recounted his previous tale and the farmer indicated the farmhouse.

'Come on in, we'll talk about it, but I warn you, I can't offer much.'
'All I'm looking for is a bed, and food for me and my horse. I'll work hard for it .'

They went into the main farmhouse. Inside, it was neat and tidy. Mr. Dives motioned Samuel to sit down at the main table which had been neatly laid with two places ready for a meal.

'Anneliese!' the man called authoritatively.
'Coming Papa.' From a neighbouring room, a tall, rather waiflike girl appeared. She was wearing similar working clothes to her father and her fair hair hung down below shoulder level. She looked demurely at the guest. Samuel

rose to his feet and extended his hand but the girl froze with shyness and did not move.

'May we have some tea?' her father asked kindly. The girl nodded her head and went back into the kitchen from which delicious smells of baking were wafting. The two men looked at each other.

'Right, tell me who you are, where you have come from, ' he was watching Samuel, 'and where you're going.'

Samuel kept it simple. He recounted the tale exactly as told to Mr. Greenacre and as he spoke, the farmer sat expressionless, but obviously thinking. Anneliese brought in the tea on a tray which she placed on the table before her father and stepped back. Samuel could not but help notice the large slices of fruit cake on a metal plate.

'Pour the tea then girl,' said her father amiably. She set a steaming mug of tea before each of them together with a slice of cake. The farmer looked thoughtful for what seemed an age before he picked up his mug of tea. Samuel didn't need to be asked a second time and savoured the cake to make it last.

'Would you like another piece?' she asked and before he could reply she heaped an even larger slice onto his plate.

Samuel had been watching the girl, she too had bronzed skin from working outside on the farm. Her features were slim without being striking and her well brushed hair hung down to her shoulders. She looked to be rather scrawny but it was difficult to be certain because of those baggy clothes. Her hands were fine, too fine for manual work but she obviously had no choice in the matter. Anneliese noticed that she was being scrutinized and blushed. She was about five and a half feet tall and Samuel thought she must be about sixteen years old.

Her father's clearing his throat brought Samuel back to reality.

'I can't offer you any more than your board and you will have to work hard for that. You'll sleep in the barn and Anneliese will make you a bed in the loft; you can take your meals with us - that's the best I can offer.' He looked at Samuel and went on,' And either of us can cancel the agreement at will; is that right with you ?'

'Thank you,' replied Samuel. He tried to make his reply sound sincere because he was truly grateful for the chance to pause in his flight and the isolated farm would make a good hiding place. The farmer moved in his chair.

' It's too late to do very much today, I'll show you some of the farm while Anneliese makes your bed.' He looked at his daughter, 'So it will be three for supper, girl.'

'Yes papa,' was the timid reply.

The two men finished their tea and Samuel followed his new employer back outside. For the last hour of daylight the two rode across the farm with Samuel making a mental note of the details. The farm was largely given over to beef cattle and vegetable crops which could be, no doubt, profitably sold in town or to the military. The farm was bounded on one side by the stream and most of the farm land occupied the flat plain between the stream and the Tabanyama hills about two miles away. The farm was presumably prosperous because water from the stream had been successfully piped into irrigation channels which ran into the man-made pastures before flowing back into the stream. Between the farm and the stream were fields of vegetables irrigated in a similar way. Samuel was impressed with the ingenuity of the farmer but felt it would be condescending to flatter him.

As they rode back to the farmhouse they passed an obvious but rough grave. Stones were placed over the grave and a rough wooden cross had been erected; there was no name on the grave.

'That's where we buried my wife.'

'What happened to her Sir?'

'She died of a snake bite; there was nothing we could do. Within two hours she was dead.' They rode on and he added,

'Life is hard and cheap out here.' Samuel could only agree.

They returned to the house and washed in readiness for the meal.Anneliese placed an appetising pot of stew on the table and all bowed their heads as Mr.Dives   said grace. The oil lamp on the table gave the room a friendly comfortable feeling and Samuel realised he could feel at home here.

That night he washed himself with soap and water from a bowl thoughtfully provided by Anneliese then   savoured the feel of soft blankets, even though the bedding itself was laid out on the hay. He felt quite safe in the loft, safe on the farm and warmly content. As the only person who knew of his whereabouts was Mr. Greenacre, the chance of anyone else   finding him here was too remote to contemplate. Just after dawn he awoke to the sound of Anneliese hammering on   a saucepan with a wooden spoon to announce breakfast, after which he was put to work.

* * * * * * * * * * * *

Late the following Friday afternoon the two men were working near the stream. They were mending a leaking trough which brought fresh running water to the house when a lone rider was seen approaching the farmhouse from the main roadway. Samuel saw him first and stood up to get a better view of the intruder.

'It's only Hogg,' said the farmer without even looking up. 'He visits here twice a month.' Realising it wasn't much of an explanation he went on, 'we talk a lot and drink some whisky which he sleeps off in the barn.'

'A friend of yours then?'

'Not a friend, more an old acquaintance from several years back, but he's about the only person who comes out here now. He works for the military arranging the black workers.' Samuel said nothing; he had learned that if you want to know something you say nothing and let the other person talk. Accordingly Mr. Dives went on.

'Hogg arranges groups of blacks to work at Ladysmith and Newcastle for the army; he gets well paid by the army but pays the blacks a pittance.'

107

'Isn't that illegal?' asked Samuel.
'Who cares!' was the blunt reply.

Hogg rode past the house and led his horse into the barn. The two men finished the repair and mutually decided that enough was enough for that particular day and, anyway, it was getting late. They began the half mile walk back to the house during which time Mr. Dives revealed that Hogg was a drifter, one of a number who had been chased out of Kimberley for illegal diamond trading.

'Hogg apparently used to bribe some of the black miners to smuggle out rough stones from the workings by offering them whisky and girls in exchange,' explained Mr Dives. 'And then, some time back, he paid one black with an old rifle in exchange for a large stone. The delighted black celebrated his prize by getting drunk and fired a badly aimed shot at an unpopular mine overseer who was leaving one of Kimberley's more dubious hotels.'
'I bet that went down well,' replied Samuel.
'Yes it did!' laughed Mr.Dives, 'The following morning the Mine Owners' Committee quickly learned the truth about the diamonds from the now sober but terrified black.'
'And Hogg?' asked Samuel.
'Hogg had already fled in anticipation,' said Mr.Dives. Samuel thought for a moment.
'So , everyone knows Hogg is wanted but no one can do anything about it ?'
'That's about it,' replied Mr.Dives.

During supper Hogg talked to Mr. Dives over a range of subjects but made a point of excluding Samuel and Anneliese from the conversation. The man's thin greying hair was matted and he obviously rarely washed. His paunch hung out over his belt and he had an infuriating habit of belching as he ate. Samuel knew when he was not wanted and after the meal gave his apologies and decided to get an early night. He did not sleep well; there was something about Hogg that made him feel distinctly uncomfortable. It was well after midnight before Hogg climbed the ladder into the loft and fell headlong into the hay. It took him some time to get into his bedroll before snoring noisily for most of the night.

When the following morning dawned; Hogg packed and left before breakfast enabling life on the farm to resume its normal pattern.

Each day Samuel learned a little more about the Dives family but he had shied from enquiring more about Mrs. Dives' death.

Many weeks later, and following an unusually heavy downpour of rain one night, Anneliese was waiting for Samuel at the bottom of the loft steps. He had, of course, noticed that she was taking considerably more care with her appearance. Occasionally she wore her hair in a bun, other days it was plaited or left loose. In the evenings she had taken to wearing a modest skirt but on Sundays she wore a dress throughout the day transforming her into the attractive young lady that she was. Samuel was also aware that on Hogg's most recent visit, he had stared at her with unashamed interest. Samuel had noticed that he could make Anneliese blush furiously by winking at her; in fact, he rather liked her. On this cool morning she was wearing her usual work clothes with her hair neatly tied in a bun.

'Pa sent me to warn you, after the rain the snakes sometimes come out from under the rocks near the house; that's how one got Ma.'

'What happened?' he asked .
'Dad and she had a row, Ma came out here and sat on one of the rocks. It was raining at the time but Ma wouldn't give in.' As Anneliese spoke they began slowly walking back to the house. 'At first Dad wouldn't come and get her but after about an hour he went out to look for her. Ma was sitting on a rock when she saw Dad coming... she was so pleased ... she stood up to go to him.' The girl began to sob quietly. 'A black mamba snake bit her on the ankle. Dad carried her in and she fainted soon after... we both stayed up with her all night but she never recovered...

she just died.'

'I'm so sorry, I really am so sorry.' He could think of nothing more to say. As an afterthought he put his arm round her shoulder. She didn't respond and a few steps later he gently pulled away. As they were about to enter the house she put her hand on his sleeve , she looked up at him and smiled,
'I'm glad you've come to help us.' Samuel felt a glow run through his body; he shared her pleasure.

He never had liked snakes and thereafter kept well clear of the rocks, whether it rained or not.

Two months passed and the routine on the farm became established. An unspoken bond was slowly forming between the two young people but as yet there had been no real opportunity to talk freely. It was time that Pagan was properly exercised again and so Samuel persuaded Anneliese to join him for a Sunday afternoon ride. Anneliese saddled her favourite pony and they set off after lunch, heading up the track to the roadway. At the junction they turned left towards the high ground of Spion Kop and after about one mile they turned off the track into the hills. They chatted as they rode and Anneliese became more animated, laughing freely at his attempts to be witty. After about an hour they reached the brow of a rise in the ground and stopped to admire the spectacular view over the plain. Some thirty miles to the west the lofty Drakensburg mountains rose majestically above the clouds. In the near distance the heat haze distorted any detail but wherever they looked, there was no evidence of any other human activity. About twelve miles to the north-east they could just make out the glinting tin roofs of Ladysmith.

'Let's rest here a while,' invited Samuel and they both dismounted. The two horses were tied to some scrub; Samuel took the cape from his saddlebag and set it on the ground. He sat down motioning Anneliese to join him; without a pause she settled down beside him.
'How long will you be staying on the farm?' he asked

without looking at her.

'Who knows,' she said, ' I'll be seventeen this Christmas.' Samuel deliberately missed the point, being fully aware that girls on the veldt frequently married very young. She persisted,

'I can't leave Dad now so I guess I'll be here until I get married.' Samuel smiled and picked up her hand.

'And I'll be leaving soon,' he teased, 'so don't get any ideas.' She flared into a blush and Samuel felt a little sorry for her. He put his arm around her but this time she snuggled towards him squeezing his hand.

'More to the point, when will you go?' she asked, and almost as an afterthought she quickly followed on, 'and where will you go ... why not stay on the farm with us?' It was a question he had vaguely anticipated.

'As pretty as you are, I have to make my own way in life.' She looked at him without comment but with a pleading expression on her face which forced him to continue. 'When my leg gets better I'll be off to Kimberley and who knows, I might just make my fortune.' He then returned her look. 'Until then I'm penniless.' She tightened her grip on his hand and asked ,

'Will you come back?' He thought for a moment and smiled at her,

'If you are still here when I next pass I'll call and see you, you'll probably have lots of children and you won't want to know me.'

She retained her grip on his hand and quietly said,

'I doubt it, I doubt it.'

She lay back on his cape and closed her eyes. Samuel wasn't sure how to react and lay beside her. That was fruitless so he sat up and looked at her peaceful face. Her lips were slightly pouting and she looked almost beautiful. He leant over her and gently kissed her mouth. She didn't react. He kissed her again and very slowly she opened her lips and responded. She pulled him closer and he could feel himself being overwhelmed as his body began to respond. Her delicate hands reach around his neck and caressed the back of his head; he slowly pulled away and

111

lay on his back. She followed him and kissed his neck and then moved down to kiss his chest. His hands went round her shoulders and he pulled her tightly to him. He could feel her heart beating and her body gave him a feeling which was almost delicious. He ran his hands round to the front of her neck and deftly undid the top button of her blouse. He imagined that he could feel every curve of her body through their embrace and his excitement rose. Kissing him full on the mouth Anneliese pulled away.

She grinned at him and whispered,
'Was that enough to make you think of coming back for me?' she ran her tongue round her lips, 'because if you do, I can do much better than that.' Samuel was speechless so she went on, 'Just imagine what I'd be like if I thought I might have a chance with you.'
'You're a tease,' laughed Samuel, 'but I might just reconsider my plans if you think I'm worth it.' Anneliese sat up,
'I think you might be; let's see how we get on over the next few weeks, 'and then added cheekily, 'if you're still here.'
They sat and gazed at the scenery until it was time to return home. Little more was said but both were becoming very aware how the other felt.

On the 2nd April, Mr. Dives asked Samuel to deliver twenty head of cattle to the army camp at Ladysmith. This suited him well because the time was right to collect the rifle and effects which had lain hidden the other side of Ladysmith since January. He readily accepted the opportunity and Mr. Dives surprised him with the gift of a sovereign.

'Spend the night at the hotel and don't rush back,' he patted Samuel affectionately on the back and watched him expertly herd the cattle towards the farm track.

Anneliese came to the verandah to see him off and both waved as he followed the cattle out of the farm. It would be a golden opportunity to collect the booty and to buy Anneliese a present from the Greenacres' store. He set off in high spirits.

After the cattle were safely delivered to the army butchers he headed on into Ladysmith. Samuel was now only interested in the present for Anneliese; the idea of spending the night in the hotel didn't really appeal to him but it was getting too late for the return journey. Mr.Greenacre was just in the process of closing the store and looked startled to see Samuel. With urgency Mr. Greenacre ushered him out of the building.

'Quickly, put your horse round the back in the store shed,' he ordered, and Samuel obliged. 'I've got a few straight questions for you my lad, and I want some straight answers.'

Samuel was then forcefully grabbed by his shirt and ushered through the back door of the store into the kitchen. Mrs. Greenacre looked mildly surprised to see him but greeted him warmly; she saw the determined look on her husband's face.

'Leave him alone Harvey, we haven't heard what he has to say,' she said.
'What's the matter?' Samuel asked curiously but with some concern in his voice.
'The military have been here asking for you.'
'Go on,' said Samuel as calmly as he could while trying to ignore the feeling of dread spreading through his body.
'Well, it might not exactly be you, but the description does vaguely fit you,' Mrs.Greenacre chipped in .
'They say someone like you left the camp at Helpmakaar without permission and for some reason they want him... or you if it's you .... back there.' They both looked at him and Mr. Greenacre continued,
'Is it you they are after? They say there was a terrible battle and no one survived so why do they want you. What have you done?'

Samuel didn't know what to say or where to begin. Mrs. Greenacre continued preparing the supper but paid full attention awaiting the explanation with anticipation.

113

'Nothing,' said Samuel simply. 'Yes, I did escape from the battle but then I got hopelessly lost for two days; the Zulus were everywhere and it was some time before I could get back. Someone from another unit must have known I was on patrol and when I did get back ...more dead than alive, I discovered they had listed me as a deserter .... I've done nothing wrong, my whole unit was killed.'

Mr. Greenacre looked perplexed and spoke quietly. 'I didn't think it could have been you they were looking for and I've said nothing. It only dawned on me after they left that it might be you.'
'I promise you both,' Samuel tried to sound as sincere as possible, 'that I have done nothing wrong, I survived the Zulus and now I can't go back, it's as simple as that.'

They both nodded their understanding and Mrs. Greenacre, obviously relieved by his explanation, gave him a hug. It was agreed that Samuel should remain with them and was offered a bed for the night. During supper Samuel related the details of the battle. The Greenacres were spellbound like small children listening to a terrible fairy tale. After nearly two hours they had discussed everything through in graphic detail. Before retiring for the night, Samuel insisted that he let himself out before dawn. Almost as an afterthought, he tried to purchase some lace handkerchiefs for Anneliese but the Greenacres insisted that they were a gift. They wouldn't let him part with his hard earned sovereign.

'And here's a present for you', said Mr. Greenacre handing Samuel a large leather bound book, two pens and a bottle of ink. 'It's a diary, you ought to write everything down before you forget what has happened. You can write can't you?' added Mr. Greenacre almost as an afterthought.
'Yes I can, I will write it down, and thank you.' replied Samuel as he examined the heavy leather binding of his unexpected gift.

It was agreed that his secret should be kept between the

three of them and if asked again, the Greenacres would state that someone of the deserter's description was last seen heading for Durban. They both knew full well that Samuel had begun to make Chaldon Farm successful and both were accordingly prepared to give him the benefit of any doubt.

Next morning Samuel directed Pagan out of Ladysmith but in the direction of the Durban roadway. He knew the local garrison numbers had recently been reduced to reinforce the new invasion force being assembled at Durban and the evidence of heavy wagons having taken this route was everywhere. The roadway had been well churned up by the combination of numerous waggons and hooves and he was obliged to ride along the side of the roadway.

It would take him about two hours to reach the hills where his cache was hidden so he settled down into a pace comfortable for Pagan. Later that morning Samuel recognised the spot where he had turned off the road and without difficulty found the large boulder. Everything was still there. He took up the rifle and eased its firing mechanism which worked well. Opening the leather pouch he unfolded the Colour. It was truly beautiful, and holding the material gave him a strange feeling ; he began to realise it was the Colour that had saved him from certain death on the battlefield and subsequently through the cold of the nights during his escape. He held the Colour tightly to his chest and closed his eyes; he could almost hear the battle , the shouting and agonised screams of the dying. He felt his flesh creep and the hairs on his arms bristled. Without another thought he purposefully refolded the Colour and placed it back in the pouch ; but it was some time before he felt warm again.

He wrapped the rifle and bayonet in a sack especially brought for the purpose and remounted Pagan. Although it would be a long ride back to the farm, Samuel guessed he could cut across country which would save being seen again in Ladysmith. It the far distance he could make out the distinctive shape of Spion Kop; he would head for this

115

prominent landmark and then turn off for the farm . He even admitted to himself that he was missing Anneliese. By late afternoon he reached the main roadway which lead to Chaldon Farm and at dusk he very quietly led Pagan into the barn. He swiftly secreted the rifle, bayonet and pouch under some loose hay, unsaddled Pagan and turned him into the paddock.

Collecting the lace from his saddlebag, he went over to the farmhouse. Supper was about to be served and Anneliese was pleased and excited with her present. She held the fine material to her face and danced like a small child.

'Thank you,' she said with affection in her voice, and her eyes seemed to pierce through to his soul.

CHAPTER EIGHT.

Several weeks went by and nothing more was said about Samuel leaving the farm. He accompanied the Dives on their monthly shopping expeditions to Ladysmith and it appeared that his presence at the farm had been generally accepted in the locality. No further military enquiries had been made about the mysterious deserter and Samuel felt more relaxed when in town. His beard was now fully grown and by wearing the same rough farming clothes readily available from the store, not even Owen would recognise him now. Their visit to the Greenacres' store was always the highpoint of the regular trip to town; stocks were replenished, gossip and news could be circulated and the Greenacres' open invitation to stay for tea was always accepted.

The rainy season came and went while Chaldon's Farm prospered. The monthly trip to town became a fortnightly excursion due to the high productivity of the vegetable farm and the insatiable demand by the British Army for fresh produce. The Zulu war had reached an inconclusive stalemate until news reached Ladysmith that Lord Chelmsford was to lead a second invasion into Zululand.

The fresh military preparations for war proved to be extremely profitable for the Dives. The Army purchased a considerable proportion of their available cattle to help feed the massive troop reinforcements being assembled at Pietermaritzburg for the re-invasion of Zululand. By the time the army procurement officers reached Ladysmith, the prices of horses, waggons and cattle were exorbitant, in most cases the price now demanded was two or three times that paid last year. More capital came into the farm from the single sale of three hundred head of beef cattle than the farm had earned in its total ten year's existence. Mr. Dives shrewdly declined to sell the whole herd, retaining sufficient breeding cows and three fine bulls to restock the farm. During this period, more time was spent on maintenance and improving the quality of the vegetable farm.

Mr. Dives was greatly appreciative of Samuel's depth of farming knowledge and their own relationship strengthened. He knew only that Samuel had left his parents' farm in Wales to join the army; the matter was not discussed further as he respected the young man's privacy.

Samuel steadily took on more responsibility. He had also noticed that Mr. Dives was growing unnaturally thin. Anneliese occasionally talked about her father's health and although he ate well and slept well, he still managed to lose weight progressively. The time was now fast approaching when Samuel wanted to insist that his employer should consult a physician. Mr. Dives might be stubborn and any such suggestion would require considerable tact on his part. Towards the end of the month, Mr. Dives weakened even more and took to having a long sleep during the midday break. Early one afternoon Anneliese agreed that Samuel should ride to Ladysmith and ascertain when the visiting physician was next due to attend the town. The two decided that he should not wait until the routine farm delivery but make a special visit. He left for Ladysmith before Mr. Dives woke.

Samuel reached the town at about 4 pm and immediately went to consult the Greenacres. They too, admitted that the appearance of their friend was causing them considerable concern. The two men sought out the physician who was, by good fortune, visiting the town on his regular circuit. They crossed the road to the Royal Hotel and were shown to his temporary clinic. Dr. Spicer was one of four British Army garrison surgeons stationed at Ladysmith. He had travelled the world extensively and supplemented his army pay by administering to the local white population. Aged about fifty five, he was a little shorter than the two men standing before him, and although slightly overweight he looked fit and well, surely a direct reflection on his profession and high standard of living.

He peered expectantly at his visitors over the top of his spectacles; and knowing that Mr. Greenacre would be

118

able to pay well for his services, the doctor condescended to smile. Samuel related his anxieties to Dr. Spicer and it was agreed that Mr. Dives should attend the hotel clinic the following noon. Naturally, Samuel was invited to dine with the Greenacres but on this occasion he felt honour bound to report back to the farm without delay.

Meanwhile, as Anneliese was preparing the evening meal she saw Hogg ride into the barn. She shivered slightly and distracted herself by fussing about her father who was sleeping on the couch. It was a good half an hour before Hogg came to the house and Anneliese wondered what he had been doing all the time. He walked straight in and looked at the sleeping Mr. Dives without comment.

'And where's the boy ?' he asked her.
'Gone to Ladysmith,' she replied icely, bristling with resentment. Hogg half smiled. The girl needed a lesson in manners.
'Bring me some hot water to the barn, and don't be long about it,' he said.

Anneliese grimaced, but felt that she ought to oblige her father's guest.
'You'll have to wait, the water's not hot yet,' she retorted.
'As soon as you're ready,' was his sinister reply.

Hogg walked back to the barn anticipating Anneliese's humiliation. He had been with many women, some white some black. Sometimes he paid for their services - some he just took as their reward for his company. He'd never married; his relationships with women were always shallow, and as he got older, his lustful contacts were becoming frequently tainted with violence. He enjoyed humiliating his conquests, the warped impression of superiority always gave him added satisfaction.

He waited inside the entrance to the barn. Looking around he saw the pile of hay in the half darkness at the back of the barn; that would be more comfortable than the floor. In the meantime he decided to investigate Samuel's bed area; it would not be the first time he'd searched through the youth's bed space. Hitherto he had found nothing of interest; he climbed the ladder and began to snoop carefully   through Samuel's possessions. He was again disappointed, there was nothing of interest.   He glanced about him and on the point of going back down the ladder,   the glint of reflected light from a belt buckle caught his eye; within seconds he'd pulled the rifle and pouch out from their hiding place in the hay. He inserted his hand into the pouch and felt around; apart from a flag and some rounds of ammunition, there was nothing of real value to be found. But the rifle - now that was curious and worth a few questions. He'd tackle the boy later, in the meantime there was the girl to attend to.

He climbed back down the ladder and sat on a wooden box to wait. He reckoned the girl was old enough not to complain to her father and as for the boy, he had special plans for him now that he'd found the rifle which was surely stolen. His find in the hay loft now gave him extra courage to anticipate satisfying himself with the girl. Anyway, it was time he moved away from the area , the army were now based elsewhere and his services could be put to better use in Durban.

Anneliese slowly walked from the house with a heavy pail of hot water held in both hands. She was wearing a skirt which was unusual for the daytime; he guessed that it was for the benefit of the boy. Her hair was tied behind her head which made her look attractive and Hogg could feel his body stirring with excitement. As she entered the barn, she paused to allow her eyes to adjust to the darkness.

'Over here,' ordered Hogg indicating the floor by the hay.

Hogg followed her and as she put the heavy pail on the ground he grabbed her from behind. He put one hand over her mouth and the other under her loose blouse. Anneliese froze . She knew he would hurt her more if she struggled, by remaining calm she might still escape. She endured his rough hands exploring her breasts and then shook her head. This, he thought, was going to be easy   and obligingly removed his other hand from her mouth.

'Please don't damage my clothes,' she said as she turned, looking him straight in the eye, 'I'll take them off.' Hogg was so surprised he relaxed his grip allowing her to sidle away. 'Sit down,' she smiled at him and indicated the hay.

He grinned and sat back on the soft hay as directed. He watched her carefully; this was going to be very different.

'Take your shirt off,' she said provocatively as she undid the top buttons of her blouse; he lay back and began to pull his rough shirt over his head. In a flash she picked up the pail of near boiling water and flung it over the sitting figure. He furiously bellowed with rage and pain but she was gone.

Back in the house her father was awake and half sitting up. She felt safer now and sat trembling by his bed .

'Are you unwell child?' asked her father.
'It's just a chill, nothing for you to worry about,' she said as she patted him reassuringly. Anneliese knew Hogg would not try anything again while she was in the house, and Samuel would be back before too long.

While riding out of Ladysmith, Samuel had remembered that Hogg was likely to visit Chaldon Farm that day, and indeed, was probably there at that very moment. Samuel despised the man and urged Pagan towards the farm with more haste than usual. The pair made good time. The day's lasting memory was of Dr. Spicer's face when Samuel related the symptoms and length of time they had existed. There was now urgent cause for concern about Mr. Dives' health.

On reaching the farm about an hour later it was already dark; Samuel let Pagan into the paddock and entered the barn. Hogg's saddle was abandoned over the saddle rail just inside the entrance and in the loft Hogg had already laid out his bedding roll on the hay.

Suddenly, a chill feeling of horror swept through his body - even before he fully realised what he was looking at; lying on the straw next to his own bedding was the army rifle and pouch. The flap of the pouch was open, the Colour was still inside and appeared to be undisturbed. It was obvious that Hogg had rummaged through the hay looking for Samuel's effects; blatantly leaving them on display indicated that the unwelcome guest was likely to provoke serious trouble.

Leaving the items where they were, Samuel descended from the loft and without attending further to Pagan, walked straight over to the house. Mr. Dives was dozing on his couch and Hogg was sitting next to him swigging whisky from a bottle. Samuel greeted the two men; Mr. Dives opened his eyes and attempted to raise himself on one elbow in order to sit up. Samuel went over to him and carefully assisted him to his chair at the table which was prepared for the evening meal.

But there was no sign of Anneliese.

'Where's Anneliese ?' Samuel demanded.
'Outside,' replied Hogg curtly. Samuel thought that odd and after patting Mr. Dives on the shoulder went outside to find her.

Anneliese was sitting on a wooden box at the back of the farmhouse. She burst into tears as Samuel approached and motioned to him to stay away.

'What's the matter ... what's happened?' She made no reply other than to burst into tears again. Being in comparative darkness her features were hard to make out.
'It's all right, we'll take your father to the doctor tomorrow ... Dr. Spicer is expecting us at lunchtime.' Still she didn't respond and he sat down beside her.
'It's not Hogg is it ?' he asked .
'I'm sorry,' she sobbed,'I'd made myself look nice and when he saw Pa asleep and you gone he grabbed me.'
'Did he hurt you.. are you all right.. what did he do?'

'I feel so ashamed, I don't want to say.'

Samuel put his arms round her and gently began to rock her.

'It's all over now, I'm here ...tell me, what did he do ... did he hurt you, did he touch you ?'

She wiped her eyes with her hands and tried to gather her composure.

'Not really, it's my pride more than anything, I was taking him some water to the barn, Pa was asleep and he came up behind me and grabbed me ...I struggled but he was too strong...he put his filthy hand over my mouth and tried to get inside my blouse... I bit his hand and kicked him all at the same time and then he let go. I poured the hot water over him so he's probably scalded. I've been here ever since...he didn't follow me out.'

Samuel felt his anger rising but he knew only too well that Hogg was very dangerous and always carried a knife. This was just the situation he'd feared most and with Mr. Dives virtually powerless, there was no telling what Hogg might do, especially when he was drunk. They were all in great danger, particularly Anneliese. He thought rapidly.

'Take Pagan, he's in the paddock and still saddled ... and put this on,' he ordered, handing her his jacket. 'Ride down to the vegetable packing shed and sleep there but keep Pagan near you just in case, I'll take good care of your father and in the morning we'll take him straight to town.' Anneliese nodded her agreement.

'And what about you, will you be all right?'

'I'll be fine, Hogg's too drunk now, I'll just keep an eye on him and as soon as its light we'll be off.' She gave him a hug and walked quickly in the direction of the barn to collect Pagan.

With Anneliese out of the way Samuel felt better, but what was he to do? The answer was to act normally and continue with the preparations for supper. He re-entered the house and attempted to be as normal as possible. Mr. Dives looked at him and mumbled,

'Where's Anneliese?' Samuel went over to him,

123

'She's not feeling very well, I think she's had too much sun today and gone to bed; now I'm going to get your supper.' With that he went towards the kitchen and out of Mr. Dives' hearing quietly said to Hogg,

'And she's gone to Ladysmith out of your way,' he angrily lied.

Hogg glared at him and took another gulp of the whisky. The bottle was nearly empty but Mr. Dives kept a special bottle in the kitchen. Samuel swiftly opened the replacement and placed it in front of Hogg; the drunkard belched and stared at his now empty glass. It was his lucky day! He took another long drink which finished off the first bottle.

The meal was the usual farm stew and , after the range fire had been stoked, Samuel soon had the pot simmering. Mr. Dives had fallen asleep at the table. The meal was ready before any further conversation took place and Samuel placed three heaped plates on the table. Mr. Dives was in no condition to eat, he rocked slowly in his chair with his eyes closed. Samuel gently lifted him bodily and placed him on his bed in the side room. He gently placed a blanket over the frail figure and shut the door.

The aroma of the meal wafting through the house reminded Samuel of his own hunger and he returned to the table. Hogg began to pick at his food but was too drunk to co-ordinate his movements, some of the food reached his mouth but as much fell in his lap. After Samuel had eaten his meal, he asked Hogg to look after Mr. Dives while he collected more fire wood. To his surprise Hogg grunted his assent but then said,

'Wait!' He took a deep breath to collect his thoughts.
'You and I have got to have a little chat,' he drawled drunkenly. Samuel sat down as Hogg peered at him through his alcoholic haze .

'You're the deserter ain't you... well, I'll tell you what you're goin' a do . Tomorrow you gets back on your horse, and takes your stolen rifle.... an' yer don't come back.

If you do,' he paused for thought, 'It's this.' Hogg dramatically drew his fingers across his throat; his meaning was abundantly clear.

'I'll give you up to the Army. Dead or alive, it don't matter - they'll hang yer anyway.' Hogg grinned sardonically.
'All right, I'll do as you say,' said Samuel. His mind was racing and he needed time to think. ' I'll get some fresh wood in for the stove. 'To his surprise, Hogg nodded and then said ,
'An' don't go gettin' no fancy ideas with that rifle,' he opened his jacket pocket and revealed the rifle ammunition which he'd removed from the Colour pouch then deftly slipped his hand over the knife hilt attached to his belt. Samuel turned and made for the door. He had no option.

The cool night air began to calm his fury but Samuel knew he didn't have much time. This repugnant man knew everything and was now much too dangerous, there was no telling what Hogg might do and the thought of him molesting Anneliese in his absence was more than he could endure. Shooting him would be quick but that option was now impossible; anyway, the Dives would hear the shot and too many complicated questions would be asked in town.

Pacing up and down in the dark he nearly tripped over Mrs. Dive's grave. He paused and then, almost unknowingly, smiled to himself. Hurrying over to the barn, Samuel armed himself with a long stick and a large sack then headed for the rocks, there was just enough light from the stars to illuminate his way over the rough terrain to the previously avoided area of rocks near the barn.

With fervour and not a little fear, he began the laborious task of overturning the lighter rocks in his search, taking great care not to get his legs too close to any lurking serpents. Rock after rock was turned over but nothing was found. Mindful of where he was, he stood on a large rock to catch his breath and to collect his thoughts. Whilst he sought inspiration he decided he must first relieve his bursting bladder.

As the steaming puddle spread, the uncovered dust appeared to come alive next to the boulder he had previously lifted. Something moved .. squirmed slowly .. hissed ... and then went still. Because the sinister creature was black and partially covered in dust, it was almost invisible in the dark.

Samuel could feel his skin creeping with horror, his hair was on end and his heart pounded away, partly with anticipation but due more to pure naked fear. He knew the black mamba could strike swiftly at any moment but in the cold night air it would be sluggish. He checked; it didn't respond to the light prod of the stick but lay coiled and still... staring at him. The mouth was slightly open and Samuel could imagine the glint of its front fangs ready to strike; the narrow slit eyes reflected the starlight as it waited for the man on the rock to step within striking range.

There was a flurry of movement as Samuel deftly cast the heavy sack over the mamba; once satisfied it was completely over the snake, he leapt down onto the sack with his feet either side of where he hoped the coiled snake should be. Using the stick, he pinned the top edge of the sack firmly to the ground. For a moment the snake was trapped, it lay still... and waiting. After what seemed like an eternity, Samuel detected movement in the centre of the stretched-out sack as the long snake slowly flexed itself in its endeavour to seek escape. Samuel hoped the venomous head was also in the centre and tried to gather enough courage to wrap the sack round the snake. He held back momentarily and silently cursed Hogg.

To his horror he saw the head of the black mamba appear at the edge of the sack next to his right foot. Immediately behind its head he could begin to make out the shape of the hooded neck as it attempted to squeeze itself free. Instinctively he stamped his left foot firmly behind the snake's head trapping it; this made the remainder of its long body writhe and squirm. The sack fell aside as the snake slowly but deliberately began to coil the tail of its six foot long body around Samuel's left leg;

Samuel fought hard to control the rising, desperate urge to scream and flee. Slowly and deliberately he bent down and picked up the sack which he carefully shook open. He then placed it in front of the trapped mamba's head and, with the tip of the stick, lifted the mouth of the sack open. By cautiously moving his foot back from the snake's head he began to ease the open sack towards its venomous head with the stick. The head was about the size of a man's fist though its long body was relatively thin. Painstakingly slowly, the head was eased into the mouth of the sack until about one foot of its body was covered. Once the deadly head was safely enshrouded he bent down and wrapped the neck of the sack tightly round the mamba, the rest of its body then fell from his leg and hung limp like a thick piece of rope. He realised it was merely feigning death. Samuel thankfully shook his leg free.

Defensively, the snake continued to hang limply. Samuel knew it was very much alive, he remembered teasing grass snakes as a child, they too would feign death and then suddenly flash away to the mock terror of any onlooking children. He gently relaxed his grip and shook the rest of the snake into the sack. Holding the top of the sealed sack well away from his body he headed for the hayloft. There was still no movement from the house and the weight of the snake in the bottom of the sack made it swing as he climbed the ladder. Hogg's bedroll was just visible in the darkness. With one hand he gathered up the mouth of the rancid bedding and shook it open.

Placing the opening of the sack inside the mouth of Hogg's bedroll, Samuel gave the sack one final shake and its lethal content was transferred; the snake slithered to the bottom of the bedding and re-coiled itself into a tight ball. Samuel firmly folded the base of the bedroll over twice to trap the snake firmly then stepped back with relief.

127

Within minutes he'd collected enough firewood from the store and hurried back to the house. Hogg was still progressively working his way through the second bottle and Samuel decided the time had come for firmness.

'Come on old soldier, time for bed.' He extended a hand out towards Hogg who instantly waved him away.

'You won't get me like that,' he hissed. It was astonishing to Samuel that he could still talk coherently.

Hogg staggered to his feet still clutching his new but half empty bottle and made for the door. Samuel moved ahead and opened the door for him. Hogg stepped outside and inhaled deeply, his inebriated exhalations hung in the cold night air like the fiery breath of some mythical dragon. With heavy measured pace Hogg drunkenly made his way towards the barn, Samuel found himself hardly daring to breathe and followed at a distance. Hogg paused outside the barn to relieve himself and then went inside.

In the still of the night, the only sound that could be heard was from the creaking rungs of the ladder as Hogg made his way into the hayloft. Then silence.

Samuel waited. Walking up and down seemed to ease the tension and every few yards he paused to listen. The night remained ominously silent. The minutes went by.

When it happened, Samuel froze to the spot. The first scream was piercing, terrible and harrowing. Then silence.

The second scream came a few seconds later, but this time it was louder and longer. Samuel shivered as he visualised Hogg trapped in his bedroll with those lethal, razor sharp fangs pumping lethal venom into his blood stream. With no escape, the black mamba would strike repeatedly and paralysis would overcome Hogg in a matter of minutes. The terror crazed screaming gradually died away.

Then, not a sound could be heard.

Even the stars seemed frozen by the sound of that last scream.

Samuel stood motionless. Perhaps he had gone too far this time, but Hogg would certainly have murdered him and Mr. Dives in the night. As for Anneliese... , whilst he pondered the now receding possibilities he noticed that he had stopped shaking. He slowly but calmly walked back to the house.

As the first light of dawn appeared in the eastern sky, an exhausted Samuel fell into a deep sleep.

CHAPTER NINE

The night began to shed its cold mantle from the farm as the first warming rays of golden sunlight crept over the hills. Samuel was deeply asleep in the house and oblivious to the sights and sounds of daybreak, only the animals stirred on the farm; nothing moved in the barn. Anneliese had spent most of the night sheltering from the cold in a fruit packing shed trying to keep warm and unhappily worrying about Samuel and her father. During the silent hours before dawn she had begun to realise that her overriding concern was not for her ailing father but for the enigmatic young man who had recently ridden into her life. It was a strange pervasive feeling. She waited restlessly by Pagan but no one came; she found herself torn between her desire to ride to the farm and waiting as instructed. At any moment she expected to see the farm wagon come trundling over the ridge; she impatiently waited on.

An hour later as the sun began to warm the ground, Anneliese was already deeply worried. She reached the point when she could wait no longer and with the skill of a girl brought up with horses, sprang lightly into the saddle. It was only a short ride to the farm buildings and she halted about half a mile from the house. From her vantage point she watched the farm and listened intently. There was no sign or indication of movement.

With growing trepidation and half expecting to discover the bodies of those she loved, she cautiously eased Pagan forwards to the trot along the track towards the buildings. She halted at the main door of the house and listened, if anyone was there they would have heard her by now and come out; no one came. She felt uneasy in case Hogg was still there, and decided not to dismount; instead she nudged Pagan towards the barn. If Hogg's saddle was still on the rail, she would have to exercise great care. Menacingly, the saddle was still there.

She knew she must enter the house. If Hogg had killed them both he might just as well kill her, life would no longer have any meaning without Samuel. She determinedly directed Pagan back to the house and tied the horse to the railpost before pushing the house door open. The table had not been cleared and evidence of the meal was still untidily left throughout the kitchen. She peered into her father's room and saw him sleeping peacefully: puzzled, she wondered where Samuel might be. She crept into her own room and discovered him fast asleep in her bed. A great flood of relief swept over her as she sat down beside him. He awoke with a start but calmed immediately he saw her.

'Where's Hogg?' she asked. 'And what about Father ?' Anneliese realised her priorities were wrong and she asked again, this time with a hint of soft teasing in her voice.

'Why are you in my bed... what has happened ?'
'I'm not sure,' he replied sleepily before the disturbing memories of the previous night began to flood back. 'I got Hogg drunk on your father's best whisky and took him back to the barn out of harm's way, I must have slept too long ... I'm sorry.' She bent down and kissed him lightly on the cheek.

Samuel's mind cleared to the reality of the previous evening's events; he leapt from the bed and looked out of the window towards the barn.
'Is Hogg still here?' he asked.
'Yes... well his horse is unsaddled in the paddock so he must be.'
'I'll go and see what's keeping him,' answered Samuel, 'while you get us all some breakfast, then we must get your father ready to see the doctor.'

Although he anticipated finding Hogg dead, the uncertainty of what he would find made him feel exceedingly nervous, almost to the point of being frightened; then the memory of the scream came piercingly back to him giving him added confidence to investigate the loft. He paused inside the barn but nothing moved. He began to climb the rungs of the ladder to the hay loft and suddenly remembering the black mamba, he now proceded with added caution.

Hogg was lying half out of his bed roll with his head and torso agonizingly arched back, his unseeing eyes were bulging and his arms reached out as if he were desperately grasping for life itself.

Samuel pushed him with his foot but it wasn't necessary, Hogg was stiff - and very dead. Greatly relieved, Samuel began to breath more easily again, but where was the mamba? He instinctively retreated towards the ladder. A quick glance round the loft showed there was no sign of the reptile. It occurred to him that it might still be in the sleeping bag so he very gingerly went back to Hogg and slowly pulled the bedding away from the body. Samuel was well aware of the black mamba's reputation for speed. It could move quickly, some said as fast as a horse because stallions had been known to die from a mamba bite; the snake could lift its head up to a height of over three feet before striking an intended victim. Death was invariably certain as the venom rapidly paralysed the whole muscular system quickly affecting the heart and lung muscles.

He warily took the bed roll to the edge of the loft and shook it over the side, nothing fell out and he couldn't feel anything unusual in the blankets. Remaining where he was, Samuel peered anxiously around the loft before he detected a slight movement next to where Hogg lay. The snake was slowly emerging from under the body and began stealthily wrapping itself round one of Hogg's outstretched legs. As it moved, its eyes were locked on to Samuel; he realised it had probably remained under the body during the cold of the night.

Samuel leapt for the ladder and with his heart pounding rapidly he jumped the last six feet to the ground and ran to the house. Anneliese came out of her father's room as he entered the kitchen.

'Where's your father's gun?' he asked breathlessly,

adding,

'Hogg's dead, a mamba's got him !'

'It's under Papa's bed,' she urged, 'and the bullets are in
the red tin box.' Samuel rapidly loaded the rifle and put
some spare rounds in his pocket.

'Stay here!' he ordered; then ran back to the barn.

He carefully climbed the ladder to where he could safely
peer over the edge into the loft. He could just see the tail
of the mamba as it began to move away from under Hogg's
leg. He eased himself to the top of the ladder and stepped
cautiously into the loft. With the rifle loaded and held in
front for added protection he peered in the direction of
Hogg's body; the light was not good and the mamba
blended in with the dark timbers at the back of the roof
space; he knew it would necessitate an accurate head shot
to kill the snake.

Suddenly it reared up about ten yards away and moved
its head back. Samuel knew it was preparing to attack and
took aim at the centre of its hooded neck. He fired. The
snake's body was thrown backwards by the impact of the
heavy lead bullet then fell thrashing to the ground in its
death throes.

Mustering his courage, he lifted the body of the snake
over the barrel of his rifle and dropped it out of the loft
onto the ground below. Now it was Hogg's turn. His body
was heavier than anticipated and Samuel heaved him by
his ankles to the top of the ladder. It occurred to him that
there was little point lifting Hogg down; with a good
push, and not a little pleasure on Samuel's part, the body
was launched towards the ground where it fell with a dull
thud across the dead snake. Hogg could stay there with
the snake for company until the wagon was ready to go to
town. He smiled to himself at the thought of Dr. Spicer
getting a dead body to look at as well as seeing Mr.Dives;
it would save a lot of formalities.

Anneliese had come running from the house at the sound
of the shot. She recoiled at the sight of the body lying
across the snake but she couldn't take her eyes away from

133

the scene as Samuel explained what had happened. She peered at Hogg's body cautiously as though he could still come to life and shuddered.

'Do you think it's the same snake that got Ma?' she asked naively.

'Perhaps,' he replied in sympathy, 'I expect there are several nests of them in those rocks.'

'I wonder what it was doing in the loft?' she mused innocently. Samuel shrugged his shoulders.

'We'll take Hogg to town with us and the Doctor can get him buried. In the meantime, let's have some coffee and then get your Pa ready.'

Mr. Dives looked better for his long sleep; and over his breakfast of a boiled egg, he listened to the account of Hogg's death. Mr. Dives thought for a while and then looked at Samuel.

'Hogg was a thief and a rogue,' he said with quiet authority. 'I wonder about the diamonds that got him into trouble, I think you should search his clothes, the horse and even his saddle because that's where those stones will be hidden. He's not the sort that would leave them in a room somewhere... You'd better do it now else others might come looking when they know he's dead.'

Samuel got to his feet and looked at Anneliese.

'I'll do as your Pa says. Be ready to go when I get back.'

As Samuel approached the body, buzzing flies were already beginning to swarm around Hogg's body. Attracted by the malodorous smell of death, they busily searched out cuts or orifices into which they could lay their eggs. Samuel bent down and checked the pockets, then pulled Hogg's shirt open to reveal a hidden hand-made belt round his fat waist. He paused as he noticed three pouches sewn into the leather. Samuel felt his excitement rise as he removed the belt from the body. Gently, he undid the cord that bound the pouches securely and held his breath with glorious anticipation.

The first two pouches contained a total of eighteen

large rough diamonds, each one as big as a sovereign. They glowed as he held them towards the light and carefully rolled them in his hands. He put two back in eack pouch and secured their draw cords, the remaining stones were carefully placed in his pocket.

The third pouch contained twenty sovereigns wrapped tightly in a small white handkerchief. He put all the coins back in the pouch and replaced the belt around Hogg's middle. Samuel knew Dr. Spicer would examine the body; it would be more plausible if he discovered the coins and diamonds.

Having next ascertained the saddle bag was empty, Samuel quickly climbed into the loft, secreted the diamonds behind a loose plank and returned to the house.

'Did you find anything?' asked Mr. Dives.

'Only some sovereigns which I left in his money belt.'

'I wonder where his diamonds are, if he ever had any; but best to leave the money where it was.' said Mr. Dives as he rose to his feet.

'Right then, let's go and see this quack of yours before I change my mind.'

After Hogg had been lifted into the wagon, Samuel covered the dead man's head with the same sack used to catch the snake. The snake itself was placed alongside Hogg as Dr. Spicer would be impressed to view the actual instrument of death. Mr. Dives sat alongside Anneliese who drove the wagon behind Samuel and Pagan.

They arrived in good time and pulled up outside the town store. Mr. Greenacre was expecting them and immediately came out to greet his friends, followed by his wife. Their expressions changed when they heard about Hogg; Mr. Greenacre insisted on viewing the body.

'Come and look at this!' he called to some customers in the store. They all excitedly gathered round and the astonishing tale began to spread among the inhabitants. Samuel lifted the dead mamba and placed it across Hogg's

135

chest for greater effect making the viewers gasp and take a few paces back.

'Get the doctor, Nigel,' ordered Mr. Greenacre; and an onlooking farmer set off across the road to the hotel. A few minutes later Dr. Spicer arrived complete with his medical bag. He examined Hogg's eyes and turned to the small crowd.

'He's dead!' he announced .

Someone laughed as if the pronouncement were a joke; no one was saddened by the event.

Dr. Spicer turned to the farmer,

'Will five shillings bury him, Nigel?' Nigel agreed it would.

'And you had better get rid of this.' said the doctor, indicating the snake.

'I think it got him on his leg,' said Samuel helpfully. Dr. Spicer pulled Hogg's trousers up towards the dead man's knees revealing several puncture wounds. The crowd gathered round to view the bites.

'Right, take him away,' said Dr. Spicer casually. He then looked at Mr. Dives who was still sitting on the wagon seat. 'And you must be my next patient. We'll go back to my room , but I think we all need a drink first.' The doctor offered Mr. Dives his hand and, assisted by Anneliese, they climbed off the wagon. The small party began to cross the road to the hotel.

Suddenly there was a loud shout from the farmer entrusted to bury the body.

'Doctor , Doctor.... come back here.... look what's on the body!' The farmer stood over Hogg pointing at the deceased's stomach. Samuel breathed a sigh of relief.

The farmer pulled the secret belt away from the body and one of the onlookers cried out,

'It's the diamonds, he had them on him all the time!'

The gathering crowd made way for the doctor who took the belt from the farmer. Dr. Spicer carefully opened the pouches and put the four stones on the side of the wagon.

He then counted out the twenty sovereigns and handed one to Nigel.

'He can pay for his own funeral,' said the doctor and everyone laughed. Hogg had never been more popular. Knowing Mr. Greenacre was a member of the Council of Elders, the doctor handed the remaining treasure to him.

'I think these had better go into the protection of the Elders; they might like to notify the Mine Owners' Association.' With that he turned and headed back to the hotel. The crowd slowly dispersed.

Anneliese assisted her father up to Dr. Spicer's room and then joined Samuel who had ordered some refreshments.

'We'll wait for Pa down here,' she said. 'He'll be a while.'

It was cooler in the hotel lounge and the two gratefully sat down on the comfortable chairs. The proprietor brought Anneliese a glass of lemon while Samuel sipped a beer. There were no other intrusive visitors in the hotel and neither felt inclined to say very much as they waited. Mr. Greenacre then arrived and invited them all to the store for a salad lunch.

'I've closed the shop,' he said, 'this is all too exciting; come over when you're ready.' Then he left for the store feeling very pleased to have been actively involved in the action.

A good half hour passed before Dr. Spicer appeared on the stairs assisting Mr. Dives. Samuel immediately went towards them.

'It's all right,' said Mr. Dives, 'we'll come and join you.' He waved an arm at the proprietor. 'A cold bottle of Cape wine if you please.' They sat and sipped the wine while waiting for the doctor to speak.

'I'm afraid I've diagnosed a stomach cyst,' he addressed Anneliese. 'He will need to rest for the next few weeks and

137

I've given him some opium to keep the pain away.'

'But Papa, you didn't tell me you were in pain,' beseeched Anneliese.

'I didn't tell you because it's not that bad,' replied her father.

'As long as he can sleep when he wants to,' intervened the doctor, 'he will be all right.'

Samuel however didn't think the doctor was very convincing. Out of politeness for Mr. Dives, the subject of his health was avoided. They chatted excitedly about the demise of Hogg and the diamonds found on his body.

'There,' said Mr. Dives reproachfully to Samuel, 'You should have checked him more thoroughly.'

'I wanted to, but his clothes were stinking. Anyway, we've gained a good horse and saddle,' he replied. Samuel put his arm round Anneliese.

'There, it's all over now, he won't bother you again.'

Anneliese shuddered as she thought of those grime encrusted hands feeling her body. The others laughingly speculated over the value and likely destination of the four diamonds.

Samuel breathed a deep sigh of relief, everything had gone to plan.

CHAPTER TEN

The group finished their wine and profuse thanks were rendered by all to Dr. Spicer. Everyone shook hands and then Dr. Spicer spoke firmly to Mr. Dives.

'Take the medicine as instructed and I'll see you next month as we agreed; in the meantime, you must rest... let the youngsters do all the work.'

They laughed; and waving their goodbyes, the family group set off to visit the Greenacres for lunch. As they crossed the road, a growing cluster of townspeople had gathered between the hotel and the store; some were there to hear the tale and share the drama while others greeted Mr. Dives. The sensational tale of the diamonds and Hogg's death had spread to every household in the small town; it was even more exciting than the outbreak of the Zulu war. Some congratulated Samuel for shooting the mamba while others expressed their pleasure at seeing Mr.Dives again. He was well known as a founder member of the Town Elders and most of the locals knew of his illness.

Following lunch, they bade the Greenacres goodbye and set off for home. There were black rain clouds building to the north and the townspeople were anticipating the flash flood which always followed heavy rain.

A cool breeze was blowing by the time they reached the farm. Mr. Dives was pleased that his energy had lasted throughout the strenuous day but already the insidious tiredness from the day's events was beginning to overwhelm him. Anneliese helped her father into the house while Samuel took the wagon into the barn and let the two horses join the others in the paddock. For an idle moment he watched Hogg's horse; it was a proud, strong looking stallion of sixteen hands. He reasoned that it would be wise to allow the animal another week or so to settle before trying to ride it. A glance at Hogg's saddle confirmed that it was well made and that too would come in handy as a spare.

He walked back to the house. Mr. Dives was busily opening a bottle of the same fine Cape wine they had earlier enjoyed at the hotel.

'I have a small announcement to make,' he smiled and Anneliese looked at her father curiously. He slowly poured the wine into three glasses and gave one each to Samuel and Anneliese.

'From today, it is my wish that Samuel becomes a part of the family.' He turned directly to Samuel. 'I want you to move into the house and we'll convert the spare room into a proper room, after all - we can't have you sleeping with black mambas or Hogg's ghost. That's all in the past.' He raised his glass and proposed a toast. 'To the family.'

They all responded and Samuel quietly thanked them both. Anneliese took hold of Samuel's hand and looked directly at him.
'You'll stay then ?' There was a degree of pleading in her eyes.
'Yes, for the time being.... let's see what happens, there's still a war on and times are uncertain... but yes, I'll be staying.' She gave him a hug and they all sat for several hours chatting over the day's extraordinary events.

The unseen cyst in Mr. Dive's abdomen continued to grow and progressively weaken his whole system. The elixir supplied by Dr. Spicer, a tincture of opium in brandy, eased his pain and enabled him to sleep for most of the time. After that memorable day when Hogg died, Mr. Dives had continued to weaken and, within the month, became virtually housebound. Anneliese devoted most of her time to caring for her ailing father.

Following the earlier bulk sale of the cattle, there was little to do on the farm and even the native farm workers only needed meagre supervision when they were cropping vegetables. On the 1st July, Samuel visited Dr. Spicer to collect a further supply of the medicinal tincture. During their meeting they discussed Mr. Dives' condition and

Samuel's fears were confirmed. With four refilled medicine bottles safely tucked in his saddlebag he returned to the farm. Knowing the seriousness of the condition made him feel a little easier, nevertheless he had already decided not to say anything to Anneliese. They could do nothing other than watch helplessly as the old man deteriorated.

The morning of the 4th July 1879 was a day Samuel would not forget. It was the day the Zulus were finally defeated by the British Army at Ulundi. It was also the day Mr. Dives died from his illness. During the previous night he painfully wrote a short note to Anneliese, then drank the best part of a full bottle of the opium mixture.

Samuel had left the house at sunrise and was busy supervising the farm natives digging out a new irrigation channel when he saw Anneliese slowly riding towards him. He walked to meet her. As she approached he could see she was crying. Without either of them saying a word he helped her dismount then held her tightly. The comfort of his firm embrace was too much for her and her copious tears began to flow followed by deep racking sobs of anguish. She remained in his arms for some time before he gently led her to sit on the sandy bank beside the stream. She produced the roughly written note for him to read.

> "My dearest daughter, I can burden you no more. Everything I own is now yours, see Harvey, he has my will. Your mother and I will always watch over you.
>
> Papa."

Samuel struggled to hold his own emotions in check but the kindness of the note was too much for him. They shared their grief by the lifegiving stream for the next hour or so, and then together they returned to the farm. The following morning Anneliese took Pagan into town to make the legal arrangements for the burial and to notify their family friends of their loss. Samuel had already decided to build a more dignified grave for Mrs. Dives and this was the opportunity. When the backbreaking work of digging through the stony ground was completed, Anneliese's parents were laid to rest together. Mr. and Mrs. Greenacre attended the makeshift burial; each read a short passage from Anneliese's bible before Samuel completed the task of shovelling back the remainder of the stoney earth. As requested, Mr. Greenacre had brought a supply of mortar, and over the next few days, Samuel fashioned a solid structure over the two bodies complete with named matching crosses.

The following Friday, Samuel and Anneliese attended town together to complete the few but necessary formalities to transfer the farm to Anneliese. Thereafter life continued on the farm. Anneliese rapidly regained her gaiety and enthusiasm for helping Samuel by spending the mornings working in the house and outbuildings and the afternoons with him out on the farm. About three weeks following the burial, Samuel was planting seeds at the vegetable plots when he saw Anneliese approaching. He was astonished to see that she was riding Hogg's horse. She grinned at him when she saw the perplexed look on his face.

'I thought it was high time I took the curse off the poor beast, he's lovely and we've both enjoyed the ride... he's so well mannered but I think you'll have to ride him... it's like riding an elephant up here.' They laughed as she slid down from the horse.
'I've done enough for today,' he said, 'let's ride back.' They chatted as always and when back at the house, Samuel finally managed to pluck up sufficient courage for the task that had hitherto eluded him.

Anneliese was busy in the kitchen when he approached her.

'Can we go outside ? There is something I have to say.'
'I hope it's not serious,' she teased .
'Yes it is ; well, it's middling serious.' His expression gave nothing away.

Anneliese felt uncertain for the first time since her father died; it was not like Samuel to be evasive. They sat down together on the verandah bench.

'Something is wrong here,' he said firmly. A hundred thoughts flashed through her mind and she could think of nothing which could possibly be wrong. Perhaps he was going to leave; a look of concern began to slowly spread across her face.

'Will you do something for me?' asked Samuel softly.

'That depends ...' she waited while he struggled to find the words so often rehearsed over the last few days.

'We're living here together and folks will soon talk ... I can see there is only one thing to do.' At that point she saw the glint in his eyes .

'Can we be married?' he asked nervously .

Anneliese pulled him to her and they held each other tightly.

'Yes,' she replied, 'I had begun to think you might not ask me, in fact I had even thought of sending you back to sleep in the barn.' They both beamed at each other.

'Wait here a moment.' said Samuel. He went into the house and returned a moment later. He was holding a small leather pouch. She had seen him purchase it on their previous visit to the town but had not queried its purpose. Her curiosity increased.

'There is something I must tell you, but first put your fingers together, like this,' he made a cup of his hands. She copied him. Opening the pouch he slowly poured the uncut diamonds and as they fell from the leather pouch into her hands, the evening sunlight played on the edges of the stones in a flight of colour.

Even through their roughness, they could both see the brilliance and energy of a million years trying to cascade out. Samuel broke the silence.

'I took them from Hogg, he stole them from the mines... I've thought about them a lot, if I give them back, some millionaire will become a little richer... I would like to think that, in a way, they are a wedding present to us... right from within the earth itself... and we'll only use them if we have to.'

Anneliese said nothing but she knew he was right.

'I agree... does this mean that we are rich?' She had never held a diamond before and any value the stones might have was beyond her comprehension.

'Well... judging by the fuss when they saw Hogg's diamonds, I expect they are worth a great deal.'

'Can you explain one thing?' she was puzzled. 'How have you got these... I mean... I saw them find the diamonds in his belt?'

Samuel explained that to have taken all the stones might have aroused some suspicion, even placed them in danger . After all, everyone had heard that Hogg was an illegal diamond dealer. They sat holding hands until long after darkness fell.

The Greenacres were delighted with the young couple's news and Mrs. Greenacre went into a whirl of excitement at the thought of all the preparations for the wedding.

On the 6th of September 1879, Anneliese and Samuel were married at the recently completed Ladysmith church. Following a simple ceremony, the newly married couple entertained their friends for the rest of the day at the Royal Hotel.

The farm prospered. Over the next few years Anneliese gave birth to three healthy sons, Winston, Cedric and Frederick. All the while, a sealed parcel containing the diamonds and the Colour flag lay deposited for safety in the vault of the Ned Bank in Ladysmith.

The package slowly gathered dust.

On the 25th August 1879, the Cardiff City Newpaper reported the end of the Zulu war. On its back page and edged in black, it listed over one thousand names of the dead from the two Welsh Battalions together with the names of their home towns. A copy was subsequently posted in the town square at Brecon; it was several days before the Carrington family learned that Samuel's name was included. For them, the news was not totally unexpected, Samuel's last letter arrived over eight months earlier and everyone knew that the Welsh soldiers had borne the brunt of numerous Zulu attacks.

The following Sunday, prayers for the fallen were said in the packed churches and chapels across the length and breadth of Wales.

At the back of the little church at Sennybridge, Bethan was unable to hold back her tears.

NQUTU PLATEAU

TO ULUNDI

ROUTE OF ATTACKING ZULUS

ZULUS FIRST SEEN FROM HERE

CONICAL HILL

G COMPANY RETREAT

1ST BATTALION

BRITISH POSITIONS

2ND BATTALION

ISANDHLWANA

HORSE KILLED HERE

GRASSY PLAIN

ESCAPE ROUTE DAY ONE

TWO NCOs KILLED HERE

ROCKS

NIGHT SPENT HERE

DEEP GORGE

BRITISH RETREAT

ESCAPE ROUTE DAY TWO

ROUTE OF ULUNDI (AND INVADING) OF BRITISH ARMY

NATIVE TRACK

TO RORKE'S DRIFT

S. Carrington. 1880

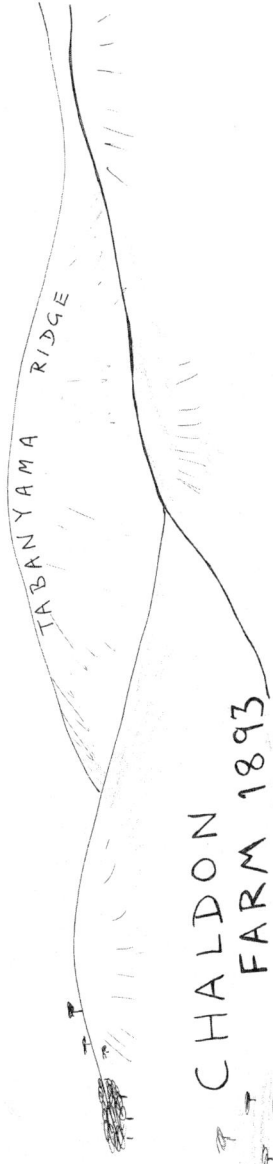

CHALDON
FARM 1893

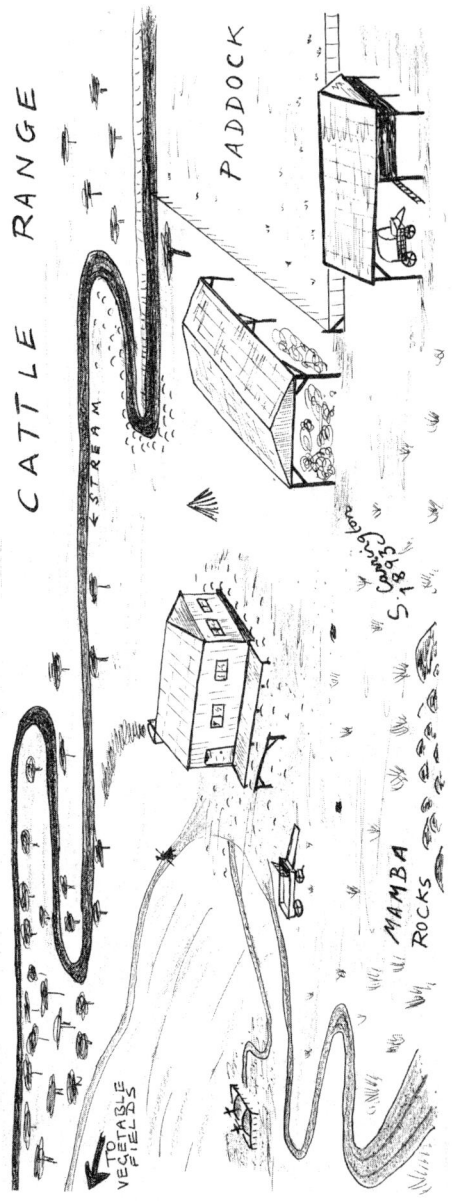

TABANYAMA RIDGE

CATTLE RANGE

PADDOCK

STREAM

TO
VEGETABLE
FIELDS

MAMBA
ROCKS

Carrington
S 1893

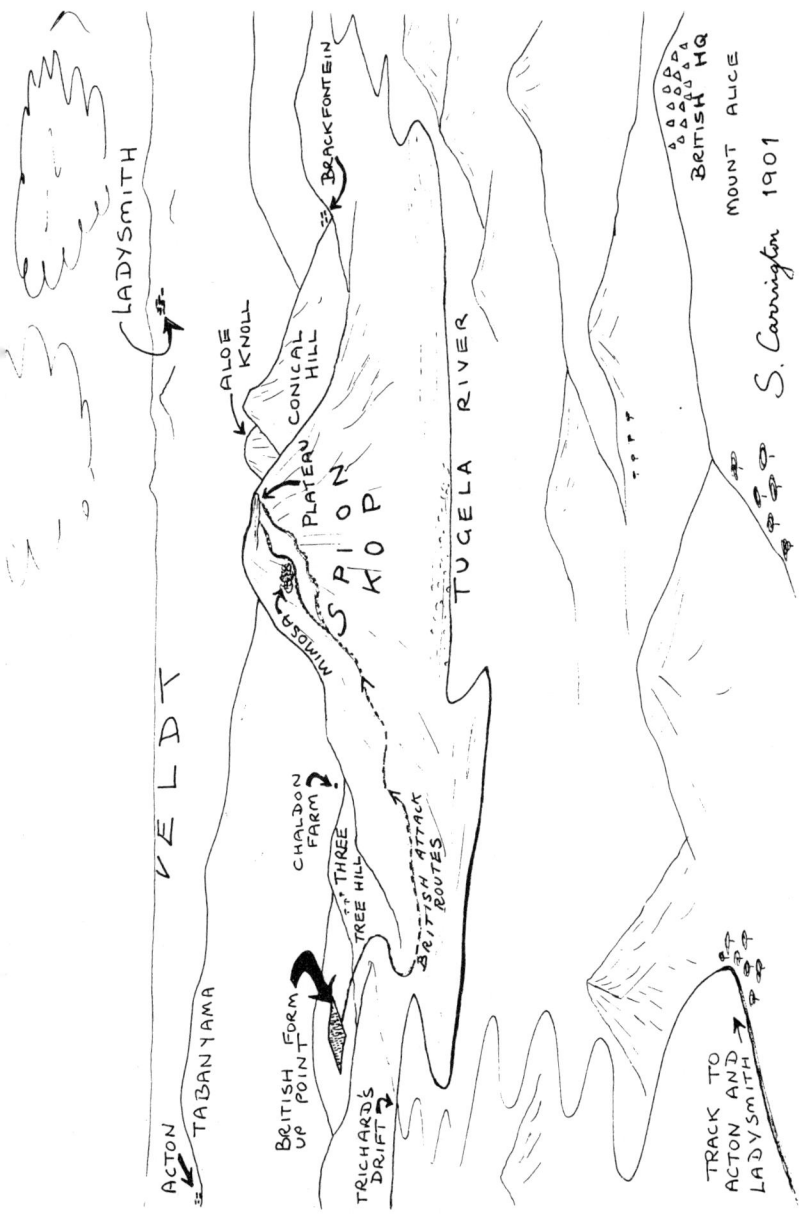

VELDT

LADYSMITH

ACTON

TABANYAMA

BRITISH FORM UP POINT

CHALDON FARM

THREE TREE HILL

BRITISH ATTACK ROUTES

TRICHARD'S DRIFT

WINMSOW

PLATEAU

ALOE KNOLL

CONICAL HILL

BRACKFONTEIN

SPION KOP

TUGELA RIVER

TRACK TO ACTON AND LADYSMITH

MOUNT ALICE

BRITISH HQ

S. Carrington 1901

PART TWO.

PART TWO.

A BRIEF HISTORICAL PROLOGUE TO THE BOER WAR.

Natal is the smallest of South Africa's four provinces and has always been widely recognised for its varied floral beauty, magnificent scenery and fertile soil. By offering so much, men have been attracted to compete for its vast and abundant resources. The inevitable result has been its long history of war, punctuated only by brief periods of peace. Apart from minor skirmishes between the Boers and British in 1881, comparative peace flourished again until the 2nd October 1899. Once more, the cause of impending war was man's greed.

In 1884 substantial deposits of pure gold were discovered in the neighbouring Boer controlled state of Transvaal. The gold rush which followed brought untold thousands of prospectors from across the world to seek their fortune. Over the next five years these 'Uitlanders' as they were known, eventually outnumbered the Boers. In order to maintain their beloved independence, the Boer government refused to grant the Uitlanders any voting rights; the Uitlanders then promptly and bitterly complained to the British government. Sensing trouble and now able to capitalise on their new found wealth, the Boers armed themselves with modern weapons provided by the sympathetic Dutch and German governments.

On the 2nd October 1899, the Transvaal leaders declared war on Great Britain. Ten days later the hotch-potch Boer army, consisting mainly of farmers, began its invasion of Natal. Anticipating the attack, Britain had already moved a considerable number of troops and artillery into Kimberley to protect the diamond fields. The same was happening three hundred miles away at Ladysmith because of its strategic importance . The British Army in South Africa was well trained but too widely spread to protect its far flung interests. The Ladysmith garrison dispatched two forces to attack the gathering Boers; the first action at Elandslaagte on the 21st October resulted in victory for the British. The second action was more ambiguous; a sizeable British force knocked the Boers off the Talana Hill near Dundee at a cost of over five hundred British casualties only to find themselves being surrounded by an even larger enemy force. They withdrew back to Ladysmith in considerable disorder.

Once refreshed, the garrison commander Sir George White, sought to deliver the Boers a crushing blow before they became too established. He sent an offensive force of two brigades complete with supporting artillery and cavalry to attack the Boers headquarters which he 'hoped' was located somewhere about four miles north of the town. The Boers cunningly changed their location and pounded the unsuspecting force with artillery and rifle fire. It was a rout with the British losing three hundred men killed and nearly one thousand captured; uncharacteristically, the British broke ranks and became a rabble intent only on seeking their way back to Ladysmith. During the 26th October, the retreating survivors staggered back into Ladysmith to the consternation of its civilian population. The main Boer force of over twenty thousand volunteer farmers then completely surrounded the garrison and brought up its artillery to bear on the town; slightly smaller forces already lay siege to Kimberley and Mafeking.

The British Army could eventually rely on a further ten thousand reinforcements currently en route from India and the Mediterranean but the war had commenced magnificently for the Boers. Once they had taken Ladysmith, the way would be clear right through to the coast and the port of Durban. The Boers sensed an overwhelming victory and so the siege of Ladysmith began.

For several years prior to hostilities, Ladysmith had been known as the "Aldershot" of South Africa. It was an ideal site for all things military. Situated in the middle of nowhere, it possessed good road and rail supply lines and communications to both Durban and the Cape. The flat dusty plain to the south of the town was eminently suitable

147

for set-piece military manoeuvres and parade ground tactics beloved of the generals, and the troops felt comfortable around the town. Even two of the local hillocks had been renamed 'Caesar's Hill' and 'Waggon Hill' after familiar features from around Aldershot. It was , however, not a suitable place to defend being hemmed in on all sides by these same hills now occupied by the Boers. Sir George White now crammed over thirteen thousand troops and all their military stores and paraphernalia into the town's school and churches. Around the town, a sea of white army bell tents had grown until, from the Boer positions, they looked like clusters of flowering white daffodils.

Over the next two months the surrounded garrison idly prepared for the possibility of action and apart from mild skirmishing and some irregular Boer shelling, little happened to raise or dampen spirits. The British were content to sit in the sun and await relief by superior forces, and while the Boers couldn't capture the two towns, their dream of extending the attack towards Durban and the sea could not materialise.

During the first part of December, the approaching British relief force steadily gathered and prepared to attack the Boers. The assault began on the 12th December 1899 at Magersfontein near Kimberley but the British under the command of Lord Methuen lost the first battle with 902 men killed or injured. In the same week, whilst attempting to break the Boer line to relieve Ladysmith, Sir Redvers Buller VC sustained 1,138 casualties at Colenso. The Boers owed their astonishing victories to their frustratingly successful hit-and- run tactics, sheer bravery in the face of a modern army and local knowledge of the unmapped battlefields. The British had marched into battle in their tight parade-ground formations only to become trapped on the open veldt by accurate rifle and artillery fire from concealed trenches.

Many British soldiers broke ranks to flee the slaughter only to be cut down by accurate cross fire from the entrenched Boer marksmen. While the withering Mauser rifle fire from the hidden Boers raked through their remaining pinned-down ranks including three kilted Highland regiments, the unremitting and intense heat of the midday sun burnt through their unprotected pale Scottish skins. By the end of that scorching December day, the Scots sustained agonising suppurating wounds on the backs of their legs leaving many unable to walk.

Captain Congreve, ADC to Buller and the Campaign press censor, summed up the day.

'No water, not a breath of air, not a particle of shade and a sun which I never felt hotter even in India.'

By nightfall, the so-called relieving Army of Sir Redvers Buller had suffered an ignominious defeat, it had also lost a tenth of its strength and many of the survivors would not be fit to fight for several weeks until their sunburnt legs healed. All were weary, bewildered and depressed. There was only one course of action; Buller led his army in retreat back the seven miles to its base at Frere.

The Boers were greatly encouraged by their defeat of two large highly professional British forces charged with attempting to relieve their besieged colleagues.

In London, events were reported by the press under the heading of the 'Black Week.'

* * * * * * * * * * * * * * * *

CHAPTER ELEVEN

Chaldon Farm , Ladysmith 1899.

During the time leading to the Boer invasion, Samuel was already sharing a lot of the routine farm work with his two grown sons, Winston and Cedric. At eighteen, Winston was a mirror image of his father, albeit slimmer and without his father's beard. Cedric was sixteen, shorter and looked more like Anneliese although he could work as hard as his older brother when he wanted to. The youngest son, Frederick was still at school in Ladysmith. He was looking forward to his fourteenth birthday and the much wished for opportunity of finally leaving school. During the school term, he lived with the Greenacres over their recently rebuilt spacious store, riding home for the weekends and holidays. Samuel had proved to be a very successful farmer as well as being a caring and protective husband and father. Anneliese was as beautiful as ever and doted on her handsome family. Their contentment was nearly complete; Samuel only fleetingly spoke of his family in Wales, it was something which had always concerned Anneliese. She knew he had refused to write to them all those years but she respected his decision.

The Boer invasion suddenly changed many things. With the Boers swiftly surrounding Ladysmith there was no school for Frederick and the town could no longer be supplied with the farm's produce. Samuel was growing more concerned for the safety of his isolated family than for the temporary loss of his trade although he and Anneliese had quietly reasoned that they were far enough from the besieged town not to be bothered by the Boers. He had already decided to let the farm continue normally , after all, the British would soon arrive and defeat the untrained Boers. Ladysmith would then be desperate for his supplies again. He also had obligations to his small but loyal native work force who relied on him for their everyday needs.

Events were soon to overtake their otherwise peaceful existence. On the morning of the 10th November 1899, two Boer officers rode onto the farm. The boys spotted them when they rode over the brow of the hill and excitedly alerted their parents. Samuel and Annelise stood waiting for them on the verandah as the riders cautiously approached the house. The boys waited respectfully behind their parents in the doorway. Samuel could not decipher the Boers' ranks as the older of the two visitors casually dismounted and courteously smiled at the anxious family.

He approached Samuel with the typical Boer greeting,
'Goeie dag Almal,' and extended his hand.
'Welcome,' replied Samuel accepting the handshake , 'But I hope we can speak in English, my Afrikaans is only passable,'
'No problem,' acknowledged the Boer, 'but we wish to talk to you.'
'Please come in,' Samuel indicated the open door, 'We were about to have coffee.'

The two visitors were wearing the classic soft brown field hats of the Boers with the raised side brim, though otherwise they were dressed in their normal farming clothes. Both carried new Mauser rifles fresh from their factory packing cases. The boys stared at the heavy bandoliers of ammunition each man wore over his shoulder as they entered the house. They all sat down except for the boys who stood back and observed the proceedings in considerable awe.

The elder Boer watched Anneliese making the coffee before turning to Samuel.
'We have no quarrel with you or your family, we will duly expel your leaders and your army, but the people can live in peace with us.' Anneliese set the cups before her husband and their guests.
'But the British will come in great numbers,' she said, 'they have done the same before.' Her mind went back those twenty years to the Zulu war.
'We do not think so,' replied the same Boer, 'they have no use for this country; once they are beaten they will withdraw back to the Cape.'

They all pondered on his words while Anneliese poured the coffee.

'But that is not the purpose of your visit?' suggested Samuel with just the hint of a question in his voice.

'Quite right, we wish to purchase some of your cattle, your fruit, your produce... we have many hungry mouths in our army and they all need feeding. We will pay you in gold if that is acceptable?'

Samuel knew that his market with the British was non-existent all the time Ladysmith was surrounded, and between his farm and the town was the bulk of the Boer army. He had no argument with the Boers; like many of the remote farmers in the district, he considered his personal enemies to be drought and disease; he'd always thought of the Boer farmers as equals trying to make a meagre living from the harsh lands bordering the edge of the Kalahari desert.

Samuel was fully aware there were no immediate options.

'Have what you need and pay me what you can, just leave the breeding stock alone so that I can re-stock. As for the other produce, send your supply wagons to the farm and I'll provide what I can.' The Boers looked at each other and the spokesman took up the issue.

'It may not be possible to pay you immediately but I give you my word that you will receive your money.' Samuel nodded and just hoped that the British would not be too long arriving; especially as they always paid hard cash for their goods.

The conversation continued with polite comments about the farm. Anneliese felt rather sorry for the two Boers so far from home; they remained in the house until no more coffee was offered then they finally rose to leave. Following some robust handshaking, the Boers departed. The boys were almost overwhelmed by the unexpected visit and it took a few stern words from Anneliese to calm their excitement.

'What does this mean for us?' she asked seriously. Samuel shrugged his shoulders.

'It means at best we get paid for our cattle, at worst they just take them; they'll probably pay for some but who knows... it depends how the war goes for them.'

'Are we safe here?' asked Anneliese. Samuel could see that she was concerned.

'I really don't know, it might be as well for us to be ready to go, although I don't think anyone will hurt us, we're too remote.' Anneliese agreed.

'To be honest,' her husband continued, 'we are in more danger from the actual fighting itself, but with the British bottled up in Ladysmith, any fighting will probably take place around the town. What I will do is take Cedric with me and scout towards the south.... and you, Winston, can ride a few miles north. Just see where the Boers are and then we'll have a better idea of our situation. If anyone stops you, you're looking for stray cattle.' Winston nodded his understanding.

Samuel and his younger son, Cedric, set off south towards Trichardt's Drift on the Tugela River. They skirted round the hills of Spion Kop and by midday they could look down towards the river which meandered below their vantage point albeit some two miles away. They could both clearly see the Boers digging trenches on the near side of the river.

'They must be Boers because nobody else would dig trenches during the hottest part of the day,' remarked Samuel to his son. Samuel also noticed several Boers on the distant summit of Spion Kop and it was obvious that another defensive position was being prepared on the commanding high ground. He reflected on the passage of time; was it really all those years ago when he took Anneliese to see the view from the summit of Spion Kop. He remembered her teasing him and smiled inwardly at the memory. But back to reality, they had seen enough for today, it was time to go home.

153

Winston had already returned to the farm by the time they arrived back. He recounted that the Boers were heavily concentrated around Ladysmith but there was no sign of any other activity between the town and their farm. Samuel decided, for the time being, that they would all remain where they were . If necessary, he would send them to acquaintances at Acton, a small hamlet some six miles to the West.

In the meantime, they could only wait and watch, but be ready to act. He also decided to undertake a daily patrol beyond the farm boundary to monitor the whereabouts of the Boers, not knowing what was happening just confused the issues but at least they could be ready to leave. That evening they each packed a bundle of clothes in readiness for a sudden departure should an emergency arise.

Thereafter the Boers visited the farm every week or so. They commandeered beef cattle and other produce according to their immediate needs, they always paid in gold sovereigns or with promissory notes signed by the local Boer commander. Samuel carefully secreted the coins but realised the paper receipts would certainly be worthless unless the Boers defeated the British. Little news of the war filtered through to the family other than what could be gleaned from the Boers who remained friendly and optimistic. Their officers considered the initial successes to be the model for any future actions and, after all, unless the British changed their tactics the Boers believed themselves invincible. And God was on their Calvinist side.

The Boers were especially jubilant when they arrived at the farm on the 17th December. By now they felt at ease with Samuel and Anneliese and over the usual coffee which accompanied the exchange of payment, Samuel learned of the latest British defeat only ten miles to the south at Colenso. The Boers were now totally confident that the British could never win but Samuel had already detected some dissent among the lower ranks. The average Boer was, after all, a farmer and he was a long way from home and family. Samuel had heard the rumours circulating among the Boers that the British had burnt several of their distant farms. This was worrying if true and such news would only serve to further sap their morale. After the Boers had concluded the transaction and departed, the family discussed the latest news together with their reaction to the lack of British progress; then they heard the sound of another horse approaching. Samuel went to the door and recognised John Debling, a cattle farmer from the far side of the Tabanyama hills to the west. Samuel welcomed his neighbour. After dusting himself down after his long ride he looked enquiringly at Samuel.

'I see you had another visit; stealing more of your cattle were they?'

'Yes, each week it's the same, are they taking yours?'

'Yes,' replied John, 'there's not much one can do about it.'

'You had better come in,' invited Samuel, 'they'll soon take all our stock at this rate, do you know what's going on, have you any more news ?'

They all sat around the kitchen table for yet another "council of war" as Anneliese described these conversations.

John was a tall man about the same age as Samuel and equally weather beaten. The two men had casually known each other for several years and although they were neighbours, their farms were separated by some seven miles of barren veldt.

'You wouldn't believe it,' began John, 'the Boers have beaten the British at Colenso forcing them to retreat for the time being .... but they'll no doubt return. In the meantime the Boers are strengthening their line this side of the river; I think they'll make a fight of it.'

'We've seen them digging trenches,' added Samuel.

'Apparently the British marched right up to the Boers at Colenso.' John paused for effect, 'It was a slaughter, and it will happen again; they're fortifying right along the river bank just south of your farm waiting for the British to

155

attack again,'

'That's what we're worried about,' replied Anneliese .

'Roz and I think you should all come over and stay with us,' said John, 'if the British get across the river, you'll be right in the middle of the fighting.... and that cannon fire is devastating.'

'We've been thinking about that possibility, and you are right,' said Samuel. Rapidly he considered the problem in his mind. If the farm was damaged, he could always rebuild it; he couldn't rebuild his family if they were hurt. John had also heard fresh rumours of Boers attacking British farms near Kimberley in retaliation for the sacked Boer farms, and expressed his concern that the same could easily happen here. That fresh information forced Samuel to face up to the deteriorating situation; his mind was now firmly made up. He addressed his family with added firmness in his voice.

'Anneliese, you and the boys will go with John this afternoon.' He turned to John, 'They have already packed, I will stay on for a few days in order to sell the remaining beef cattle to the Boers. If we all go now they'll be suspicious and take everything.' They all agreed.

Samuel gave the boys their instructions. Winston and Cedric hurried off to collect their horses and prepare the farm wagon while Frederick assisted Anneliese to pack food and clothes into some wooden farm crates.

'Can you stay awhile and ride with them?' asked Samuel. John nodded and asked,

'And what about you, how long will you stay here?' Samuel was already thinking beyond the immediate situation, he needed some extra time to deal with another problem nagging his mind.

'A few days, then I'll ride over and see you all. I'll keep an eye on things here for as long as I can but I will feel a lot easier if the family are out of harm's way.'

'We're ready,' announced Winston as spokesman for the departing family.

Anneliese and Frederick climbed onto the neatly packed wagon as the other two sons mounted their ponies. Samuel watched from the verandah and began to feel strangely remote from his family.

'Take care of yourself,' said Anneliese with obvious concern in her voice, 'and don't be too long before joining us.' They all waved and within a few minutes they were hidden from view by the rising dust of their departure. Samuel realised he was alone again for the first time in many years. Slowly that old feeling began to take a hold on him. He could feel his skin tingling and the pounding heart within him felt near to bursting. Memories of that long forgotten escape from the Zulus began crowding back into his mind, he shook his head to rid himself of the deepening feeling and gradually the sensation began to ebb away. He felt completely drained of energy.

He then began to think about the other major problem he must resolve.

Sitting in the bank vault in Ladysmith was his secret fortune in diamonds, together with the Colour. If the Boers eventually forced the garrison to surrender, they would certainly ransack the bank before retreating home.

He must somehow get through the Boer lines and into the town. Once there he could withdraw the diamonds and conceal them out of harm's way. He secured the house and saddled his horse while his mind struggled to form a plan of action. He had accepted Winston's assertions that there were no Boers this side of the Platrand hills overlooking the besieged town; however, it would be safer to make sure. If he could get close to the outskirts of the town without being challenged, there was the distinct possibility that he could slip through the Boer lines and reach the town under cover of darkness. He knew that the moon was waning but tonight might just be dark enough, if the clouds remained.

It was late afternoon when he set off towards the town

but keeping well clear of the roadway. He rode cautiously, taking time to scan around for signs of patrols or Boer revettes, the route appeared to be clear. When he was still only half way, it became obvious that to approach nearer would be very dangerous as the Boers were sited in large groups around their main artillery positions, they would easily spot a lone rider. Dismounting in the lee of a small hill, Samuel took his telescope from the saddlebag and scanned his proposed route. The Boers appeared to have carefully sited their artillery around the town utilising the high ground. They were able to look down on the town and all its radiating roads but they did not appear to be concerned with protecting their rear supply lines. Samuel realised the Boers didn't need to protect their own supply lines; behind them was their own main force which had recently prevailed against the British. Seen through the telescope, the Boers were obviously relaxing. Their horses were unguarded and the men were sitting in groups smoking or in conversation. Occasionally a gun would randomly fire a shell into the town, otherwise there was no activity. Samuel saw his chance.

Riding back to the farm, he spent the final hour of daylight placing the family's more valuable possessions in the underground cool store behind the house. After replacing the wooden lid, he heaped manure on top to discourage a casual searcher if the Boers decided to ransack the farm. After checking the cattle with his headman and securing the house, he set off back towards Ladysmith. It was getting dark by the time he reached the observation point of the earlier afternoon. The Boer positions were now softly illuminated by lanterns; and through the telescope, he carefully scanned between the gun sites for signs of any new guard positions.

The Boers were masters of concealment; but so was Samuel and there were no visible signs to concern him. By nightfall, it was obvious that there were no apparent lines of communication between the Boer artillery positions. In front and to the right of his observation point was an unguarded gap about eight hundred yards wide between two gun emplacements. Samuel decided it should be reasonably easy for a brave man to walk through the line in darkness but his horse would certainly be discovered by the Boers in the morning. Pagan was well trained, so Samuel decided the horse could walk with him.

After untying two specially packed empty sacks from the back of his saddle, he carefully cut each in half. Pagan obediently lifted each foot in turn for his owner to fashion a muffling pad of sacking over each hoof and the pad was then firmly bound with cord. Samuel led Pagan for a few paces and was immediately impressed with the silencing effect, the horse was now nearly as inaudible as any man on the sandy soil. By about 7 pm sounds of singing carried across from the Boer positions; their evening hymns echoing shamelessly across the darkened veldt. Now was the time.

The slow moving figures of the man and horse merged invisibly with the night. Samuel decided to lead Pagan on foot until they were through the lines and by using the lights of the two selected Boer positions as his guide, they cautiously but steadily made good progress. It took longer than anticipated to draw level with the Boer line but gradually the pair made headway. After an hour they paused.

The two positions were now definitely behind them so Samuel warily mounted Pagan and eased the horse towards the lights of the town. It was surprising that it had been so easy; but after all, the Boers were only interested in enclosing the garrison, they wouldn't consider that anyone would want to get into a town under siege. Half an hour later he was challenged by a sentry of the Liverpool Regiment who insisted on taking Samuel to the Officer of the Watch. Following some curt questioning, he was then escorted into the town by a suspicious sergeant for his identity to be verified by the Greenacres. With that formality over, he was released to his delighted friends.

There was much to talk about and it was late before all the news was exchanged. He explained his presence to the Greenacres as an intelligence mission to provide the garrison commander with details of the Boer positions. He would do exactly that tommorow.

In the morning he presented himself at the bank and withdrew the precious package of diamonds. The pouch containing the Colour could remain where it was for the time being; it would be of no interest to looters in the event of the town being taken. He placed the diamond pouch inside his jacket pocket then sought out the duty officer of the Liverpool Regiment which supplied the forward guard picquets. Arrangements were then and there made for Samuel to report to the guard commander at 8 pm that evening when he would be escorted through the British front line. In the meantime, and to his surprise, the staff officer to the garrison commander was rather indifferent, expressing total disinterest in any information Samuel might have.

He headed back to town and peacefully spent the rest of the day with the Greenacres. To their surprise, Samuel informed them that he would leave that night. Just after 7 pm they said their farewells; he slipped out of the house and   walking Pagan behind him, went to a neglected grave in the corner of a nearby churchyard. He noted from the inscription that the selected grave was the final resting place of one,

"John Roy Lance. Born 1844 . Died of dysentery 1889".

After loosening the stones and earth from around the headstone he secreted the small pouch containing the diamonds and carefully replaced the disturbed earth. After waiting some ten minutes to ensure that his presence was unobserved, he headed out of town to the camp of the Liverpool Regiment.

He arrived on time to find a guard already detailed to guide him to the forward position. Pagan was already 'silenced' and at the furthest outpost, the guard wished Samuel well.

His eyes were now well accustomed to the black of the

night and the same two Boer gun positions were easily distinguishable some three miles away. Samuel adopted the same routine for the return journey carefully picking his way forward on foot to avoid any stony terrain. This time he was gently ascending toward the hills and it took over an hour for him to draw level with the Boers' positions.

He paused and hoped that the singing would soon start. Nothing happened; he moved slowly forward with Pagan shuffling behind him. About half an hour later Samuel reasoned that he was clear of the Boers. He was just about to mount up when he heard the unmistakable 'click' of a Mauser being cocked ready to fire. He froze.

'Wie is daar?' questioned a young voice ahead.
'The farmer,' answered Samuel. A young Boer approached him through the darkness and Samuel was then aware of other Boer guards circling around him.

'Hande Op!' ordered the guard and Samuel obediently raised his arms. The Boer youth cautiously approached to ascertain that his captive was unarmed; he indicated that Samuel should follow in the direction of the nearest Boer position. He was led to one of the illuminated tents followed by half a dozen curious Boers.

Samuel remained calm. It was just bad luck to be caught and, after all, he was nearly back on his own farm; he just hoped they would oversee the muffling on Pagan's hooves. The officer in charge swiftly ascertained that Samuel had been caught between the two positions and looked at him enquiringly but without speaking. Samuel seized the initiative.

'I am a farmer, this is my land and I'm looking for lost cattle.' There was no reaction from the Boer so he continued, 'Your quartermasters buy my cattle; they have bought nearly all of them so now I must bring in the strays,' he was feeling more bold, 'otherwise your men don't eat.'

The Boer called for one of his men by name. A big man

161

replied immediately from the direction of a camp fire and ambled over to the tent. Samuel was impressed by the informal respect the Boer leader commanded. He spoke to the big man in English for the benefit of Samuel.

'Take him back to the farm, if it is his farm.... let him go. If it is not , then he is lying,' he looked coldly at Samuel, 'so shoot him.'

'Ja Oom Kommandant,' replied the tall Boer. He grabbed Samuel and tied his wrists firmly behind his back. The Boer was brought a horse and Samuel was lifted back on to Pagan by some of the gathered onlookers.

'Vorvarts!' ordered the Boer and Samuel used his heels to guide Pagan back towards the farm. About an hour later they reached the darkened farmhouse. During the journey the Boer had begun to talk; and on reaching the farm, he was evidently pleased that Samuel was obviously the rightful owner. After releasing the binding on Samuel's wrists, Samuel unlocked the door and lit a lantern. The Boer followed him inside.

'Would you like some food or a drink?'

'Only if it will be quick, I must get back and report.' The Boer remained only for a mug of coffee then set off back to his unit.

Samuel breathed a huge sigh of relief and pondered what to do next.

CHAPTER TWELVE

The farm was unnervingly quiet without the everyday bustle of family activity; the unusual stillness gave the house an empty, eerie presence. Samuel could almost envisage one of his family walking into the room at any moment. He sat down at the kitchen table and closed his eyes, with a little effort he could imagine the laughter and incessant babble of their voices. As he opened his eyes, the voices melted away just as his beloved family had melted away a few days ago. So much had happened since then and he realised now how exceedingly tired and hungry he was. In the store room next to the kitchen hung row upon row of cured biltong; one of these strips of dried beef would make an excellent stew. He took one down together with a selection of vegetables from the storage bins and began methodically to prepare his supper. It was especially at moments like this that he realised how much he had hitherto taken Anneliese for granted. Always cheerful and happy, she had been the focal point of his life and their home for so long; now he felt isolated and empty without her. A deep involuntary breath brought him back to reality and he smiled inwardly as he found himself staring at a row of vegetables on the chopping board. He chided himself about his feelings; a good hot meal followed by a sound night's rest would quickly restore his composure. Tomorrow he would ride to Acton and pay his family a surprise visit.

Samuel awoke early according to the usual pattern of life on the farm. The dawn was already well advanced and today was going to be another typical December day, swelteringly hot long before noon. The water channel to the remaining cattle needed to be checked before he could be on his way, but first some coffee and two of Anneliese's renowned biscuits for breakfast. After the house was secured and Pagan saddled, he set about delegating the few outstanding farm chores to the farm's resident natives.

The residue of his herd were contentedly sitting in the sun lazily engaged in the involuntary routine of flicking flies with their long tails. The fruit and vegetable fields were a truly sorry sight. The Boers had randomly helped themselves leaving the usually tidy land looking more like an unsightly rubbish dump. The once neat rows had been repeatedly ridden over and trampled by careless soldiers; discarded rotting produce lay steaming in the hot sun. So be it, he thought. There would be no new planting until this wretched war was over: once the Boers had scavenged his farm they could all go hungry. He left the foul smelling fields behind him and rode steadily towards Acton and the Deblings' farm. It was a two hour ride. Anneliese was at work in the main house when Samuel arrived and her joy at seeing him was a pleasure to behold. She had been spending her time helping John's wife, Rosalind, with chores aided by the two Debling daughters, sixteen and thirteen year old Catherine and Jennifer. Samuel's sons were spending their time eagerly following John about the farm and occasionally making themselves useful.

They all met again over lunch and everyone was hungry for news. Samuel recounted his observations of the Boer positions but omitted any mention of his visit to Ladysmith. He would tell Anneliese later but now was not the time to heighten her uncertainty. During the meal, John insisted that Samuel should remain as their guest until after the Christmas period. Everyone agreed, and Samuel's intention immediately to return to Chaldon Farm dissolved under the weight of their combined persuasion.

The two families began to blend as they all gaily set about making Christmas a success. Samuel and John occasionally discussed the progress of the war, but nothing was going to dampen their spirits. On the 23rd December both men rode to a safe hilltop vantage point overlooking the Boer positions along the river bank. Nothing had changed and of the British, there was no trace. Back in the comfort of the Debling home the boys teased the girls who in turn reciprocated by demurely flirting back. Anneliese and Rosalind busied themselves baking bread and cakes.

Christmas came and then the celebrations gave way to the uncertainty of the steadily looming war. On the 27th December, Samuel bade his hosts and family a temporary farewell and set Pagan off at the trot back to Chaldon Farm. This time he varied his route and headed south east towards the river; by tracking along the Tugela he could observe the depth and strength of the Boer defences before turning north near Trichard's Drift. Once the river came into view, he kept high on the hill line to avoid any Boer scouts. Turning north near Trichard's Drift he could clearly see a party of Boers working on top of the dominating peak of Spion Kop. On rounding a hillock he nearly rode into an unexpected Boer gun position under construction. He instinctively brought Pagan to a halt and saw about thirty Boers gathered around one of three field guns; it appeared that the group were receiving gunnery instructions. They were less than fifty yards away and his presence was clearly unwelcome. As they menacingly turned and stared at him, one slowly picked up a rifle and indicated that he should advance towards the group. Samuel obliged.

The Boer with the rifle purposefully moved to the front of the group and waited. Samuel brought Pagan alongside the man and dismounted.

'Wie is je, wat doen jy hier?' asked the Boer.
'I'm a farmer, this is my land and I'm rounding up my stray cattle.' Another Boer walked round Pagan looking for any weapon, he merely said 'Nichts' to the man with the rifle. There followed a rapid conversation in Afrikaans which Samuel could not understand. He was then instructed to remount. A youth appeared with two more horses and the armed Boer and another man mounted up.

'Kom saam met ons,' said the Boer and Samuel nodded his assent. He couldn't help observing the implacable faces of the Boers; their weather beaten faces looked sternly at him. They rode off and then rejoined the main track from Trichard's Drift to Ladysmith which in another two miles would lead back to the farm. They rode in

165

silence for about another mile until a campsite of white bell tents unexpectedly came into view directly north of Spion Kop.

It was obviously the temporary headquarters of the new gun positions and for the troops manning Spion Kop. As they rode into the camp, Samuel estimated there were some fifty tents and up to one hundred heavy wagons positioned around the camp in the defensive laager so beloved of the Boers. Numerous horses were railed together and he reckoned there must be over two hundred men encamped on the site. On the far side of the tented area were another three field guns with their barrels unaccountably pointing directly towards Spion Kop.

The party came to a halt outside the most central tent. The Boer with the rifle dismounted and went inside. Samuel could hear men earnestly talking and then their conversation stopped. Several Boers came out of the tent and stood about ten yards away, one looking vaguely familiar. He stepped forward of the group and looked at Samuel.

'So English farmer, you're still looking for your cattle?'

Samuel recognised the man as the cold eyed, brown suited, Boer who had ordered him back to his farm only five days earlier.

'Hello again, yes it's true, but I'm also on my way home from visiting friends over Christmas,' he replied honestly. Samuel thought it best to be truthful as the Boers may have observed his going to Acton.
'Don't you think it is a coincidence that you are once more following me?'
'Sir, it is indeed a coincidence, but that is simply because you are still on my farm.' The Boer smiled. He had a pleasant round face when he relaxed.

'My men would like to shoot you,' he paused. 'They are understandably suspicious but I accept we are here as your guests.' He looked thoughtfully at Samuel and continued. 'Go back to your farm and this time, stay there. There is nothing here for a farmer so the next time you 're found near me, you really will be shot. Do you understand?'

'Yes of course, but am I permitted to know who I must avoid with such care?' asked Samuel quietly.

'My name is Louis Botha,' replied the Boer, 'General Louis Botha, now go before I change my mind.' Samuel smiled and nodded; and nudging Pagan they walked back through the Boer lines.

'Interesting,' he mused to himself. After all, it was not every day he would meet a Boer army commander in person. Perhaps he really ought to keep out of the man's way in future.

On returning to the farm, Samuel found the house exactly as he'd left it. He now felt the full frustration of the war and its disrupting effect on their family life. He spent the day cooling his anger by catching up on repairs to the two main barns. His mood was not enhanced when a party of Boers came on to the farm and loaded two wagons with fruit and vegetables without reporting to the farmhouse. Such inconsiderate action did not bode well for the future.

Over the next few days no one visited the farm but on the morning of the 4th January, Samuel was returning to the house after having taken the farm natives their weekly meat supply. On tying Pagan to the verandah rail, a sparkling glint of reflected light from an overlooking hillock caught his eye. It was obviously from a telescope and he realised the Boers now had him under constant surveillance, perhaps they were just wary of his proximity to the headquarters. He decided to be careful and avoid the south side of the farm for the time being. Using his binoculars from the inside of the kitchen he quickly spotted two Boer scouts on the hillock leading to the main track. He felt like a springbok being watched by a pride of lions but decided against taking any action; the most appropriate action would be simply to ignore them. The days passed slowly but little changed other than a short visit to Anneliese and the boys on the 11th January. He spent the night at the Deblings' farm and returned on the following day. The ever watchful Boers continued their surveillance of the farm from their hilltop observation point.

That night Samuel felt strangely uneasy. The horses had been unusually fractious throughout the evening and there had been intermittent barking from the distant native dogs until long after dark. It was possible that the Boers were moving more men up to the front; or perhaps they were retreating. The thought even crossed his mind that the British might be about to attack the Boer positions. Even when he retired for the night, teeming thoughts plagued his mind but sleep eventually took its inevitable hold on him.

The crash and splintering of the front door being smashed down brought him instantly awake. He lay there in the confusion of the moment with his heart already pounding in anticipation of action, but what action would be appropriate? He waited and held his breath. Flickering lantern lights rapidly advanced from the kitchen and three heavily armed Boers rushed into the bedroom.

'You are arrested!' said one of the Boers pointing a revolver at him.
'You, come with us, get dressed!' said another. Samuel did as he was ordered reasoning that this was perhaps why they had been keeping him under observation.
'Where are you taking me?' he asked.
'Where you can't talk to the British,' answered another voice.
'Can I leave my family a quick note?' he asked. One of the Boers agreed.

Samuel dressed rapidly then wrote a short note to the effect that he was being taken by the Boers. He left the house as secure as possible given the circumstances then saddled Pagan under the watchful eyes of his captors. They set off in the direction of General Botha's camp which they reached just before dawn. Samuel was ordered into a guarded tent and Pagan was lead away. Already his mind was contemplating the possibility of escape but for the time being, he was probably safer where he was. If he attempted to escape, the Boers would certainly shoot him on sight. He decided to wait and see what they had in mind for him.

Life as a prisoner was frustratingly boring, hot and dull. Apart from meals and walks to the latrine he was kept isolated; there were no other prisoners and the Boers deliberately ignored him. On asking for a book he was given a Boer bible written in Dutch; his requests for writing material were bluntly refused. The Boers who brought him his meals or exercised him were clearly under orders not to engage in conversation. He spent his time sitting on a box at the door of the tent watching the incessant camp activities; Boers came and went about their duties but it was difficult to guess what exactly was happening. It was three days following his arrest before he was taken before two Boer officers in a tent full of maps. To his surprise he was offered a seat and a jug of hot coffee was brought into the tent. One of the officers filled a mug and offered it to him. Samuel's curiosity began to stir.

'We were going to shoot you,' smiled one of the Boers 'but then we decided to offer you your life in return for a small task.' Samuel looked at them but could detect no clue from their faces as to what was coming. 'We are going to release you , but only on condition you go straight to the British and inform them that you have escaped. You will then tell them you escaped through our lines at a point which is poorly defended , then you are a free man. The alternative is simple, we shoot you. Do you agree to perform this simple task ?'
'Yes, I agree ... but surely the British will attack you.'
'Ja, that is exactly what we want.'

Samuel realised that he was being coerced into luring the British into a trap but for the time being any alternative eluded him.
'I agree, but what if the British won't listen, or I tell them the truth?'

'Then we burn your farm, burn the Deblings' farm and take your women and children prisoner.'

Samuel immediately knew that the Boers must have followed or observed him going to Acton, and they could so easily carry out their threat with only John to protect them. He shuddered at the thought.

'You see,' said the Boer officer, 'you really must persuade the British otherwise you will have the lives of your family and friends on your conscience.' He opened a rolled map of the area and Samuel saw that it was a relief map of the Tugela River, Spion Kop and extended on to Ladysmith.

'You will be released here at Trichard's Drift,' said the officer pointing to the river fording place. 'You will tell the British that it is undefended except for a mere two hundred Boers at the base of the cliff. You will also inform them that we intend placing heavy artillery on Spion Kop to control the access to Ladysmith. They will then attack the Kop. If they do so, your family and friends will be safe , I give you my word.' He looked coldly at Samuel. 'And if the British don't take your advice, you will suffer the memory of your family for the rest of your life.' said the Boer sitting back and looking away from his prisoner.

'I don't have much choice do I ?' said Samuel.

'Neither do I,' replied the officer who appeared to relax a little. 'None of us want to be here, we just want this war finished and then we can all go back to our farms. Once the British are defeated they will leave us alone.... for good I hope.' He surprisingly held out his hand to Samuel,

'Good luck, I hope you will be convincing.'

During the dark moonless evening of the 16th January, Samuel rode Pagan under a watchful Boer escort through their lines and on to Trichard's Drift. The night was black as pitch but as the two riders neared   the water's edge, Samual could make out the ribbon of meandering river glistening silently with the reflection of the stars.

'Where are the British?' he asked the Boer leading him.

The man pointed in the direction of Colenso.

'If you head toward the town, you'll meet one of their

patrols.' The man turned his horse away and disappeared back into the night.

Samuel urged Pagan across the rock strewn river, the chilly water reached the horse's belly and made it shiver at the unfamiliar cold touch. On the far bank he headed toward Colenso which lay ten miles to the east. Since fleeing with the Colour all those years ago, Samuel had felt indifference to the British. Now he began to feel guilty that he could be instrumental in yet another defeat for the British Army, many innocent young men would certainly die.

'None of this is of my making, my family comes first,' he muttered crossly to himself.

About ten minutes later Pagan began to twitch, it was always a good indication that other horses were nearby so he reigned in and listened. He could hear approaching horses and walked on to meet them. They were four young British troopers escorting a lieutenant to the local headquarters, they inquisitively gathered round and listened intently to Samuel's brief report of escape. When he mentioned that he knew where the Boers' positions were sited, the lieutenant took the bait.

'Come with us Sir,' invited the young officer, and they all headed off toward the headquarters of the Lancashire Brigade at the nearby British camp sited about a mile south of the river.

Samuel learned from the officer that the whole brigade was about to launch an attack on the Boers and even though the hour was late, the camp was still alive with the buzz of earnest activity. He had not seen so many tents since the Zulu war; they extended over a square mile and in the light of their camp fires he saw a variety of uniforms that were unfamiliar to him. It was obvious that the British would be attacking in considerable force; Samuel hoped they had learnt the art of flexibility after the defeats of the last few weeks. They arrived at the Brigade Headquarters and the lieutenant disappeared into an illuminated tent.

171

Several minutes later he returned with a more senior officer who informed Samuel that he would be questioned the following day. He was then taken by an orderly to the nearby field hospital where there was a row of empty beds.

'Sleep here,' said the orderly, 'you can put your horse in the hospital stables at the rear, breakfast is at five sharp.'

Shortly after eating an excellent army breakfast of cold meat, bread and coffee, Samuel presented himself outside the same tent where he was asked to wait by a clerk sergeant.

'Colonel A'Court's staff officer will see you shortly,' said the sergeant. Samuel waited and casually observed the bustle of noisy activity that always surrounds soldiers before marching into battle. His own thoughts drifted back to the time when he too was part of an invading army; he understood their feelings and felt both excited and yet sad for those who would not return home. There were soldiers, horses, dust and noises everywhere, groups were forming into units and the apparent chaos was slowly marshalled into line. Orders were shouted and a slow but steady movement began in the direction of the river; the battle would not be long in coming, the big question now was, where was that battle to occur? The sun rose and the day became hotter.

'Mr. Carrington, come this way sir,' invited a young subaltern. Samuel followed him and together they entered a large imposing tent; sitting at a field table were a number of officers. He thought it looked remarkably similar to the Boers' intelligence tent, there were maps everywhere with serious looking officers discussing fine details. A young man rose to meet him, Samuel was surprised to see that he was wearing the rank of Colonel, he looked far too young for the rank.

'Please sit down, my name is Colonel A'Court; I am the staff officer here. I understand you escaped last night

172

through the Boer lines?'

'That's correct. My farm, or what is left of it, lies between the Boers and Ladysmith. I couldn't get to Ladysmith so I came this way.'

'Can you show us what you know of their positions?' The colonel pulled a large map of the area round to face Samuel.

Samuel began by pointing out the position of his farm and related exactly where he had seen the Boer positions surrounding Ladysmith. His story flowed logically including why he had sent his family away; he mentioned the Boers taking his cattle and farm produce and finished with his annoyance at the farm being constantly under observation. Samuel noticed the other officers were now listening intently; after all, here was a real source of the current Boer positions, what first rate luck for them. The tale concluded with his decision to escape at the weakest part of the Boer defences, and here he was. Their questions followed thick and fast.

'Where is their artillery?
'How many guns?'
'How many men at this position ?'
'Are they dug into those damned trenches ?'
'How long is their line?'
'Where are their supplies kept?'
'What are they doing on Spion Kop?'

Samuel answered their questions truthfully but made a point of heightening their awareness to the likely tactical advantage of Spion Kop.

'What you can't see from here,' he explained, 'is that Spion Kop dominates all the ground for miles around including right down to Ladysmith. If you don't take it, the Boers will put their guns on the top which will wear you down and forever deny your men the two roads into Ladysmith. '

'From here, the face of the Spion Kop appears sheer ...and it must be over a thousand feet high.' The Colonel was serious as he voiced his thoughts. 'How do we get to the

173

top ?'

'Climb it,' said Samuel simply, 'It's not so steep when you get there, in fact it's only a stiff walk to the top.'

'Can we get our guns up there?' asked another officer.

'Once the position has been taken, yes,' acknowledged Samuel; he went on, 'and the Boers won't expect you to attack from this direction. At the moment they use it as an observation point to watch you but within a week or so they'll have their guns on top; they're making a track to the top and already a team of Boers is preparing the site,' said Samuel.

'We have, as you would probably expect, ignored the possibility of taking Spion Kop,' said the Colonel quietly. 'It's too late to change our plans now but I will advise General Warren to consider securing the Kop within the next few days.' He looked at Samuel. 'Would you be willing to guide our advance up the cliff if we decided to take it?'

'Yes,' replied Samuel before he had time to consider what he was accepting. He felt a sudden pang of fear; he was having to put his life at risk. He knew he had no alternative.

'Good, I understand you are billeted at the hospital, please remain there. I will call for you when I have briefed the General, thank you and good morning.' The Colonel rose, he and Samuel shook hands.

All through the day, several thousand infantrymen together with cavalry and artillery crossed the river. There was no resistance from the Boers who had withdrawn from the river bank. Once across, the whole British force turned due west following the river bank. Samuel wondered why they didn't advance directly towards the trapped garrison and quite logically reasoned that they were making a detour to attack the Boers from behind. Two days later he was called back to see Colonel A'Court.

'General Warren sees no merit in anyone taking the hill, on the other hand, I do.... accordingly I have taken the unusual liberty of mentioning your views to the Column

Commander, General Buller who wants to see you. You will ride to his camp at Mount Alice; do you know where that is?'

'Yes, near Potgieter's Drift,' replied Samuel.

'Make haste. My orderly officer will take you through the lines to his headquarters; you should be there in about an hour.'

The two men rode off without delay and reached the Army Headquarters tent of General Buller during mid-afternoon. The site was perfect; it afforded an unrestricted view across the river to Spion Kop itself some six miles to the north. From this position, the face of the Kop looked exceedingly severe and steep; no wonder the British plans to attack the Boers avoided those cliffs. Samuel was taken through the guards directly to General Buller in person.

The General, an imposing large figure sitting at his desk, looked curiously at Samuel standing in front of him. He motioned him to sit down opposite.

'So, you are the farmer from the other side of Spion Kop?'

'Yes sir.'

'I understand that all we have to do is march up that cliff and roll down the other side into Ladysmith ?'

'Yes sir; the Boers are all dug in along the hills overlooking the river, they are obviously expecting you to march against their prepared positions again.' He paused to let his apparently innocent words remind the general of his previous defeat. 'The only part of the line they don't have to defend is the Spion Kop hill.'

'We'll see how the infantry get on during the next two days so don't go far, I may be needing you.' He turned to his adjutant.

'Look after this man.'

Samuel was billeted with the headquarters non-commissioned officers. For the next two days he walked freely around the camp and observed the battle's distant progress. The British opened their offensive by attacking the Boers from the furthest end of the Tabanyama hills and everyone could hear the far off crump of artillery and occasionally see the flash of exploding shells on a distant hillside. The whole scenario of the war seemed totally incongruous with the beauty of the scenery as seen from the headquarters on Mount Alice. The Tugela river continued flowing on its life giving course, the warm scented African air encouraged a myriad of exquisite butterflies and birds to take to the wing while the ever stretching golden veldt totally swallowed up the tens of thousands of struggling men intent on slaughtering each other.

While Samuel waited the day's outcome, he tried unsuccessfully to keep his mind free of the dangerous game he was being forced to play. His thoughts constantly examined the tactics of his subterfuge; if the Boers won the battle, then the British would probably have to withdraw from South Africa. If the Boers were defeated there was always a chance they wouldn't be able to harm his family; he had already accepted that the farm didn't matter.

During the day, news began to trickle back to the Headquarters that progress was being made albeit at an excruciatingly slow pace. The Boers were once again outmanoeuvring the British; now, reasoned Samuel, they would have to accept the idea of attacking Spion Kop.

General Buller's impatience at his mounting casualties and with his hesitating subordinates finally expired. Samuel was summoned to his tent and duly informed by General Buller himself that he had, at last, ordered General Warren to take Spion Kop under the cover of darkness.

'I hope I am right, for your sake as well as mine ... as you may have already guessed, you will be guiding the troops leading the assault.' General Buller smiled at him. 'If we are successful, the nation will be well pleased, if not, you probably won't survive anyway.'

Again Samuel was wished good luck. He thought it

ironic that so many people had recently wished him good
luck.

CHAPTER THIRTEEN

By advancing into the Boer held hills on two narrow fronts, General Warren had failed to break through the enemy's lines. For four days now, his front line infantrymen had been pinned down by accurate rifle fire from high above the valleys. The supporting British troops were unable to advance and their morale began to slip once more. General Buller's waning patience   finally expired. On the 23rd January he rode over to General Warren's camp and after a short one-sided conversation, Warren submitted and gave orders for the attack against Spion Kop. Tactically it made good sense; the British believed the Boers were not defending the peak which dominated their intended   main supply   route   to Ladysmith.

That same morning, General Buller's intelligence staff dispatched Samuel to join General Warren's headquarters' staff at the forming up point   west of Three Tree Hill. He rode across the gentle slopes to the new rendezvous point and on his arrival early in the afternoon, let Pagan run and feed with the other horses in their temporary compound. He then reported to the headquarters staff.

The new advance on Spion Kop, under the command of General Woodgate, was to be spearheaded by Lt. Col Alec Thornycroft and two hundred battle hardened Uitlander scouts; all were veterans of numerous skirmishes with the Boers. Over two thousand British troops would immediately follow these scouts, troops from three full strength battalions of the Lancashire Brigade supported by mounted infantry and engineers. At 2 pm Samuel was introduced to Col. Thornycroft, a large red faced man who in turn handed him over to the two scout commanders detailed to guide the attack. From the protection of a nearby concealed gully, Samuel carefully indicated the easiest ascent up the boulder strewn slopes to the summit of Spion Kop. The two scouts drew a rough map of the slope and nodded their satisfaction with the plan. The temperature had been steadily dropping since lunchtime and low cloud began to form conveniently around the top of the objective; this would partially blind the defending Boers and give the attack a greater chance of success.

The scouts briefed Col. Thorncroft who was optimistic that the combination of low cloud and darkness would sufficiently obscure the assaulting units; the attacking troops could then sweep the Boers off the top with a decisive bayonet charge. It was agreed that Samuel's role was to lead the two scouts through the lower rocky slopes until a prominent copse of yellow mimosa bushes was reached two thirds of the way to the top. The scouts would then assemble the following Uitlanders and regular infantrymen before guiding the combined mass assault up the more gradual summit incline for the final attack. Following the briefing, Samuel was free to stroll about the area watching the preparations. There was an air of excitement running through the assembled British army; the soldiers were determined to seize the hill and drive the hated Boers down onto the far plain below, there the waiting cavalry and artillery could sweep round to harass the Boer retreat.

Samuel was sitting watching the Quartermaster's staff issuing ammunition to the soldiers at the rate of 150 rounds per man when a native labourer approached and casually stood beside him.

'Mr. Samuel isn't it?' asked the native secretively. Samuel was taken aback .

'Yes , what do you want?' The man was typically dressed in a mixture of uniform and native apparel. He was tall and looked very fit.

'I've a message for you,' he said confidently as he casually glanced around him before continuing, ' you are to stop at the first ridge at the top...it's in thick fog so they won't know... that's the message.'

'Where are you from?' asked Samuel as calmly as he could.

'From General Botha ... and he told me to tell you that your family are all safe ... so long as you do as you're told.'

The black Boer messenger casually picked up Samuel's

ration pack, grinned at him defiantly and walked off. The man naturally blended in with the other bustling natives carrying stores and equipment and disappeared.

So, thought Samuel, the crafty Boer general knows exactly what's happening; but the significance of stopping at the first ridge temporarily eluded him. He was greatly relieved to learn that his family were still safe, but deeply concerned they were still vulnerable to threats from the Boers.

At 5 pm the troops queued for their supper and afterwards, began to form up in columns under the direction of their NCOs. The weather progressively deteriorated and the damp mist now extended all the way down the mountainside to envelop the whole forming-up point. By 8.30 pm the officers had assembled and to everyone's relief, General Woodgate finally gave the order to advance.

In the misty dark of the night, men cursed as they slipped and stumbled across the rocky terrain over which they were now clambering. Many ignored the order not to talk; it was difficult to see the man directly in front, and a little banter always raised morale. Samuel easily led the two scouts to the base of the hill where they waited for the following troops to catch up. He was astonished to see the soldiers still attempting to march in their tight ranks of four abreast but at the base of the steep slope they were ultimately obliged to break their formations and pick their way individually over the rough scree. It was now after midnight and the scouts became concerned lest the assault should lose its impetus. Inexorably the column gained height.

At about 3 am Samuel and the leading scouts reached the mimosa bushes, the following Uitlanders quickly spread out and the heavily breathing troops assembled behind them. Everything was ready for the final assault. The mist was still thick and visibility was reduced to twenty yards. As silently as possible , bayonets were anxiously fixed. The men were now well spread out and, shoulder to shoulder, crouched down for added protection for whatever awaited them on the nearby silent summit.

On the whispered order from Col. Thornycroft, the troops cautiously but blindly set off towards the crest line. Suddenly a startled German voice called out through the fog .

'Wer is da ?' For a moment there was silence then a British officer shouted back.
'Waterloo !'

There was a crash of Mauser fire less than fifty yards away and the British hurled themselves flat amongst the rocks. The firing continued until the British could hear the sound of Mauser rifle bolts being worked to reload, then an English voice shouted out,

'CHARGE!'

And charge they did. But the token detachment of Boers guarding the small summit plateau had already fled into the dense mist leaving behind one injured man. The British were jubilant as they poured onto what they thought was the summit and gave three rousing cheers; their voices were heard in the valley below. The news was immediately relayed to General Buller at Mount Alice and on by telegraph to Capetown. It would reach England and Queen Victoria herself the following day. With the Boers fleeing at last, Ladysmith would surely be relieved within a day or two. However, Samuel was well aware that the British were not on the actual summit as they believed, but occupying a small plateau a mere hundred yards beneath it. He had completed his mission but Samuel had mixed emotions, he suspected the Boers had engineered a deadly trap for the unsuspecting British and now deeply regretted his complicity.

In the meantime, the accompanying engineers began half heartedly scratching a woefully inadequate trench in the rocky ground along what appeared to be the flat top of Spion Kop. It was only at this juncture that it was discovered that most of the shovels had inadvertently been left behind. There were only twenty five shovels to dig a trench for over two thousand men; but the hill had been taken and the Boers had fled. Accordingly no-one was much bothered about a trench, and anyway, the ground was strewn with small boulders should a defence ever become necessary. Soldiers slept where they fell with exhaustion from the long climb.

The fog was by now even thicker. The British relaxed, talked, drank coffee and those asleep slept on. Samuel politely took his leave from Col. Thornycroft who thanked him profusely, then, without looking around he slipped away whence he came.

Just after dawn the thick mist slowly began to clear. Suddenly, and totally unexpectedly, the Boer counter attack commenced just as the British settled down to breakfast. Unseen by the British, they mounted a full counter assault against Spion Kop with units from the Pretoria and Carolina Commandos and, as the cloud lifted, other Boer units could be seen preparing defensive positions on the adjacent high ground of Aloe Knoll and Conical Hill. Because of the mist, the British had been totally unaware that this other high ground, only four hundred yards away, even existed. They were also now painfully aware that they were not on the actual summit of Spion Kop but exposed and in full view of the gathering Boers immediately above them.

The confused British suddenly came under sustained fire from the nearby summit as well as devastatingly accurate enfilading fire from Aloe Knoll and Conical Hill. There was nowhere for the British soldiers to hide; their defences were too shallow, inadequate, in the wrong place and the Boers were now firing directly from Aloe Knoll into the men desperately trying to take cover in the crude trench.

Then the Boer artillery fire commenced. There were now over two thousand British soldiers attempting to take cover in an area hardly the size of two football pitches.

The British lay in amongst the rocks as the sun began burning off the protective mist foretelling another scorching day. The air was alive with the incessant zipp zipp of Mauser fire interrupted only by the regular explosion of Boer artillery shells. Heroism was spontaneous, groups of British soldiers desperately charged on numerous occasions and each time, every man taking part fell dead or seriously injured. At 10 am General Buller received a call for urgent assistance from Col. Thornycroft; two fresh battalions were dispatched to the hill with the order "No surrender".

Around the summit, men on both sides were understandably wilting, the Boers from heat - the British under the assault of heat, accurate rifle and artillery fire. The horrendous carnage was everywhere with arms, legs, heads and torsos littering the scene; injured men were crying out and screaming in agony. There was no relief from either the heat or devastating Boer shelling. At 1.15 pm a group of British soldiers could take no more, a white flag was waved and a group stood up; for a moment the unremitting firing stopped.

A furious Col. Thornycroft bellowed at the men to get down just as a line of reinforcements from the Middlesex Regiment came over the crest with bayonets fixed.

The Boers rapidly ushered their prisoners away as both sides simultaneously resumed fighting. More British troops reached the summit plateau during the afternoon. Just after 6.30 pm darkness fell and with it came the blessed cessation of artillery fire. In the eerie still of the evening, the cries and groans of the mortally wounded continued to humiliate the bewildered British survivors.

Neither side could be aware of the battle's progress or of the actual strength of the opposing enemy on the other side of the hill. Unbeknown to the British, the Boers already considered themselves defeated and began to steadily withdraw from Spion Kop. Col. Thornycroft had been promoted to General during the day yet he too viewed the day as a complete disaster. He had been without sleep for nearly three days and naturally felt personally responsible for the appalling carnage wrought on his men. Neither side felt able to withstand the inevitable onslaught which would surely occur the following day.

General Thornycroft succumbed to his disorientated feelings and personal exhaustion; he reluctantly initiated the tactics of defeat and gave the order to withdraw from Spion Kop. As the survivors began to make their way quietly away from their position, a young reporter from the "Morning Post", one Winston Churchill, brought the General fresh orders to hold the position.

Churchill found him disconsolately sitting on the ground surrounded by his men amidst the unforgettable scenes of mass butchery. It was too late; the General had made up his mind and the new orders only served to add to his confusion. Spion Kop was rapidly abandoned; the dead and injured were left where they lay .

A truce was arranged the following day, the 25th January, for both armies to bury over six hundred dead; the British had additionally incurred more than 1,200 wounded casualties and a mile of waggons was needed to evacuate them all. The Boers had lost 345 men, mainly injured, during the action.

General Buller yet again resumed direct command of his whole but dispirited army. They were also back where they were two weeks earlier, still south of the Tugela river. A number of painful lessons had yet to be learned.

In the meantime, Samuel had collected Pagan from the horse pound and eventually rode back onto Chaldon Farm at about the same time as dawn was breaking. Apart from the smashed front door, the farm appeared intact. He let Pagan loose to graze and wearily walked back to the house. A thin film of veldt dust had blown through the damaged door and settled on the furniture, otherwise everything appeared to be in order. In the daze of tiredness, Samuel prepared himself some coffee whilst collecting his thoughts. Having complied with their orders, the Boers would now hopefully leave him alone. On the other hand, if they were forced to abandon Spion Kop, the farm would lie directly in their path; they might well be tempted to devastate the buildings out of spite or shell it to deny the British its amenities.

By now the explosions of artillery shells could clearly be heard from the direction of Spion Kop so he knew he had time to think. First things first; he hadn't changed his clothes for well over a week and he desperately needed a bath. He took some soap from the kitchen and headed for the waters of the stream behind the house.

'Hey boss!' called a familiar voice from a nearby thorn thicket. His native headman appeared wearing a broad grin, 'Ah thought you'd gone forever boss.'
'Hello Headman, no I'm still here... go and find some eggs and make me a real breakfast.'

Headman bounded away delighted that Samuel had returned. Whilst relaxing in the refreshing stream waters , he logically thought through the current situation and decided to move the family further away to safety. Headman and his family could easily look after the house and cattle in their absence. He soaped himself, dived under the cool stream waters then walked back to the house. The smell of frying smoked bacon hung around the house and the prospect of seeing his family again brought his optimism surging back.

His mind then turned to Anneliese and the boys .

CHAPTER FOURTEEN

As Samuel entered the house, he saw Headman had cleaned the kitchen table and was now busy frying bacon and eggs. The kitchen range was clicking and hissing from the heat of the burning wood and the sounds flooded his mind again with memories of his absent family. The coffee pot began to simmer in the background as Headman placed the platter of eggs and bacon in front of him. Headman was whistling happily as he busied his way around the kitchen, Samuel sat back in his chair and began to take stock of the situation, things were definitely improving. In the course of light banter with his servant. Samuel was able to ascertain that no Boers had visited the farm since he was last there more than a week ago; he turned to Headman.

'I'll be off again in about an hour ... but I should be back in the next day or so; in the meantime get your wife and her sister to come and clean the house. And you can try and fix the door to stop the sand blowing in.' Headman grinned; he felt pleased that Samuel should trust him with such responsibility and his chest swelled with pride.

'Are the cattle all right?' asked Samuel,
'Yes boss.'
'Have the Boers left the breeding cows alone?'
'Yes boss, they all fine.'
'And the horses?'
'They all there boss.'
'Right , I hope to be back shortly. When you've fixed the door, get the rest of the Kraal boys to begin clearing the fields ... we've a lot of work to do.' Headman grinned with pleasure that normality was returning.

Samuel rose to his feet and stretched his aching limbs; he realised that he'd not slept for several days but the luxury of sleep could wait until he reached the Deblings' farm. He collected some ammunition and a rifle from the bedroom as a precaution; there was no telling what was happening between here and the Deblings. As he paused at the door, the crump of artillery fire from around Spion

186

Kop could now clearly be heard. He strode across to the paddock and whistled; Pagan trotted to the gate and stood waiting to be saddled. Ten minutes later they were both ready, with a casual wave to Headman he was off.

He had already decided to exercise caution and do his best to avoid the Boers. Remembering the warning from General Botha, he headed away from the farm towards the Fairview track; once there he could swing north to Acton and hopefully avoid both the Boers and British troops by keeping to the gullies and scrublands which characterisd the area. The artillery fire from Spion Kop was now constant. He felt sorry for those on the receiving end but then, the war wasn't of his making. After riding for about an hour he approached the Fairview track, spotted another new Boer laager less than a mile away, and reined in. He dismounted and, after removing his telescope, carefully ground tied Pagan's reins to a tuft of grass.

He climbed a nearby ridge and lay down to secretly observe the Boers. There were several hundred waggons down on the plain and as many horsemen; it was obvious that he could have stumbled upon another major Boer position.

It was difficult to see what was happening, the waggons were facing away from Spion Kop in three long lines yet the horsemen appeared to be milling aimlessly round them. This was a blow to his plans, it would be folly to attempt to ride round them with such endless visibility across the veldt. A lone rider would be easily spotted even if he could reach the gullies, and undoubtedly the Boer scouts would investigate just out of curiosity. He would have to wait until dark; in the meantime there was no telling what the Boers were up to and it would be much safer to find a more secluded hiding place. He scrambled back to Pagan and slowly rode to the protection of a patch of scrub he'd seen about a half mile back. The scrub would safely hide them as well as affording limited protection from the blistering heat of the sun. The sounds of battle continued to rage in the distance. Samuel tied Pagan under the shade of a thorn tree and lay down on his saddle blanket. There would be little danger here and he could safely doze until nightfall; he settled down and within a few minutes was fast asleep. Pagan was used to standing still in the approaching midday heat and rapidly adopted the trance like state of idle horses the world over by standing on three legs with one resting. The hours went by.

The cooler air of the early evening woke him with a start. He had to think for a moment to remember where he was and then stretched his muscles. He stood up and had a good look round; there was no sign of any immediate danger. Leaving Pagan where he was, he took his telescope and set off back to the ridge. He peered cautiously over the rim; little had changed. The Boer waggons had not moved but there were less horsemen. He watched the cluster of men and waggons for about an hour during which time two groups of about a hundred riders each rode off in the direction of Spion Kop. The artillery barrage was now less intense and because it had been going on for so long, his mind had almost overlooked the regular far off explosions.

As he lay watching, about half the waggons began slowly making their way down toward the plain in the direction of Ladysmith. Samuel was even more mystified by the Boers' actions; it would only make sense if they were retreating but all the signs indicated that they were winning the battle on Spion Kop. He decided to wait until it was dark. Carefully, he made his way back to the protection of the scrub.

At about eight o'clock he set off. Pagan's hooves were already muffled to prevent any undue noise and the pair made steady progress. Samuel paused frequently to listen for Boers but heard nothing. Instead of making for the track and following it, he crossed it and then turned in the direction of Acton. Having seen so many Boers on the main cart track, there remained the distinct possibility that others would still be in the vicinity.

Now he could see the lantern lights from the Boer waggons receding behind him as he progressed. Just before he reached the Acton road he paused again to listen. Nothing stirred. He dismounted and removed the padding from Pagan's hooves to give the horse better grip on the ground. They set off at walking pace with Samuel constantly peering into the dark; an hour later he could see the faint lights of Acton about six miles away. He approached the hamlet with caution but could see nothing untoward, nevertheless, he skirted the homes and made directly for the Deblings' farm. He arrived shortly before midnight and finding the farmhouse was in darkness, he dismounted and walked quietly to the stable. All the Debling horses and some of his own were there which indicated that everything was in order, he unsaddled Pagan and left the horse in the stable. He walked directly over to the house and knocked on the main door. After a pause, the glimmer of a lantern appeared and John's voice called out from behind the door. Samuel acknowledged him and then he was safely inside. Within seconds, Anneliese, the boys and the whole Debling family all rushed from their rooms and hugged Samuel. The questions came thick and fast and it was another hour before everyone calmed down.

Samuel gave a brief account of recent events but it was some time before they went back to bed. He and Anneliese eventually fell asleep. They were still asleep in their embrace long after John and the boys left the house to attend to farm chores. By breakfast time the questions were again flowing fast; Anneliese was concerned to get back to Chaldon Farm, the two older boys wanted to remain with the Deblings and Anneliese recognised the budding romances between her teenaged boys and the Debling girls. Their boys' reluctance to return home was becoming more understandable. After breakfast Samuel and John took their coffee out on the shaded verandah, and noticed the sound of artillery was absent.

'There's been no firing now since yesterday evening,' said John.
'That means the battle is over; the question now has to

189

be, who won?' replied Samuel. The two pondered the situation; then John spoke.

'There's only one way to find out, let's go and have a look. We should be able to see the whole of Spion Kop from Bastion Hill without getting too close to the Boers.'

'Right,' replied Samuel 'and I'll be interested to see what has happened to all those Boer waggons.'

The two men left about half an hour later and rode directly to Bastion Hill. They dismounted immediately below the summit ridge and walked their horses up to the top. John held their mounts while Samuel looked through the telescope .

'There's nothing on Spion Kop ... no men moving ... lots of craters, it's almost as if nothing had happened there.'

'Perhaps we're too far away?' suggested John.

'I don't think so,' answered Samuel, ' and if one side had won, why aren't they being shelled by the other?'

'Can you see the waggons?'

'No , but I don't think we can see them from here, we'll have to ride over to the top of Tabanyama, then we'll be able to see everything.'

The two men remounted and carefully descended the hill; they then rode the mile across the veldt and began the ascent of the rounded Tabanyama Hill. At the top they could see the glinting roofs of Ladysmith about ten miles to the north east.

'There!' said John, 'what's that?' He pointed to a long column of dust rising from the plain to the east of Ladysmith. Samuel took the telescope from the saddlebag and quickly picked out the retreating Boer waggons.

'My God!' he exclaimed, 'the Boers are running away; they've abandoned Spion Kop and are heading home .... perhaps they've had enough.' He handed the telescope to John then asked as an afterthought,

'But where are the British? Surely they 'd harrass the Boer on the plain; he's a sitting target down there.'

'Nothing,' replied John as he scanned the endless veldt,

'just hundreds of waggons and horses and no sign of the British.'

'Can you see Chaldon ?' asked Samuel.

'Yes , the farm's still there... have a look yourself.'

Samuel took a long look at the farm, it was too far away for him to be able to make out any detail but it was definitely still there; the tin roofs of the house and barn glinted in the heat haze.

'The Boers must have been in a great hurry to leave,' said Samuel.

'Perhaps it's all over, the Boers aren't heading for Ladysmith, maybe the British have outsmarted them for once.' The men felt greatly relieved.

'Let's get home,' said John .

They all remained at the Deblings' for another day, then on the morning of the 27th January Samuel and John rode to Chaldon Farm to make sure the Boers had completely left the area. There was no sign of any activity during the journey and they reached the farm by midday. Samuel saw that Headman had made a good attempt at patching the door and inside the house it was obvious that his wife had cleaned everything. Within minutes Headman appeared and confirmed that the Boers had indeed retreated along the Fairview track in the course of the previous day.

'Right,' said Samuel, 'let's get back and packed up, we've been your guests far too long.' John laughed.

'It's been our pleasure, and anyway, I think we'll be seeing quite a lot of your two lads from now on.'

'In that case,' replied Samuel, 'I hope we'll be seeing more of Kate and Jenny.'

The two weary men arrived back at the Debling farm at dusk and Samuel was pleased to see that Anneliese had almost completed the packing in anticipation of their departure. It was agreed that they would stay one more night and then depart the following day.

By 7 am. they were on their way. Frederick rode in the cart with Anneliese, the menfolk riding alongside. There was much waving and handkerchiefs were very useful for dabbing young girl's eyes. They took the Ladysmith road for six miles and then turned right along the Fairview track. They reached home just after noon and Headman, his wife and some of the kraal women were there to greet them. The house was immaculate inside and Anneliese thanked Headman with the gift of a small knife. By sunset the farmhouse was nearly back to normal, the boys had properly repaired the front door and one of Anneliese's stews was bubbling on the stove. The smell of fresh bread made everyone feel hungry and supper turned out to be a joyous feast.

The following day, work began clearing the vegetable fields and the ox plough was soon at work under Headman's exaggerated supervision.

On the 30th January Samuel and Winston set out for Ladysmith, partly for some supplies but mainly for confirmation that the Boers had lifted their seige. They were bitterly disappointed; the seige around the town remained in full force. When they were still seven miles from Ladysmith they saw the waggon laagers and then heard the Boer guns fire the occasional shot into the town. Samuel was confused; the Boers had obviously been beaten on Spion Kop so where were the British, and why was the siege being maintained? They returned disconsolately back to the farm.

The siege of Ladysmith was to continue for nearly another month. The surrounded British garrison eked out its dwindling supplies to both soldier and civilian alike. The civilians were provided with the occasional treat of army horse meat, much to the indignation of the cavalry who still enjoyed beef. Any bread available was now having to be made from ground maize. Eggs were two shillings each but only if the civilians could keep the troops from stealing the hens. Unity between the military and civilians was rapidly breaking down; whatever the army thought it needed it requisitioned. Sadly it became necessary for the townspeople to hide everything of value. The army had taken over every useful building as well as many houses and the damage caused by the new occupants was generally considered worse than any damage caused by Boer shelling. The civilians were virtually starving and typhoid had begun to spread throughout the town; those civilians that were still fit were pressed into service in the military hospitals. There was no escape for anyone; only hope of relief by the slowly advancing British column kept many alive.

It only remained for the British to fight their way through the remaining Boer positions still around the town. The British had failed to seize the opportunity to follow through after the Boers abandoned Spion Kop, so the war dragged on. Finally, the sheer force of numbers and superior artillery forced the demoralised Boers to retreat.

On the 28th February 1900, the 119 day siege of Ladysmith was lifted.

On the 2nd March, Samuel took his family to Ladysmith for the day, mainly to check that the Greenacres were still alive. They left at dawn and by 10am they were all having tea with their friends. During the afternoon, Samuel slipped away and strolled into the town cemetery. He easily located the grave of John Lance and deftly scooped away the loose chippings; within seconds he felt the soft touch of leather. Everything was intact and after quickly refilling the small hole he departed with the diamonds safely in his pocket.

It took several months for Chaldon Farm to recover its normal level of productivity and at the end of the year Samuel used the Boer gold coins towards the purchase of two small but dilapidated beef farms on the outskirts of Ladysmith. The new farms were eventually managed by Winston and Cedric who in 1903 married the two Debling girls. In 1909, Frederick graduated from Capetown university and became an engineer. Samuel and Anneliese carried on farming at Chaldon Farm until 1919 when they sold it for a nominal sum to their two eldest sons. They retired to a spacious bungalow overlooking Ladysmith.

On his sixtieth birthday, Samuel left the house at dawn and rode one of his horses to the Tabanyama Hills. At a point near the summit overlooking Chaldon Farm, he carefully paced out a spot on the ground then buried the ten remaining diamonds in a small metal box. Later that day he placed an envelope addressed to each of his sons in the safety of his bank in Ladysmith. Each envelope contained one large uncut diamond. That night Samuel wrote down the exact co-ordinates of the buried diamonds in his diary, taking the precaution to record the details in Welsh. The remaining diamond was cut, polished and mounted as a pendant which Samuel presented to Anneliese on her next birthday.

* * * * * * * * * * * * *

Samuel died in his sleep on the 1st June 1936 at the age of 81. Anneliese outlived Samuel by another seven years. Their considerable property was equally distributed between their three sons but Samuel's diary, together with the family trunk, was left without any comment to the eldest son, Winston. A few days later Winston flicked through the diary and replaced it in the trunk which he eventually passed to his only son Philip. Apart from a casual glance through the papers and diary one rainy afternoon, Philip took no real interest in the trunk or contents until his son, Peter, was born. The trunk was placed in the child's room for him to sit on as he grew up.

Footnotes.

1. Samuel's original escape from the Army remained a secret to the outside world but in September 1905 something happened which he never fully understood. Whilst collecting provisions from the Greenacre Stores, an assistant informed Samuel that an attractive and obviously rich English lady had arrived in Ladysmith and taken two rooms at the Royal Hotel for two days. She was, unusually for those days, accompanied by a man servant. At one point during her short visit she had specifically made enquiries after anyone with the name Carrington. Apparently she had smiled at learning of Samuel, Anneliese and Chaldon Farm. She had immediately rushed off to inform her servant. They departed for Durban the following day. When Samuel subsequently learned of the mysterious pair and curiously examined the hotel register, the name "Mrs. Smith and servant", divulged no clues. Though by then, Bethan and Owen had already embarked on their ship back to Britain.

2. Had Samuel returned to his native Wales, he would have learned a great deal about the family and friends he left behind. He would undoubtedly have been devastated to learn that his youngest brother, David, had joined the Army Service Corps in 1885 and in 1899 sailed as a Company Sergeant Major with his regiment to the Boer War. He was mortally wounded on the summit of Spion Kop and died two days later at Colenso where he lies buried, almost in sight of Ladysmith.

3. The Army spelling of "waggon" changed to "wagon" after the Boer War. The author has retained this usage.

PRETORIA Saturday 30th May 1992.

The evening was slowly cooling as the first guests began arriving at the palatial Sachs home at Carrington Hill. As cars swept into the acacia tree lined drive, they were halted next to the family's tennis courts by a group of armed police officers while the security staff courteously checked vehicle registration numbers and occupants against the official guest list. White gloved domestic staff then led the guests onto the spacious and manicured lawns behind the house; there was a natural tendency for them to gravitate towards the swimming pool where Peter Sachs and his elegant wife, Helena, were greeting new arrivals. One guest in particular created a special ripple of interest as he arrived. Cyril Ramaphosa, the young ANC negotiator, was widely believed by both white and black politicians to be a future leader of the country. The softly spoken and immaculately dressed black man exuded a cultured charm and presence and, after a genuinely friendly welcome from the minister, circulated easily with the other guests.

By contrast, Robin and his brother Andrew arrived almost unnoticed. Robin was, however, immediately spotted by the Sachs daughters who made a direct line for him. Robin greeted the girls with his usual good-natured teasing and introduced his brother, Andrew. Andrew was still slightly bemused after the long flight from England and had not expected to be suddenly thrust into a high society function within hours of arriving in South Africa. The girls bustled around the two and then, with champagne glasses in their hands, took Andrew to meet their parents. Robin was very relaxed as the minister turned to greet them.

'Hello Robin, and this gentleman must be your brother.'
'Minister and Mrs. Sachs,' Robin put on his more formal voice, 'may I introduce you to my brother, Andrew.' Peter

Sachs beamed at the brothers and extended his hand to Andrew,

'Welcome to sunny South Africa, did you have a good flight?' asked the minister. Uncertain how to respond to such an important figure, Andrew had to force a positive

'Yes sir , thank you.'

'We've heard a lot about you from Robin,' intervened a smiling Helena Sachs, 'perhaps we'll be able to chat later when things quieten down... in the meantime the girls will look after you both, help yourself to some food and find a seat, you must be very tired after such a long journey.'

As the two brothers were led away by Elizabeth and Annie, Peter Sachs found himself staring at the back of Andrew Penny. Andrew was a tall man in his early thirties with an obvious military bearing and the clipped speech associated with an officers' mess. Thinking hard, Peter Sachs decided he would make time to speak to him later. By eight o'clock there were over one hundred guests at the braai and the warm night air was further softened by the hum of contented voices and laughter. The discreet background classical music was progressively being challenged by the increasing cacophony of mating crickets in the surrounding gardens.

Andrew was very impressed with the company his brother now enjoyed and the bounteous food was truly excellent. The fillets of beef and salads were sumptuous while the seafood buffet was as picturesque as it was delicious. As soon as any guest's wine glass was empty a waiter appeared to refill it but Andrew had already switched to orange juice; fine champagne and exhaustion didn't mix. A voice at his shoulder stirred his thoughts,

'May I join you?' asked the minister as he sat down beside Andrew.

'I understand you have come to visit the battlefields; do you have a particular interest in the Zulu war?'

' Yes minister, I'm hoping to fulfill a long held ambition from my distant army days...it was my regiment that was annihilated by the Zulus at Isandhlwana and for many years I have felt the psychological pull of the battlefield...

197

perhaps it's just the romantic sound of the place but, after all, it was a massive defeat for the British Army... in fact the worst ever.' Both men were quiet for a moment. The minister broke the silence.

'I've not been there for many years, perhaps we could arrange to go there as a group, I'll try and re-arrange my diary; one of my relatives was killed there and it's high time I paid my respects again.'

'Do you have any information about this relative?' asked a surprised Andrew.

'Sadly little,' lied the minister.

A government aide quietly interrupted the conversation.

'Minister, Mr. Ramaphosa is about to leave.'

'I'll get my secretary to telephone you Andrew; no doubt we'll meet again shortly,' said Peter Sachs as he rose to his feet.

Andrew was suddenly wide awake and excited by the brief exchange and sought out his brother who, with Elizabeth on his arm, was engrossed with another group of guests. After yet more introductions and the inevitable invitations to meals, Andrew at last related his conversation with the minister to his brother.

'He's a dark horse,' said Robin thoughtfully, 'I had no idea he even knew about Isandhlwana; now it appears one of his relatives fought there.'

'Died there.' corrected Andrew. The party continued and it was nearly midnight before the brothers returned to their hotel in central Pretoria.

April Okawa had been a junior housemaid at the Sachs' household since leaving school four years ago. Helena Sachs had always made a point of employing local staff and April had been selected for domestic training during her final year at school. The terms of her employment required her to reside at one of the central hostel blocks for government domestic staff, which was located about two miles from the minister's house. She enjoyed the daily walk to and from work. April was permitted to visit her family most weekends, subject to the domestic requirements of the household.

That evening she had welcomed the opportunity to earn some extra money waitressing and she took an almost childish pleasure being at the beck and call of the kitchen staff. It was always exciting when her employers entertained, the ladies' fashions fascinated the young black woman and the time flew by all too quickly. She was half way home and lost in her own thoughts when she became aware of the old red and white van slowing down beside her. The nearside black passenger leaned towards her and casually asked for directions to the town centre; before she had time to think, two black youths darted from behind the van and swept her off her feet and bundled her heavily into the back of the van. The van accelerated away. It was all over in five seconds.

She tried to sit up but found herself firmly restrained by one of the youths. She peered round the confined space of the jolting van as her eyes adjusted to the dark. The vehicle smelled of petrol fumes and unwashed bodies, she saw there were five black men curiously watching her. She immediately feared that she was about to be the victim of a gang rape and began to sob. The man holding her down relaxed his grip and ordered her to be quiet. She did her best to overcome her welling terror and courageously attempted to comply with the order. After about ten minutes, the van pulled off the road and stopped. The two men in the front of the van climbed into the back and the front seat passenger who'd asked for directions shone a torchlight into her face.

'Are you April Okawa?'
'Yes,' she replied nervously wondering how they knew her name, 'what do you want...I've done nothing wrong.' She was sat upright to face her interrogator.

'That's right,' said the man calmly,'but instead of feeding off the white man and enjoying his comforts, you are now going to do something useful for your own people.' She began to calm down whilst still hoping desperately that

199

she wasn't about to be violated.

'We know you have access throughout the minister's house; from now on we want you to record the names of all his visitors , especially black people, particularly Zulus. Their names, their addresses and anything else that may be of use. We are looking for someone and we need to find him urgently ...you will help us,' he ordered. April nodded. 'If you don't help us, or if you tell anyone, you will die.... that is, after we have finished with you.'

April shivered with renewed fear at the thought. She was very aware of the men's salacious eyes looking over her young firm body with considerable interest.

'Do you agree to help us?' he asked.
'Yes.' she replied, but her mind was still in a whirl from the shock of her abduction.
'Now listen carefully,' said the same man, 'someone will meet you once a week and ask you for your shopping list, you will keep details of the names, dates and times and pass it over at the meeting, don't cheat us because you are not the only one doing this for us.... we will know the truth, and you are too young and pretty to die.' April nodded in agreement.

The two men climbed back into the front of the van and the driver started the motor, a few minutes later they dropped their still terrified victim outside the hostel. April went straight to her room and burst into tears.

The following morning Robin flew his brother back to Durban in the Cessna hired for the weekend from the Durban flying club. On arriving back at the flat there was already a message from the minister's secretary waiting on the answerphone. The message intimated that the minister was proposing to accompany the brothers to Isandhlwana for a private visit. Robin telephoned her immediately and arrangements were made for the minister to be met by them at Durban airport early on the forthcoming Friday. They discussed the details then Robin put the telephone down and smiled at Andrew.

'Not only is the minister coming, he's bringing George Barber with him; he's a retired professor of Zulu studies from Pretoria University... you should be able to get all the information you need from him.'

Andrew was well acquainted with Professor Barber's name. He decided to do some quick reading over the next few days in order to be able to make full use of this unexpected opportunity of meeting an expert of Zulu history.

'The site is about a two hour drive from the airport.' interrupted Robin, looking at his map. 'We can leave the landrover at the airport and all travel by road in the official cars; I've got to organise the lunch... I think a picnic hamper will do nicely, especially as the minister is paying.' Andrew was already deeply engrossed in thumbing through his well worn copy of "The Washing of the Spears", by Donald Morris.

The minister's flight to Durban arrived on time and with him came his daughter Elizabeth and George Barber. Elizabeth had twisted her father's arm to take her along and she spotted Robin in the arrivals hall, she waved gleefully at him as the two groups converged.

'We have two vehicles waiting for us somewhere.' announced the minister as the professor was being introduced to Andrew. A smartly dressed police captain appeared and after a brief conversation with the minister, began escorting the entourage to two Toyota Landcruisers parked immediately outside the airport main entrance. Robin had already transferred the food hamper and had watched anxiously as one of the accompanying police officers conducted a security search through the carefully prepared luncheon basket.

'My guests will accompany me in the first vehicle,' instructed the minister indicating the professor and Andrew, 'you and your men can follow behind with my daughter and Robin.'

The captain saluted and he and two hovering white police constables armed with sub-machine guns escorted Robin and Elizabeth to the second vehicle. The minister took the wheel of the leading Landcruiser and the party set off north east along the N3, through the outskirts of Durban, then took the road to Pietermaritzburg and Dundee which lay en route.

Andrew was sitting next to the professor and the pair were already in deep conversation and oblivious of the police motor cyclist clearing their way through the usual early morning Durban traffic.

The vehicles sped on through the lush bush forests and well maintained farms of Natal. As they entered Zululand, the scenery changed to the wide open space of the arid veldt and scattered native kraals. Three hours later, the small convoy turned off the now empty road and slowed down as the vehicles wended and bumped their way cautiously along the stony track leading to the rock outcrop known as Isandhlwana. The professor broke the silence of anticipation which had taken hold of the travellers.

'We'll be there in about a quarter of an hour,' he said, 'just round the next bend is where they made the film 'Zulu Dawn', you'll then see a very prominent and isolated lump of rock about five miles away.... that will be Isandhlwana.'

Still at the wheel, Peter Sachs felt strangely calm. He had now decided to somehow divest himself of the Colour and with some careful manipulation; the visiting Englishman would assist him. Ideally, it should be returned to Wales where it belonged, but it needed to be achieved without his family involvement becoming public knowledge.

Right wing South Africans would relish the story of his great grandfather's murderous flight from the British with the Colour; on the other hand his political enemies would dearly love the opportunity of a scandal. He was also shrewd enough to realise that relics from the Zulu war fetched outrageous prices on the international market notwithstanding the constant attempts by the authorities to prevent the battle sites being illegally plundered. Nothing like the missing Colour had ever come on the market and he guessed its financial value would be enormous. Peter Sachs didn't need the money but he would enjoy the intrigue of driving a hard bargain for its release.

'There it is!' exclaimed Andrew. The hairs on his arms prickled with excitement. 'No wonder the British felt safe with their backs to that cliff, they could see all around themselves for miles,' he added.

Indeed, it had been the perfect defensible position; dominating, elevated and commanding the now empty surrounding plain.

'And there's the Nquto Plateau where the Zulus hid before the attack,' the professor pointed to the distant high hills off to their right.

The party chatted on and several minutes later the small convoy came to a halt in the empty carpark marked out by neatly laid out rows of small white painted stones. The steep cliff face loomed menacingly above them less than two hundred yards away and the professor methodically indicated where the British positions had been as the Zulus attacked. He then indicated a small ledge half way up the cliff face.

'That's where the last British survivors met their deaths about two hours after the battle started, there's a memorial plaque up there.'
'Can we get to it?' asked Andrew.
'Easily,' replied the professor. 'But before we look round the battlefield, we should make the short climb to Stony Hill, so called by the Welsh soldiers who defended it. There's a bronze diorama that will give us all a good overview of the site and the special points of interest.'

They walked the two hundred yards up a gentle slope to

a small dais protected under a tin awning which protected an intricately crafted bronze scale model of the battlefield. The professor spent some time explaining details to his attentive audience, matching the battle tactics with the actual panorama which lay before them. He described the extent of the British defences, the route of the attacking Zulus and indicated the white painted mounds of rocks dotted over the plain under which the British still lay buried. The questions came thick and fast until a little later the party headed back down the path towards the battlefield itself. Andrew walked off a short distance until he was under the cliff and sat down on a rock to absorb the aura of the site, he had thought about this moment for many years. The minister approached Andrew unnoticed and quietly sat down beside him.

'It's eerie isn't it?' said the minister.
'Yes, it's almost as though one can still feel the spirits of the dead... it's as though the battle was only yesterday...they were so young... so far from home,' replied Andrew.

Both men breathed in the atmosphere of the silent battlefield and gazed at the miles of brown grass waving gently in the breeze.

'It's a Zulu legend that when the wind stops blowing up here, the spirits of the dead will return,' said Peter Sachs.
'At this high point it's unlikely, though wouldn't it be spectacular?' replied Andrew, both men smiled at the thought of such a mass resurrection.
'Minister,' asked Andrew cautiously, can you tell me more about this relative of yours, which unit was he with ...we know where the individual units fought... perhaps we can then identify the exact spot where he died.'

Peter Sachs was silent for a while, almost as though he was lost in his own thoughts. Could this be the right time to take this earnest young Englishman into his confidence? No, he decided, at least not just yet although he came with the right credentials and he appeared to have just the right blend of integrity and adventurousness to undertake the task forming in the minister's mind.

'Actually,' Peter Sachs paused for effect, 'he was with your regiment, he was a rider and scout with 'G' Company; there's no telling what happened to him... come on, let's catch up with the others.'

Both men rose to their feet and worked their way over the rocks towards the others who were all listening to the professor's tales of gory death and destruction as the Zulus overwhelmed the soldiers. Andrew's mind was already working overtime, how did the minister know of his great grandfather's role in the battle? After all, hardly anyone survived the Zulu attack and all records were destroyed when the victorious Zulus sacked the base camp; Andrew was very curious.

Their visit to the battlefield lasted for nearly two hours after which they attacked the luncheon hamper with relish while sitting on the banks of a dried up stream overlooking the plain towards Conical Hill. Peter Sachs knew from the secret diary in the trunk that it was from Conical Hill that his grandfather had first seen the Zulu regiments decend from the distant Nqutu Plateau. At one point during lunch, he was aware that Andrew was casually watching him but he didn't feel concerned or at all uneasy.

'Time to go,' he said with his usual ministerial authority and rose to his feet.

Robin and Elizabeth had been wandering about on their own but had condescended to join the main party for lunch. They undertook the clearing up as the party slowly walked back to the cars. A small party of Zulu children had gathered in expectation of some sweets or ten cent coins but kept their distance being in awe of the police officers. A few minutes later the cars slowly made their way off the battlefield and back along the track. Andrew was now deeply intrigued by the growing mystery which appeared to surround the minister's enigmatic relative. The journey back to the airport was uneventful and at the departure gate, promises for a speedy reunion were exchanged.

Over dinner at a local Durban restaurant, Andrew casually questioned his brother about the minister and also ascertained that the Office of Public Records was conveniently located in Durban city centre. He then decided to cancel his plans for the following day and instead, attempt to trace the minister's descendents through the registry of births and deaths.

* * * * * * * * *

At the same time in a smoke filled room of a Soweto drinking den, a group of ANC activists were sifting through the latest reports from their field agents. Of prime interest was the list of visitors to both the home and office of Minister Sachs. The new agent April had proved to be very useful, she was not only bright but kept neat notes of all the comings and goings at his residence. The ANC were already aware that the minister was flying to secret destinations, they knew that he was always flown by the same pilot, but to where and why? If it was, as they suspected, to meet the Zulu leadership, the ANC political negotiators would be most interested.

'Let's target the pilot,' said one voice.
'Only one problem, he lives in Durban; we'll have to get someone local to organise it, but I think you're right,' said the group leader. 'It's possible that this pilot may hold the clues we need.' The others nodded their agreement. Their talk and plotting went on late into the night, then they slipped away as silently as the dawn itself.

The following morning, Robin and Andrew left their Durban flat and drove into the city centre. Neither noticed the black youth following discreetly behind on a motorbike. Andrew arranged to meet his brother for lunch then easily found the archives building on the main street. It was a large colonial style building which had been built in 1899 to house the district administrator's staff. After two hours of pouring over ledgers, microfiche film and

206

with the occasional question to the helpful staff, Andrew had learnt a lot about the origins and descendents of Peter Sachs.

Peter Sachs's great grandfather, Samuel, had died at Ladysmith in 1936. The records revealed he had three sons. One of them, Winston had died following a fall whilst hillwalking in 1966. He in turn had one son, Philip, who had been killed in a motoring accident in 1968 but not before he had fathered a son, the present minister Peter Sachs. As Andrew's enquiries progressed, it began to dawn on him that he was on the verge of discovering something interesting; but where to look next ?

That same evening, Minister Peter Sachs received a telephone call from his senior security advisor, Brigadier Van Mervwe. The brigadier related that someone had spent the morning at the Records Office in Durban researching the minister's personal background. The name of the enquirer was recorded on the search forms as Andrew Penny, a visitor from the United Kingdom.

Peter Sachs thought quickly. He didn't want his own security staff meddling accidentally with his scheme, so he replied that he was fully aware of the Englishman's activities being a visiting friend of the family. The Brigadier readily accepted the explanation and apologised for disturbing him. Peter Sachs complimented him on the efficiency of his staff and thanked him for his call. He replaced the receiver and slumped back in his chair with a deep breath ; why was this visitor making enquiries about his forefathers, what was going on? It began to occur to Peter Sachs that Andrew Penny might just unwittingly be ahead of him.

Tomorrow he would act.

CHAPTER SIXTEEN

The following morning Andrew was quietly finishing his breakfast prior to leaving the flat for a tour of the Durban museum. Robin had already left to supervise some routine maintenance of the aircraft prior to another mission with the minister. Andrew was still keen to track down some elusive data dealing with the Boer siege of Ladysmith. The telephone interrupted his thoughts and to his surprise it was Helena Sachs wishing to speak to him personally.

' Andrew, I have a message for you from my husband, he has found some interesting material which may assist your research; would you like to come up to Pretoria on Sunday with Robin and stay with us at Carrington Hill. You could then carry out your studies while the others go off on their duties?'

'Yes, thank you , that would be very kind!' he replied, wondering what the minister was up to.

'Good, you can both come and have dinner with us on Sunday evening, that will give you time to talk to my husband. I'll arrange for you both to stay in the guest suite, you can then come and go as you please until your brother goes back to Durban.'

They chatted for a while then Andrew sat back and smiled to himself. Perhaps he was getting close to solving the minister's secret, Peter Sachs was definitely getting jumpy. Something strange was going on but Andrew felt confident and excited.

The brothers flew to Pretoria that Sunday morning then drove a hire car to Carrington Hill arriving in the early afternoon. Andrew was excited but kept his feelings to himself. He had not shared the mystery of the minister's background with his brother just in case there was a valid explanation. On their arrival at the house they were met by the whole Sachs family who displayed their usual relaxed but genuine hospitality. Robin led the way to their rooms in the guest annexe next to the main house. They unpacked their cases then joined the family for tea on the verandah with its superb views overlooking Pretoria.

Afternoon tea was served in the English style complete with silver service and bone china crockery. The African housemaid, April Okawa, had been well trained and discreetly served cool cucumber sandwiches followed by thick slices of her soft cherry cake. The Sachs' daughters kept the conversation bubbling while the minister sat back and bided his time to take Andrew to one side. At a gesture from the minister's wife, April began clearing away the table.

'Come for a swim!' invited Elizabeth holding out her hand to Robin.

'What a good idea,' intervened the minister ,'but you all go along, I've got one or two things to show Andrew; by the way Andrew , when are you due to go back to the UK?'

'Sadly, in three days time,' he replied, 'I don't want to go but I've a job that's waiting for me.'

'Perhaps you should consider coming to live out here like your brother, we still welcome foreigners,' said Helena laughingly. Andrew smiled and quietly admitted to himself that it was an attractive idea.

'Right, off you all go, we'll join you later,' said the minister indicating the house to Andrew.

The inside of the house was pleasantly cool compared with the glowing afternoon heat outside. Andrew followed the minister along the path to the house wondering what the next hour might bring. The pair went directly to the minister's study and Andrew was offered the armchair opposite the minister's desk. Andrew sank down in the soft leather and spread himself out as nonchalantly as he could.

Peter Sachs sat back and looked at Andrew.

'Andrew, I'm fully aware that you have been conducting some research into my past... now I don't mind at all but I think you owe me something of an explanation.'

Andrew took a deep breath, this was the last thing he'd expected, and how on earth did the minister know he'd been checking up on him. His mind went into a spin and for once he was lost for words.

'Well it doesn't matter because I've a shrewd idea we might both be looking for the same thing,' smiled Peter Sachs.

Andrew was relieved and began to breathe more easily. Peter Sachs rose from his chair and went to the drinks cabinet, he poured two large whiskeys and gave one to Andrew without saying a word; he resumed his seat. Slowly he opened the top drawer of his desk and drew out a book which at first glance looked like an old family bible. Andrew saw that it was aged but still in very good condition, he then guessed rightly what it was.

'This is my great grandfather's diary,' said Peter Sachs reverently as he unwittingly stroked the book's polished leather cover. 'It is very special to me for reasons which will become obvious to you as you read it. I would like you to work through it over the next day or so, when you have read it we can begin our conversation in earnest.'

Peter Sachs was enjoying Andrew's obvious disadvantage. He also knew that his proposed offer to the Englishman would be even more attractive once Andrew had read the diary. Peter Sachs held the diary out to Andrew with both hands, almost as a gesture that he was offering his own life to this young Englishman.

'No one, not even my own family, has ever properly read this diary, it's very existence is my one big secret.'

Andrew could feel the emotion behind the words and stared at the brown leather bound book. He carefully took it from the outstretched suntanned hands.

'I want you to read it carefully. When you have finished I propose to enlist your help with a project, but before I do, I need to know how you react to my great grandfather's actions,' said the minister.

Andrew saw that the minister looked more cheerful again which only served to intensify his own curiosity. Before Andrew had time to say anything Peter Sachs continued,

'Let's go and have that swim now, you can read to your heart's content while Robin and I are away tomorrow. If you've finished it by the time we return, we can talk then.'

That evening April Okawa slipped out of the house and at the bottom of the drive sidled up to the figure lurking near the main gate, without a word she passed the neatly written note containing full details of the two new house visitors to her ANC contact. Included in her report were several interesting pieces of information which she had culled from a quick search of the new guests' rooms; that Robin was the minister's pilot, his brother from the UK had held a secret hour long meeting with the minister and they had all spent a whole day somewhere in Zululand the previous week.

* * *

Boipatong . Sunday 14th June 1992.

'Could he be from the British Government?' asked one of the ANC committee members through the smoke of the township drinking den.
'We don't know yet, but we do have him under constant observation,' replied another, 'We can eliminate him or the pilot at any time.'
'Perhaps the deal with the Zulus is more advanced than we realised,' added another.

The political aide from Nelson Mandela's team had said little during this weekly meeting, it was usually his role to listen or, when necessary, contain the younger militant commanders from mindless violence but it was increasingly obvious that some action was becoming necessary. The talks between President De Klerk, Nelson Mandela and the Zulu Chief Butelezi were indeed

211

progressing, or at least they appeared to be progressing. But something was not quite right. It was becoming increasingly obvious to the ANC hierarchy that there appeared to be growing evidence of a secret plan being formulated between the white government and the Zulus. The Zulus were, uncharacteristically, taking a passive role in the negotiations as if they had been bought. And all the while the white negotiators were becoming too confident for comfort. If this was the case, the collective voting power of these two groups would cast the ANC into political oblivion. Something had to be done to discredit the Zulus.

The discussion between the ANC area commanders continued without any progress being made until the sector leader from Boipatong indicated he wished to speak. Junior members usually kept quiet at such meetings so everyone in the dimly lit room turned curiously to twentysix year old Omo Leroke as he rose to his feet.

'For several months we have tried to provoke the Zulus, clearly they are under orders not to retaliate even though we kill two or three of the vermin most days. Certainly they are getting angry but they obey orders, this confirms my feeling that something strange is going on which we don't know about. Anyway, I have an idea.'

The room fell silent, it was rare for a speaker to hold everyone's attention. Somewhere in the distance a child could be heard crying otherwise the atmosphere was charged with silent expectation. After all, here was one of the military commanders showing rare initiative as well as daring to express his view. With all eyes on him, Omo continued,

'The Zulu compound near Boipatong is only separated from the main township by some waste ground about two hundred yards across. We will spread strong rumours that the Zulu compound is to be attacked by our ANC guerrilla fighters at a certain time and date. There is a distinct probability that the Zulus will pre-empt the attack by staging an assault of their own.' He could see he had their full attention, he continued with his soft but carefully thought out delivery.

'Now this is what we do, instead of waiting for the Zulus to attack, we send our own fighters to destroy a small part of our township next to the Zulu compound, we can then shout for help. The police will search the Zulu compound and discover enough Zulus in a state of readiness with weapons, ammunition and best of all, no excuses. The whole world will then blame the Zulu Inkatha party, and best of all, De Klerk and his white government can also be blamed for allowing the massacre to take place.'

'What massacre?' asked the political agent, his voice tinged with surprise. Up to this point he thought the plan was brilliant.

'The massacre of enough of our men, women and children,' replied Omo coldly. The room was silent, he waited a few moments for maximum effect before continuing,

'We have seventy, eighty or who knows, ninety thousand souls living in Boipatong, we move some sick, some aged, a dozen beggars, a houseful of prostitutes together with their children into selected houses near the Zulu compound - then do ourselves a big favour by killing them in the cause of discrediting De Klerk and the Zulus.'

The room remained silent. There were over fifty seasoned and politically astute ANC members gathered and not one moved as much as an eyelid. Omo prepared himself for his finale and took a deep breath.

'Even some of you don't know where Boipatong is, certainly the rest of the world has never even heard of it. In two years we've killed over a thousand Zulus in Boipatong, they've killed or maimed about the same number of our people yet not a single line has ever appeared on the back page of even a South African newspaper. Give me your approval and within two weeks the name of Boipatong will be famous round the world and De Klerk and his Zulus will be discredited for ever. We then kill Minister Sachs who is trysting with the Zulus and no one will even notice his loss, except the white government and his Zulu lapdogs.'

Omo Leroke sat down. All eyes went to Mandela's political agent who sat looking at his folded hands. Slowly he stood up and turned his eyes towards Omo .
'You will have your answer within the week, in the meantime make your initial preparations. Others will consider the ramifications of such an event before final approval is given.' He raised his arm in the clenched fist salute and his bodyguards twitched involuntarily. He spoke quietly but firmly,
'Everyone in this room is sworn to total secrecy, the meeting is closed.'

During the early Wednesday evening of the 17th June 1992, over seventy specially selected Zulu warriors armed with pistols, machetes, spears and knives assembled in the Zulu hostel nearest the township which housed the workers and families from the pro ANC tribes. Those assembled knew at 2 am that night they were to be attacked by ANC guerrillars, their role was to repulse the attack and inflict maximum casualties on the attackers. The South African police had been tipped off about the impending attack but they were satisfied that the Zulus could take care of themselves.

At 10 pm that night on the edge of the main residential area of Boipatong, a force of thirty five ANC fighters wearing imitation Zulu headbands and carrying stolen traditional Zulu fighting sticks and assegais, silently approached a cluster of houses previously indicated to them.

They paused and listened in the direction of the Zulu compound but nothing moved. At a whispered signal they rushed forward attacking some twenty carefully marked houses. That morning, each house had been cleared of its usual residents and replaced by a similar number of unsuspecting misfits who were only too happy to have a decent roof over their heads. Not one had questioned his or her good luck , no one in any township dared asked questions when ordered to do something by the ANC. The doors were kicked down and the ensuing slaughter was noisy, rapid and total leaving forty seven bodies of men, women and children scattered about. Not one of the new residents survived and the attackers disappeared in less than a minute. Instantly the well briefed waiting mob of youths began approaching the unsuspecting Zulu quarters. Their orders were to approach but not to attack the Zulus so that the police and the world's press could examine the scene of the slaughter.

The police on duty in the area at the time were taken completely by surprise by the speed of events. What had happened was completely unexpected and now the township officials were calling on the police to search the Zulu compound. Two hours later, wary police captain Huw Crouch eventually approached the Zulu compound but was ordered away at gunpoint. The armed Zulus were trapped between the growing mob and the police but they had already begun trying to burn or destroy their weapons. Neither they nor the police were yet aware that they had both fallen into a well orchestrated trap. Whilst the police were awaiting instructions from their senior officers, a small patrol of white police officers was surrounded by black stone throwing youths from the township. The police opened fire over the heads of the youths but several frightened officers fired into the fleeing youths killing two. Within hours the name of Boipatong was spreading even faster round the world.

All the efforts of the South African government over recent years to regain respectability and credibility began to melt away. In the offices of the ANC, the jubilation was immeasurable.

That same night, Andrew was progressing through the diary of Samuel. He was riveted by what he read and especially interested that Samuel's original surname, prior to settling in Ladysmith, was Carrington. Perhaps, thought Andrew, Samuel had feared being discovered and sought anonymity using the assumed name of Sachs.

By 2am he decided that he must reluctantly sleep for a

while. He was still fast asleep when the Minister was telephoned and urgently requested to attend at his office due to a serious disturbance at one of the townships. Shortly after 7am, April brought Andrew a cup of tea and he blinked at the diary to make sure it was still there, that it had not all been a wild dream. As he dressed, Robin came into his room with the news that the minister had been called to his office and that he was therefore free that day. Andrew decided to let his brother into the secrets of the diary and afterwards, both agreed that Andrew should finish reading it before they considered their position.

The brothers were now fully aware that the disclosure of the diary contents could cause serious political damage to the minister, on the other hand, if the Colour could be recovered it would be world news. Robin decided to think of other things and announced that he would take Elizabeth out for the day instead. After breakfasting on the verandah, Andrew went back to his room to continue with his reading. As he progressed he took copious notes, these would form the basis of a number of questions beginning to build in his mind.

By lunchtime he had finished the task. Now he knew that the Colour had survived the battlefield but did it still exist and if so, where was it now? He was both stunned by what he had read and excited. The main question in his mind concerned the Colour. What had happened to it? Andrew half guessed that this was going to form part of the discussion he was to have with the minister. There were many questions burning through his mind which the minister could answer but there was another mystery. The diary entry dated the 25th September 1915 was written in what appeared to be Welsh. Andrew's knowledge of Welsh was non existent.

He sauntered over to the main house and found the minister's wife unloading her car following a shopping trip. After some light conversation, Andrew asked if he could telephone a friend in the UK during the afternoon. Permission was granted with a smile, Helena chided him for even bothering to ask for such a small favour.

'You are our guest, treat our home as if it was yours; and how many are we for lunch, is Elizabeth back yet?' Andrew genuinely had no idea where anyone was.

The two of them were served lunch by April Okawa during which Helena took a call from the Minister to say that he would be home at the normal time. Apparently there had been some unpleasantness in one of the townships, somewhere she hadn't heard of. They chatted over the possible menu for dinner and Andrew decided to do some personal shopping for himself that afternoon before returning to the UK. Before setting out for the shops, he telephoned a long standing friend, David Heather at Llandinam in Wales, to arrange for him to receive a fax and hopefully translate the Welsh text he had copied from the Diary. Andrew impressed on David the urgency of his request and David agreed to telephone him back as soon as he'd managed to get the text translated.

During his walk around the shops he had the distinct impression he was being followed but the idea was so fatuous he dismissed it from his mind. He found a business centre and faxed the Welsh text to David together with a reminder for David to telephone him back immediately with the translation; with that urgent task completed he turned his mind to the necessity of finding some souvenirs to take home.

CHAPTER SEVENTEEN

Later that afternoon, Andrew made his way back to Carrington Hill to find Robin and Elizabeth lazing in the shade by the family swimming pool. Walking back the two miles from town in the heat had tired him and he waved at the pair as he headed towards the guest room to collect his swimming trunks. For the next hour or so the three of them swam and dozed by the poolside. Helena Sachs joined them just before 6 pm with her youngest daughter Annie, followed by April Okawa who was carrying a silver tray of iced Pimms.

'Peter will be home shortly and we'll eat at eight. Has everyone had a good day?' asked Helena. Everyone had and they chatted while they sipped their drinks. A few minutes later, April reappeared and hurriedly reported to Helena Sachs.
'Madam, there is a telephone call from the UK for Mister Andrew.'

Andrew excused himself and walked quickly to the house. As he'd expected, it was the awaited return call from David Heather and the telephone line from Wales was crystal clear. Andrew listened carefully to the translation as David relayed the details in his soft Welsh accent. Andrew then picked up a pen and asked David to repeat certain items which he carefully wrote down. He thanked his distant friend and promised to explain everything on his return to the UK, he slowly replaced the receiver. Andrew read the note again and then thoughtfully folded the piece of paper. He went immediately to his room and secreted the information in his research documents before returning to the poolside.

'Is everything Ok?' asked Robin.
'Yes, just a call from the office checking when I'm returning home,' he replied.

They all laughed and the matter was soon forgotten by everyone except April, she diligently recorded what she knew of the call for the benefit of her ANC masters.

218

Peter Sachs returned home just after 7 pm and joined the sun drenched group for a cooling swim. Shortly afterwards Helena decided it was time to change for dinner and suggested her daughters and husband accompanied her back to the house. As Peter Sachs climbed out of the pool he turned to Andrew.

'We'll meet at a convenient juncture this evening, I've discovered some more material to show you, that is, if the others don't mind us hiding away for an hour or so.'

With that the minister picked up his towel and strode off after his wife. Andrew thought it was more of an order than a suggestion and the comment left him wondering how the evening would progress, he noticed his heart beginning to beat faster with anticipation.

After dinner the two men excused themselves and headed off towards the minister's study. Neither spoke as they crossed the wide hallway and entered the cool spacious room. Andrew sat down opposite the minister's desk, made himself comfortable and prepared himself for whatever was to follow. The minister closed the door behind them then poured two drinks from the well stocked cabinet, he handed one to Andrew then sat down in his leather bound captain's chair. He sipped his drink before unhurriedly turning to Andrew.

'Have your past two days here been interesting?'
'Yes minister, but having now read the diary, I 've got a feeling that it won't be long before I return to Africa.' Andrew tried hard to contain his excitement; the minister looked at him without changing his expression.
'May I now have the diary back?' requested the minister.

Andrew had already placed it under his chair in the study before dinner, he picked it up and carefully handed it over. The minister took the diary to his wall safe, unlocked the outer door and clicked the combination lock tumblers to release the inner safe door and deposited the diary inside.

'Tell me then Andrew, what is your considered reaction to the diary?'

'To be completely honest minister, I'm excited by the memoirs recorded by your great grandfather and also very intrigued by the fact that the account appears to be an original piece of history. The diary now poses one particularly important question, the Regimental Colour was obviously saved by your great grandfather, where is it now?' The minister lightly shrugged his shoulders but said nothing.

'In itself, the diary is a wonderful find, on the other hand I'm a little concerned for you,' said Andrew. 'Your own family history could be construed as being murky and your possession of the diary proves you knew all the time about Samuel and, I presume, the present whereabouts of the Colour. Your political opponents will most probably use it to discredit you.' He paused, the minister continued to observe him closely but kept his thoughts to himself. 'But most important of all minister, where is the Colour now, I presume you have it ; that's what our conversation is going to be about isn't it?'

'You're quite right of course,' replied the minister calmly. 'I have thought about it many times over recent years but now the time has come to return the Colour. My reasons are, of course, of no concern to you. The crucial question is, who is most interested in owning it now?' Andrew was more than slightly taken aback.

'Surely its rightful place is back with the Regiment that lost it at Isandhlwana,' he retorted.

'In a perfect world, yes. On the other hand, the Colour would be extremely valuable to a collector, or a military museum. In financial terms, I estimate its value to be in the region of a quarter of a million pounds, maybe even more.'

Robin was almost lost for words, he had always thought of the minister as being honourable, now he suddenly saw him as being mercenary and unscrupulous.

The minister sat upright; he realised Andrew was offended and sought to redress the balance.

'Andrew, I have taken you into my confidence, you have read the diary and I am now in a position to prove that I do indeed have the Colour.'

The minister leaned forward and handed Andrew two polaroid photographs. They were slightly out of focus but clearly depicted the lost Colour flag spread across a table. In the corner of the photograph was a copy of yesterday's Pretoria Times resting against the table leg.

'You won't get any more up-to-date and conclusive evidence than that,' added the minister. Andrew stared at the photographs while the minister continued. 'I want you to approach the Regimental Association through their Museum at Brecon and offer them the chance to purchase the Colour. If you so wish, you can act as my agent. Your commission will be twenty per cent.'

'What if they can't afford it, or won't pay?' asked Andrew ignoring the obvious bribe.

'Then you offer it through an international auction house, Sotheby's or Phillips would do. In the meantime, of course, the Colour will be safely stored away from the house. There is one further condition to the arrangement - you will never disclose my interest in the sale, you will act independently and following the sale, the money will be paid into a numbered account in London less your fee. Now because I like you, I propose to offer you an additional contract which will give you the rights to market the diary on a fifty per cent basis. Because my great grandfather's and my surnames were different when he deserted, no one will be able to associate me with the diary.' He smiled at Andrew, 'You will become quite well off and famous with your coup.' The minister smiled and hoped he had persuaded the young man .

Andrew sat silently. His thoughts were racing around and he clearly had to say something; an idea was nevertheless beginning to form in the back of his mind .

221

'Minister, I am inclined to think that the Colour should be handed back to the Regiment, but as you have obviously decided to sell it, I will certainly see what I can do for you. It would assist me if I could borrow the diary to give my negotiations credibility.'

'Agreed.' replied the minister. 'You may take the diary with you when you leave tomorrow, but please take great care of it.'

Andrew breathed a sigh of relief. If his plan was to work, he had to deny the unsuspecting minister access to the Welsh text hidden in the diary. The minister stood up and extended his hand,

'I'm pleased to have you as my business partner Andrew; I think we'll both do very nicely from this venture. Please keep me in touch with your progress.' Andrew put the photographs in his pocket and followed the minister from the room.

* * * * * * * *

UK July 1992.

From the comfort of his secluded batchelor home at Tenterden in Kent, Andrew telephoned the South Wales Borderers' Regimental museum at Brecon. He ascertained that the museum would be open from 9 am the following Monday for research purposes, and yes, Colonel Lloyd, who had been a company commander with the regiment during Andrew's service was now the curator of the museum and would be there from 10 am. He then telephoned his secretary to rearrange his appointments for the beginning of the week and made a second call to Brecon to book himself into the Wellington Hotel for two nights. During the rest of the week he busied himself sorting and filing the material he had collected during the previous two weeks in Africa.

The drive to Brecon was uneventful and the Wellington

Hotel proved to be well up to standard but comparatively unoccupied. The UK economic recession was obviously biting deeply, even in deepest Wales. Having placed Samuel's diary in the hotel safe, he spent the remainder of the Sunday evening walking round the town and in so doing, also discovered where the museum was located. Andrew was enjoying the anticipation of meeting the museum staff yet he was also aware that he was now in the very same town which had once been so much a part of Samuel's life. Andrew doubted if it had changed that much and the feeling of 'deja vu' when he came across landmarks mentioned in the diary was vaguely unsettling.

The imposing Assize Court where Samuel was sentenced was now the town museum. Andrew entered the building and was directed to the large spacious room once used as the court. Everything was still in place and Andrew went and stood in the self same dock where Samuel was sentanced.

'This is unreal,' he muttered quietly to himself.

He then followed the official down a long flight of steps to the cells. He stood at the door but declined to enter the small cell. By now he felt he was imposing too much on the memory of Samuel. He left the building and walked to the site of the old market place where Samuel met Bethan. Andrew was intrigued to find it was still a market place, and the neighbouring "Tavern Hotel" was still in existence. If he had time tomorrow, he might attempt to discover if there were any of Samuel's family still living in the area; a quick perusal of the Voters' Register might prove to be a good starting point and there couldn't be too many Carringtons in such a small community. There was no hurry, once the diary was published he anticipated finding relatives galore.

At exactly 9 am the following morning, Andrew drove along the broad Watton Road to the military museum and parked immediately outside the Regimental Museum of the South Wales Borderers. It was a sign of the current troubled times, he thought, that all the roadside windows were bricked up against the possibility of terrorist attack. He was still uncertain how he would approach his task and decided to let events unfurl themselves. The regimental museum looked like any other Victorian military establishment, it was built of local stone and looked rather formidable being set to one side of the main barracks. He sat in the car for a few moments looking at the buildings surrounding the parade ground and wondered how Samuel would have felt when he was brought here for duty all those years ago; at this point South Africa seemed very distant.

He took a deep breath, patted his breast pocket which contained the photographs and picked up his briefcase containing the diary. After carefully locking his car, he set off across the road for the long awaited meeting. It would no doubt be best to be straightforward with Colonel Lloyd when the time came.

Andrew spent a good hour looking round the museum which contained an excellent section specifically depicting the Zulu war. He was facinated by the Union flag on display which had flown over Rorke's Drift during the battle and the battered bugles and drums recovered from Isandhlwana. He was mildly surprised that so many original photographs displayed on the walls had survived the war, obviously some enterprising war reporters had taken cameras into the field. He was busy studying a photograph of troops queueing for their lunch when a voice interrupted his thoughts.

'Captain Andrew Penny, or should I say Mr. Penny now?'

Col. Lloyd strode through the archway from his office with a big smile on his face, he was as tall and distinguished as Andrew remembered him those ten years ago. The two shook hands warmly. It was rare for someone of real interest to visit the museum and he was genuinely pleased to see someone he knew.

'It's been a long time,' he enthused. 'Come to the office

and we'll have some coffee. We must have lunch.'

'We'll see,' thought Andrew as he followed the Colonel past the displays back to his office.

'So, how are you and what brings you here?' asked Colonel Lloyd. Andrew explained that he was writing a book about the Zulu war and told the Colonel of his recent visit to his brother in Africa. The Colonel's eyes lit up.

'Did you go to Isandhlwana, to Rorke's Drift?'
'Of course,' he replied good naturedly .

He opened his case and took out some photographs of the battle sites. The two talked for a while over their coffee until Andrew thought the time was right to ask some more pertinent questions.

'As a matter of interest, what happened to the Regimental Colours of the Second Battalion?' Andrew asked nonchalantly.

'Lost,' replied the Colonel thoughtfully. 'Last seen at Isandhlwana, at breakfast I think, and presumably burnt by the Zulus when they sacked the camp. On the other hand we probably destroyed them when Lord Chelmsford ordered the artillery to shell the camp in case of a Zulu ambush.'

'But wasn't the Colour Staff found in a nearby Zulu kraal?' countered Andrew knowingly.

'Yes,' replied Col. Lloyd, 'but we don't know what happened to the actual Colour.'

'If it had survived, what would the Colour be worth today?' asked Andrew. Colonel Lloyd looked puzzled.

'Priceless I suppose, the museum would want it back but probably couldn't afford it.' He looked quizzically at Andrew, 'You haven't come all this way just to chat with me or browse round the museum; what are you up to Andrew?'

Andrew took the envelope from his breast pocket and handed it to Colonel Lloyd. He looked at the polaroid photographs of the Colour in quick succession then examined each one more carefully. He pressed a button on the corner of his desk and continued to study the

225

photographs. A young lady assistant knocked and looked round the door.

'Audrey, can you please bring me the Regimental Mess Journal, 1876 I believe, that's immediately pre South Africa.' The girl nodded and disappeared. The two sat in silence. In less than a minute she reappeared with a heavy ledger, placed it on the desk and smiled sweetly in Andrew's direction.

'Is that all?' she asked the Colonel.
'For the moment thank you. Oh yes, can you book a lunch table for my visitor and me at the Wellington for one o'clock?' The girl nodded and closed the door behind her.
'Have you seen the Colour, is it genuine?' asked the Colonel.
'No, I've not seen it but I have every reason to believe it is genuine. The owner is reluctant to produce it until he knows how interested you are.'

Colonel Lloyd quickly found the page he sought and opened the ledger for Andrew to see. It was a colour lithograph of the missing Colour. Andrew leaned forward and placed the polaroid photograph next to the lithograph.

The pair were identical in every respect.

'Actually, we do have a forgery here in the museum,' volunteered the Colonel. 'Back in 1894 the Marquis of St.George claimed to have found the missing Colour and offered it for sale. Some of the officers investigated the matter but it was found to be a forgery, it had been woven on one side only, otherwise we would have been taken in.'
'Where is it, can I see it ?' asked Andrew.
'Follow me,' replied Col. Lloyd.

The two men went back into the Zulu Room and the Colonel stopped in front of a large framed exhibit containing the faded fake colour. Andrew peered at it.

'It's exactly like the one in my photograph,' he added

confidently.

'Yes,' replied the Colonel thoughtfully, 'now Andrew, can you tell me what is going on, where is the Colour in the photograph and how did you come to be involved?' They returned to the office.

Andrew went on to explain how his research had brought him into contact with the Colour's secretive owner and then told Col. Lloyd about the diary. The Colonel sat quietly and listen attentively as Andrew related the tale of Samuel. It took Andrew a further ten minutes to outline briefly the contents of the diary and when the account was finished he opened his briefcase and carefully took out the elderly diary wrapped in a brown paper bag.

'And this truly is the real thing. We can also very quickly ascertain that there was a Private Carrington, whether or not he was a forced recruit and what happened to him. I fully expect that everything in the diary is true, and furthermore, the owner of the Colour and the diary is the actual direct descendant of Samuel Carrington.'

'Why doesn't this mysterious owner approach us direct, why the secrecy?' quizzed the Colonel.

'Because he is a VIP in South Africa, the public disclosure that he concealed the Colour all these years would ruin him politically. He wants the next best option, to return the Colour secretly, but at a price.'

The Colonel flicked through the diary pausing to look at Samuel's ink drawings.

'You realize that the diary alone could well be of great historical significance?' asked the Colonel. 'This Carrington fellow not only survived the battle but recorded exactly what happened at Isandhlwana.'

'Yes,' answered Andrew, 'and his interpretation of the Spion Kop defeat is totally new.'

'What will you do with the diary?'

'The owner has given me the marketing rights to the diary but before I do anything, I would very much like you to authenticate Private Carrington. As for the Colour, I'm supposed to give you the first offer.'

'This is quite a shock,' muttered the Colonel, 'Let's first check up on this Carrington fellow and ponder the Colour during lunch.'

Audrey brought in the Regimental Register of enlistments and, as they both expected, recorded against the date of the 4th January 1878 were two names.

Private Samuel Carrington.
Gaer Farm, Sennybridge ; Assize enlistment.

Private Owen Thomas.
4 Church Cottages, Sennybridge; Assize enlistment.

'Do you have a record of the dead and wounded?' asked Andrew.
'Lots of dead, not many wounded,' replied the Colonel who pulled out another heavy ledger from his bookcase and opened it out on his desk.
'This is the roll of Isandhlwana,' he said as he ran his finger down the page and stopped.
'Here he is!' the book was turned round to face Andrew who leaned over the desk.

Private Samuel Carrington. Killed in action
Isandhlwana, South Africa 22nd January 1879.

Later that afternoon, Andrew sat quietly in Col. Lloyd's office while the Colonel made a number of telephone calls. He and Andrew then worked on a new plan, they also agreed on a tentative price for the Colour; this was to be a quarter of a million pounds subject to satisfactory negotiations. Andrew departed from the museum shortly before 5 pm feeling very pleased with himself.

CHAPTER EIGHTEEN

From Heathrow, Andrew flew to Milan then took the Alitalia flight to Gaborone in Botswana. He had pre-booked a hire car which was ready and waiting for him. The drive to the South African border took him nearly two hours and it took a further hour of queueing before he reached the actual customs and passport checkpoint. The border officials asked him the usual questions to ascertain the reason for his visit. The standard "research" answer again sufficed, he then swiftly completed the tourist information form and handed it back to a red faced official who was intently studying his passport.

'You have only just left South Africa, why are you back so soon?' he asked.
'I had to return to the UK on business; I have come back via Gaborone, it's a cheaper flight and I want to enjoy the drive down to Pretoria,' lied Andrew calmly.

He was hoping that the minister had not placed him on any 'suspect' list, or if he had, that it was only at the main airports. Andrew guessed correctly that by returning to South Africa via Gaborone, his presence would go unnoticed. With his passport stamped, he returned to his car and drove on towards Pretoria not stopping until he reached the Sun Hotel on the city outskirts. He had been on the move for nearly twenty hours and urgently needed to sleep. The hotel was not full and he was quickly booked into a comfortable air conditioned room looking out over the city. After he had dined, he went back to his room and made a telephone call.

He was in luck, his brother was still at the flat. Andrew rang on the pretext of thanking him for the recent holiday but he was more interested to learn what, if anything, the minister had told Robin. It was evident that nothing had been said; Robin was his usual cheery self and the brothers chatted amiably for a while. Andrew felt guilty not telling his brother he was back in Africa, he also felt ashamed that he had to fake the two second pause in conversation normally associated with long distance satellite calls.

Andrew was sure his brother would understand when the time came.

The following morning he returned the hire car to Johannesburg airport and took the next domestic flight on to Durban being the nearest airport to Ladysmith. There he hired another car, transferred his luggage into the car boot and headed out of Durban towards Ladysmith.

Andrew now felt refreshed after catching up on his sleep. He enjoyed the drive while trying to envisage how the first explorers must have felt as they headed inland away from the safety of the coast. The undulating landscape of green hills and sunburnt veldt probably hadn't changed for thousands of years - apart from the small farms and the occasional native village haphazardly dotted about. He stopped for petrol and a quick snack at Pietermaritzburg, otherwise the journey was uneventful.

Not having previously been to Ladysmith, Andrew expected to find a large thriving town. He was therefore surprised to come over the brow of a hill and see the town nestling some five miles ahead in the bowl of the dusty plain. The distant corrugated tin roofs of Ladysmith glinted in the sunlight.

It occurred to Andrew that the view he was now beholding was identical to that which Samuel had recorded in his diary all those years ago. He drove steadily towards the town which appeared deserted, he then remembered that it was still early in the afternoon and everyone would keep out of the fierce sun until later that afternoon. Almost straight away he saw the Royal Hotel and pulled into a parking space directly outside. Andrew had taken the precaution of pre-booking a room for two nights and presented himself at the hotel reception. The hotel looked exactly the same as the ink drawing in Samuel's diary, it was quaintly old fashioned with its external pillars and shuttered windows. On occasions, it appeared that time stood still in Africa.

His room was comfortable but the bed appeared to be a specimen from the Boer War, although it had   survived reasonably well. The room   reminded him of his childhood holidays when the Penny family stayed at seaside boarding houses at resorts such as Worthing and Eastbourne. Anyway, it was only for two nights. He decided to take a nap until the outside temperature cooled to a more tolerable level, then he would find a general store for his proposed purchases. He turned the air conditioning on and fell asleep.

He woke just before 4 pm and after sluicing his face with cold water, set off to walk round the town. Andrew quickly discovered that all the shops were located on the main street and to the right of the hotel; and Ladysmith was even smaller than he had first thought. There was no sign of the Greenacre's store or even where it might have been but he quickly found the current general store. He purchased a spade and a pickaxe which he placed in the boot of his car then walked over to the Town Hall where he bought a local map. Andrew decided to reconnoitre the road out to the Tabanyama Hills which the map indicated as being some twelve miles away. He drove out of Ladysmith and followed the sign to Acton; according to the map, the road he was on skirted round the very hill he sought.

He nearly missed the dirt track leading off the road to the hills and reversed back to the turning. The hire car bumped slowly along the dusty track and Andrew reckoned the peak was now less than two miles away. The track petered out after another mile. Andrew locked the car and pondered what to do, he was so close and he could feel the growing urge to see his plan through. He took a deep breath and gathered up the tools from the car boot.

'No time like the present,' he told himself.

With the implements balanced over his shoulder, he set off to climb the final half mile slope to the top of

231

Tabanyama. He looked around but there was no sign of anyone else in the vicinity.

On gaining the hill summit he paused for breath and looked around. The surrounding hills seemed so peaceful and he could see Ladysmith to the north with the Tugela river behind him to the south. Less than a mile away the peak of Spion Kop stood remote and shimmering in the early evening heat, Andrew could clearly see the large stone memorial placed near the summit in memory of those who gave their lives on the peak in that long forgotten battle.

He turned his mind to the task in hand and moved to the highest point of the grassy rounded summit, there was a gentle breeze blowing otherwise the silence was complete. He felt the excitement beginning to rise within his body and his heart rate responded. Andrew took a compass bearing from his notebook and the reading took his eyes directly to a large farm complex some five miles away, this was indisputably Chaldon Farm although it was much enlarged since Samuel's time. He carefully checked his notes and made sure he was standing on the highest point. Andrew then took fifteen measured paces to the north and kicked the spot with his foot to mark the point. He set to with the pick and chipped away at the stony surface, it was exceedingly hard and according to his notes, he needed to dig to a depth of two feet.

The sweat began to pour down his face and Andrew paused to remove his shirt before continuing to attack the rock hard ground. Alternating between the pick and spade, the mound of spoil slowly grew next to the deepening hole. At a depth of two feet he used the pick to tease away the stones. There was nothing else there and a feeling of deep disappointment began to well within him.

'Think, just think,' he muttered to himself.

He took the piece of paper from his trouser pocket and checked over the details; they were correct in every respect so he must be in the right place.

Andrew began to calm down as he took up the pick and stepped down into the hole. Again he peered round the base of the hole.

'Nothing for it but to continue,' he told himself out loud and began cautiously to prise out the rocks from the soil.

The faint scrape of metal on metal together with the glint of reflected sunlight from the scratched corner of a metal box combined to strike his senses in unison. He stopped and stared at the revealed metal object now slightly protruding from the soil in a corner of the hole; he had so nearly missed it. Carefully he knelt down and using his fingers, flicked the soil away from around the object. Andrew grasped the corners and pulled, the small metal box came free. Andrew then hugged it to his chest with sheer relief as he sat on the edge of the hole and stared at his prize. The box measured only six by four inches and was some three inches deep; Andrew was reminded of the child's tin money box he once owned. As he held the box he could feel the weighty contents slide to one end. The box was not locked and he almost dared not open it lest he was disappointed.

The temptation, however, was too much to resist, he opened his penknife and painstakingly teased the lid away from the box. His actions revealed a leather pouch with a bootlace drawstring sealing the mouth. He lifted the pouch into his hand and was immediately impressed with its considerable weight; excitedly he untied the bow knot and tipped the glassy contents into his hand. He curiously moved the rough glass like stones with his fingers to confirm that his imagination wasn't deceiving him. The sun caught a sharp edge on one of the stones which released a piercing flash of brilliant light into his eyes. Andrew shakily and slowly counted the diamonds, there were ten large uncut stones. Each one was big as a blackbird's egg; they were exactly as recorded in Samuel's diary. Andrew took a deep breath and whooped with joy.

'Minister, I've got you!' he shouted for all the world to hear.

So far, his plan was working well. He enthusiastically refilled the hole and made his way back down the hillside to the car.

The following morning found Andrew waiting outside the Ladysmith branch of the Ned Bank when it opened. He informed the girl behind the counter that he wished to see the manager and, being the only customer at this time of day, he was politely shown into the manager's office. Any potential new customer was always the highlight of an otherwise boring day for the three staff; new customers were few and far between in Ladysmith, indeed, any customer was a rarity in this town. The manager was a polite young man about the same age as Andrew and the two quickly established a rapport.

Andrew left the bank half an hour later having opened a personal account with one of his own UK cheques to the value of five hundred pounds together with the promise of further funds from London; he also placed a small parcel for safe keeping in one of the bank's safe deposit boxes. The manager believed that his new client was a businessman looking for a house in the area and promised to speak to a friend of his who was the local housing agent. Andrew settled his bill at the Royal Hotel then set off on the journey back to Durban.

'Sorry to take you by surprise,' grinned Andrew as his brother opened the door of the flat. Robin looked at Andrew in sheer astonishment.

'Good grief,' he exclaimed, 'come on in, what on earth are you doing here, I thought you were in London!' he exclaimed.

'It's a long story,' said Andrew as he entered the familiar flat, 'and I owe you a big apology! I couldn't say anything on the telephone in case it was bugged. By the way, is anyone watching your flat?' Robin shook his head.

'Not as far as I know,' he replied thoughtfully.

The brothers talked through the events of the last few weeks with Andrew doing most of the talking. Later that evening Peter Sach's secretary telephoned Robin with details of the minister's flying requirements for the following two weeks. Andrew accordingly made arrangements to accompany his brother in the hope of confronting Peter Sachs in the comfort of his own house.

Two days later they set off from the flat for the airfield at Umhanger from which they would fly to Pretoria. It was only 8 am but the traffic on the city approach was already heavy. Robin drove as usual and he slowed as they approached the roundabout outside the airfield. Andrew felt he was about to lose his balance as his body anticipated taking the turning into the airport, but the landrover continued round the roundabout, the tyres squeeled under the pressure then they headed back whence they came away from the city.

'Don't turn round but I think we're being followed,' said Robin nonchalantly, 'there's a scruffy black on a motorcycle behind us; he's been behind me a few times too often during the last two days for it to be a coincidence.'

'What are you going to do?' asked Andrew.

'Ask him a few questions,' said Robin laconically as he accelerated away.

The black motorcyclist was only one car behind and as Robin pulled away the rider quickly chased after them before slotting in behind Robin's car. Both vehicles were soon heading fast out of Durban along the dual carriageway towards Stanger, Robin casually watched the motorcycle in his mirror whilst waiting for the traffic to thin out. Some five miles further on he seized the opportunity, noticing a lapse in the rider's attention as the chasing rider came to within fifteen feet of the landrover. At over seventy miles per hour Robin fiercely stood on his brakes causing his tyres to squeal in protest . Before he knew what was happening, the motorcyclist impacted his machine onto the landrover's tow bar; there was a simultaneous dull thud as the rider left his machine

235

and struck the rear door panel throwing him upwards; there was a second loud crack as the rider's unprotected head smashed against the landrover's anti roll bar breaking his neck. Andrew watched in horror as the doll-like body spiralled lifelessly through the air and then smacked onto the road some twenty yards in front of them.

In a flash Robin halted the landrover and leapt from the vehicle, he ran to the motionless form and knelt beside the body - then rummaged through the motorcyclist's jacket pockets until he found what he was looking for. Triumphantly he waved a small notebook at Andrew then sprinted back to the car.

'Let's get out of here!' shouted Robin as he gunned the engine back to life.

Another motorcycle flashed past the scene but did not stop, other vehicles were already approaching the scene from the direction of Durban.

'What about the rider?' asked Andrew anxiously.
'We'll go straight to the police, they'll sort it out. If we stay to help him the next lot of blacks will probably attack us out of revenge so let's get the hell out of here.'

The duty officer calmly recorded details of the accident which he relayed by radio to the nearest police patrol; the officer then thanked Robin for reporting the accident.

'Is that all that happens?' asked Andrew as they left the police office.
'For the time being, yes, but that little bugger was definitely following us. Look at this, he's kept a meticulous record of everywhere I've been over the past few days, I think the minister and his security staff might like to hear about this.' Andrew took the proffered notebook and saw that his own visits to the flat were also recorded.
'Unless he was watching us on behalf of the minister,' added Andrew.
'I doubt it, but someone's following us with grim

determination, let's hope it's not the government or we really are in trouble,' answered Robin as they got back into the landrover. 'Look, I'm due to have supper with the Sachs's anyway this evening, you had better come as well and while we fly up to Pretoria, you can get your story right for the ladies; the minister will find out soon enough why you're back.'

* * * *

An hour later the telephone rang at the EXPO office in Johannesburg where Omo Leroke worked as a cover for his ANC activities. He enjoyed the use of the telephone and photocopying machine which enabled him to efficiently control his network of fighters. Omo was still basking in the glory of his presentation at the recent committee meeting and stiffened when he heard the unmistakable voice of his controller. He listened intently as he learned of the death of the agent ordered to follow the minister's pilot. His anger stirred as he heard how this man and his brother had smashed into the defenceless agent with their vehicle and were then seen afterwards robbing his lifeless body.

'Kosa was careless,' said the anonymous voice, 'but they obviously know we are following them - kill them both as soon as you can, and also make your plans to kill the minister.' He continued, 'The maid was also careless, she informed us that the brother had flown home but he is obviously still here, so get rid of her.'

Omo was pleased with the long awaited authority to eradicate the brothers. Their deaths and that of the maid would certainly rattle the minister and Omo would enjoy playing cat and mouse with such an important person. Perhaps a small bomb under the minister's wife's car or the kidnapping and murder of one of the Sachs daughters might be a suitable prelude to his ultimate sport - the eventual assasination of the hated minister. Omo reached for the telephone and dialled a familiar number; he then arranged a meeting with his two lieutenants to discuss tactics.

* * * *

'I have a surprise guest for you this evening.' Robin was speaking to Helena Sachs on the telephone from his room at the Pretoria Sun hotel. 'Andrew has been sent back by his editor to finalise his research; they are even considering a television programme for the BBC. Can you by any chance accommodate us both for supper tonight?'

They chatted awhile then Elizabeth Sachs took over the call from her mother. A short time later Robin and Andrew took a taxi to Carrington Hill where Elizabeth was excitedly waiting for Robin.

'I hope our plan doesn't screw up your relationship with Elizabeth,' said Andrew teasingly.
'I've already mulled that one over but I don't think it will,' replied Robin as he opened the door to greet Elizabeth, 'I'm banking on the minister keeping his head down about his dastardly deeds.'

Peter Sachs was working at home that afternoon and he was intrigued to hear from his wife that Andrew was already back in South Africa. Undoubtedly his plan was working as intended and he looked forward to the imminent arrival of the earnest young Englishman. He leaned back in his chair and pondered his forthcoming good fortune. With South Africa on the possible brink of the anarchy which invariably accompanied black majority rule, it would be a wonderful stroke of luck to have all that money safely in London. Peter Sachs was fully aware that his beloved country was following the tragic course of events already experienced by countries such as Rhodesia, Uganda and Kenya where whites were no longer welcome. Many of his friends once resident in these countries had lost their farms, businesses or capital when their currencies became worthless. Already his own government was partially freezing the cash assets of its

238

white and Asian population to discourage them from emigrating.

From his study he heard the sounds of happy voices and pushed his papers to one side. He enthusiastically greeted the brothers and called for April to prepare drinks on the verandah as he ushered his guests outside to the poolside. He waited until the enthusiasm of their arrival subsided then invited Andrew to the study.

'Let's leave these two to their romancing,' said the minister, indicating Robin and Elizabeth.

Helena and his other daughter Katie were skylarking around the pool and hardly noticed Andrew and the minister heading for the house.

'So, how are you getting on, or should I ask you what brings you back to Africa so suddenly?' asked the minister as he closed the door. They both settled down in opposite chairs.

'I've come back because I've got something to show you; I've also got some very good news for you and we will need to negotiate the finer details.'

'Excellent, well done - tell me more,' replied the minister with genuine pleasure.

'I've been to Brecon - and in principle the Regimental Association would probably agree to your asking price - subject to independent varification of authenticity of the Colour.'

'That's no problem,' answered the minister quickly.

'Good,' replied Andrew, 'which brings me to the next point, I have been asked by the chairman of the Regimental Association to act as agent on their behalf. Being an ex-officer of the regiment, I am the obvious person to act for them.'

'Agreed,' nodded the minister, 'we can arrange for a contract to be drawn up during the next day or so.'

'There's just one final matter that's been puzzling me , and that concerns Samuel's diary - did you ever think of translating the section which Samuel wrote in Welsh?' Andrew watched the minister's reaction.

'No, it didn't seem relevant - why?' The minister sensed that a new development was about to unfurl and looked at him quizzically.

Andrew handed him a photostat of the translation .

'Well minister, it appears that your great grandfather buried some diamonds on the top of Tabanyama then for some strange reason recorded the details in Welsh; he possibly hoped one of his relatives would bother to translate the text. I had wondered why no one had gone up there to recover them,' said Andrew.

'I inherited a polished but uncut diamond from my grandmother which we sold about ten years ago,' said the minister, 'hence our reasonable standard of living - but I wasn't aware that there were others.'   The minister was thinking fast , this whole operation was getting better by the minute. He re-read the translation.

'We must go and get them, we can arrange it for the weekend,' his words came out uncharacteristically flustered.
    'Actually, it's too late minister,' replied Andrew savouring the moment, 'the diamonds are no longer there, I have already recovered them.' Andrew paused for a moment before delivering the final blow.

'On behalf of the Regiment which lost the Colour, I am authorised to offer you your family diamonds in full settlement for the Colour, subject to all the safeguards previously mentioned, and that includes verification for you that the diamonds are genuine. In the meantime, as a gesture of my goodwill, I can give you a small momento to whet your appetite.'

Andrew handed the minister a small carrier bag containing the metal box he had exhumed from the hill top. Peter Sachs slid the corroded box from the bag and cautiously lifted the lid; he carefully removed the empty leather pouch and examined it closely. He knew the diamonds it had once contained would be worth far in excess of the price agreed for the Colour but having to pay for them with what should have been his own property was a twist which began to amuse him.

'It looks as though we both recover what we lost,' smiled the minister.

'Lets hope so,' replied Andrew, 'as soon as I hand the Colour over to the British Ambassador, I will make a call to the UK and the regimental curator will fly out - he's ready to come immediately. As soon as he has authenticated the Colour, the diamonds are yours again.' Andrew sat back and relaxed.

'No need to wait,' was the minister's sharp reply. 'There's the telephone, call him now.

CHAPTER NINETEEN.

It was about 10 am when Omo Leroke's red and white van slowly drove along Churchill Drive on the fashionable outskirts of Pretoria and stopped opposite Number 214. The house was typical of the comfortable, stylish properties favoured by government officials and successful business men with its walled garden and security gates to the house. The van moved on and parked some fifty yards further along the road nearer a small junction. Omo's two assistants left the vehicle and walked off down the road before disappearing round the corner, one of them held a camcorder firmly under his arm. Omo looked at his watch and settled down to wait the agreed five minutes, that was more than enough time for them to get into position. At the appointed time, he sounded the horn once. Omo got out and walked round to the back of the van, carefully took out the large bunch of flowers wrapped in their shiny cellophane paper and headed back along the road to No. 214. At the gateway, he pressed the house intercom button and waited; after a short pause, a young woman's educated voice responded.

'Yes, who is it ?'

'Interflora,' answered Omo. 'Flowers for Mrs. Kathryn Brignall.'

There was a puzzled pause before the buzzer released the locked gate. Omo waltzed up the paved path with the flowers held across his chest. The house door opened and a young woman wearing crisp white tennis shorts and top stood in the doorway with a thoughtful look on her face.

'Mrs. Brignall?' asked Omo holding out the flowers.

'How nice, are they really for me; who are they from?' she asked, beginning to smile.

Omo flamboyantly looked at the accompanying card.

'From a Mr. Brignall, must be your father,' he teased. 'You don't look old enough to have a husband.'

The young mother laughed and took the flowers. She looked at the inscription on the card but couldn't recognise the writing.

'Thank you,' she smiled at Omo as he jauntily sauntered

back towards the gate where he turned and waved Mrs. Brignall goodbye. He shut the gate and calmly walked back to the van just as his two accomplices jogged back round the corner towards him.

'OK?' asked Omo.

'OK, just as planned!' was the breathless reply as they climbed back into the van. Omo started the engine and moved off towards Johannesburg.

An hour later the van drove into the public carpark of the Johannesburg General Hospital. A young black hospital orderly, resplendent in his white uniform smock, was ostensibly waiting at the nearby bus stop. On seeing the van arrive, he looked at his watch then casually sauntered over to meet his contact. He nodded at Omo in recognition.

'He's just gone into his office,' said the orderly, 'he'll be eating his sandwiches there until one o'clock, then the staff will return from the canteen ; you'd better hurry.'

'Room 34?' asked Omo as he stepped from the van with the camcorder.

'That's it man,' said the white smocked orderly as he passed a shopping bag to Omo.

'And here's what you want, there's always some in the pre-med room.' The orderly discretely handed Omo a piece of paper; typed on it were the words, "Morphia 10 milligrams". Omo looked at the note then put it in his pocket, he set off alone towards the hospital main entrance.

Omo entered the main foyer of the hospital and headed for the gentlemen's toilets. Once inside he went into an empty cubicle and removed the neatly folded orderly's coat from the bag. He quickly put it on then concealed the camcorder in the bag. Omo looked at himself in the mirror, straightened the forged security tag on his lapel and returned to the foyer. Walking with the confidence of someone who had worked in the hospital for years, he went unchallenged past the two security officers and headed up the stairs to the third floor. He had memorised the relevant section of the hospital layout from the plan supplied by the orderly informant; everything was in its right place.

* * * * * *

Omo quickly found Room 34 which was next to the corridor leading to the operating theatres. Ignoring the prominent "NO ENTRY" signs he walked straight in. Dr. Dennis Brignall, a newly qualified Consultant Anaesthetist, was "on call" for any emergency and was required to remain in the office over the lunch period. He was reading a newspaper at his desk as he worked his way through his lunchbox. He looked up with mild irritation at the young black orderly who obviously lacked the manners to knock before entering his office.

Omo held his hand out indicating the doctor should remain seated as he closed the office door behind him. He went to the desk and placed the camcorder immediately in front of the bemused doctor. Omo instantly flicked the machine to "play" and the small monitor screen flickered into life and began to replay the mornings events at No. 214. The doctor sat bolt upright as he recognised his home, he had already received a call from his wife querying the flowers; they were both mystified. After a few seconds, the picture changed to the doctor's garden behind the house. His two small boys were playing in their sandpit. His wife, Kathryn, was sunning herself on the nearby swingchair sipping a cup of coffee. For no accountable reason, he saw his wife look up and go into the house, and then remembered that today was the maid's day off. The children played on unsupervised. The metalic taste in the mouth that invariably attends the onset of real fear began to make itself apparent to Dr. Brignall.

The picture on the screen then swung to the back of the garden as a black youth appeared from behind the flowering bushes. With obvious confidence, the intruder calmly walked towards the children who looked up at the stranger then froze with curious uncertainty. The youth

244

unhesitatingly picked up their youngest son and held him up to the hidden camera. The boy began to cry. After a pause, the youth gently put the child down and nonchalantly walked back to the cover of the shrubbery and disappeared. The screen went white, as did the face of Dr. Brignall.

'Your wife and children are at home and perfectly safe,' said Omo reassuringly, 'and they will remain so in exchange for a small gift.'

'What do you mean?' asked the horrified doctor.

'All I want, and I want it this instant, are some ten milligram phials of morphine and a needle.' The doctor's mouth went open in surprise.

'I can't give you that, I mean....' Omo leaned forward to within inches of his face.

'Yes you can, and I want it NOW!' Omo relaxed and smiled at the stunned doctor.' You have seen how easily we can get to your children, we can just as easily return, perhaps not today or next week, but sometime when it suits us. NOW GET IT!' he hissed menacingly.

With resignation on his face, Dr. Brignall slowly rose to his feet. He knew he had to comply for the sake of his family; he hoped the Hospital authorities and the police would understand.

'What do you want it for?' he asked naively.

'New ANC policy,' replied Omo facitiously. 'We dose our agents before they get taken into police custody, then they won't feel the beatings.' The doctor shrugged his shoulders, he was defeated by this arrogant young black. He took some keys from his desk,

'Wait here,' he said to Omo.

'No chance,' was the immediate reply. Omo followed the doctor to the door.

'Seriously, please wait by the door, you can watch me the whole time. If you enter the room,' said the doctor pointing to his covered feet, 'it will require complete sterilization.' Omo now saw the sterile coverings over the doctor's stockinged feet, nodded in agreement and stood by the open door to the pre-med room. These things were all a mystery to Omo but the doctor's request had a ring of logic so he obliged.

Omo watched the doctor closely; he was intrigued by all
the unfamiliar machines, cylinders and dials waiting in
readiness for the afternoon's surgery. Doctor Brignall
entered the strange smelling room and unlocked a large
white wall cabinet. He removed a small packet containing
ten phials of morphine, and, on returning to his office,
handed it to Omo along with a pack of hypodermic
syringes.

'You'll need these syringes as well, now will that be all?'
asked the doctor.
'Yes. Now for the sake of your family, do nothing for ten
minutes. As long as I get away, you can do what you want.
And tell your wife not to worry, you won't hear from us
again. Enjoy the rest of your lunch!' Omo put the packs into
his smock pockets, picked up the camcorder and, after
closing the door, walked swiftly back along the corridor.

At the bottom of the stairs, staff were beginning to return
from the lunchbreak and Omo easily mingled through them
while heading back to the toilet. Once the smock was
dumped in the bin, he casually walked out of the hospital
then headed for the main drive to the road. The van would
collect him once the others were satisfied Omo wasn't
being followed. At the end of the drive he paused and
looked back. Apart from some nurses obviously going off
duty, no one was behind him. A few minutes later the van
approached and from the cover of some trees, he climbed
back into the relative safety of the familiar vehicle.

That evening in Boibatong the team van slowly cruised
the shopping district until Omo spotted a likely volunteer
for their experiment. Through the steel security mesh of a
liquor store, a middle aged black man was intently
peering at the goods on display as the van stopped beside
him. In seconds, the team pulled the unsuspecting man into
the back of the van. While they held their struggling victim
down, Omo injected him in his backside with one of the
phials of morphia and set his watch. Within half a minute
the man was smiling and relaxed. By the time one minute

246

had passed, he happily lapsed into a glorious anaesthetised dream. Omo was delighted with the rapid effect of the injection and inserted a ten rand note into the unconscious man's trouser pocket by way of compensation. The unfortunate black was then laid on the pavement outside the store to sleep off the experience. It was nearly another hour before, confused and very angry at his undignified treatment, he could stand up unaided.

The following morning, Omo's carefully selected kidnappping team assembled in the Boibatong children's Victory Playgound situated on the edge of the township. The playground consisted of a derelict patch of land scattered with rusting oil drums and the warped skeletons of several swing frames. The swings and any other item of use had long since been unbolted and carted off with the exception of the half dozen steel benches which had been set in reinforced concrete. Omo's team of five sat on one of the benches and listened intently as he briefed them. Omo then asked questions until he was completely satisfied that each member fully understood his individual task.

They then rehearsed the plan. Lifting one of the team into the back of the van, they quickly discovered it was not easy to lift and carry a relaxed body; it would bend at the waist or the lolling head would impede the carrier's knees. The arms invariably flopped to the ground getting in the way of the van doors. On one occasion there was a yelp as one of the doors were slammed on unsuspecting fingers; but after nearly an hour's practice, they could speedily pick up, jog with and then dump a 'body' in the van without complications. Had it not been so deadly serious, the participants would have been highly amused at the proceedings.

Omo's master plan's first intended victim was April Okawa. She would be the easiest to eliminate and her death would serve as a timely warning to others in service with prominent whites. Omo was fully aware that as soon as the minister or his staff became alert to the possibility

247

of any pending threat, a massive security operation would be initiated. All domestic staff would be interrogated and April would swiftly confess, even under gentle questioning.

The unsuspecting housemaid was due to leave work that evening and then liaise with her informant on the way home. They would deal with her then. The second level of the plan was to kill the two Penny brothers with a car bomb, such methods were always spectacular and commanded maximum publicity in the media. Omo had thought of varying the theme by placing an explosive charge in the minister's aircraft but that was too risky, and success would be hard to claim. The airport was well staffed with mechanics and security officials and anyway, no one on his team had the technical ability to rig an altitude fuse. There was little risk with a car bomb; people were very lax about their personal security. Even following a bombing, any vigilance soon melted away and indifference once more became the norm.

That evening, and half an hour before April was due to leave Carrington Hill, the red and white van pulled into the darkness of an alley way near to the junction of the main road with Jubilee Way. It was a few yards from April's rendezvous point. The back door opened and as silent as the night, figures climbed out and melted away into the shadows. April's link man strolled to the corner of the junction and casually leant against the trunk of a huge wild fig tree, he knew that the first roving police vehicle would stop and check him thoroughly, they would certainly search him so he deliberately carried nothing incriminating in his pockets. Now that he was in position the young black African, unarmed in case he was challenged, had a genuine reason for being in such a prestigious white area. He was simply waiting to escort his girlfriend home. The team settled down to wait, each member rehearsing his individual role in his own mind.

During dinner that evening, Peter Sachs decided to collect the Colour from his office safe immediately following the meal. His mind was not on the familiar dinner conversation but concentrated instead on the possibility of trying to coerce Andrew to take the diamonds to Amsterdam where they could be cut and sold. Collectively, they were worth a fortune; his discreet enquiries to the Kimberly Diamond Board suggested a figure approaching half a million pounds sterling. First things first though, he needed to recover the Colour from his office so that Andrew could deposit it safely at the British Embassy. He then found himself thinking about this high minded young Englishman, how he had discovered the existence of the diamonds and then displayed the initiative to recover them. Peter Sachs mentally kicked himself for not having bothered to read the diary carefully. But he had to admit to himself, even if he had read it properly, he was not sure he would have bothered to have the Welsh text translated. Andrew had indeed served him well.

As soon as a reasonable time elapsed after dinner, Peter Sachs sought out his wife to excuse himself for half an hour - in the line of duty. Helena was surprised that he only anticipated being away for such a short time; usually when he departed with such an excuse, he would first take a shower and then she knew he would be absent for at least two hours visiting one of his lady friends.

April was already in the process of bidding her mistress goodnight as he walked out of the house.
'I'm going your way April, let me give you a lift,' offered the minister.
'That's very kind Sir, but I would rather walk.'
'Nonsense, it's no trouble - just wait by the door, I'll take you home.' For a moment Helena wondered if her husband was now dallying with their housemaid but that was too preposterous, that really would fire him further than gunpowder could blast him - if he was discovered. No, on this occasion his excuse appeared to be genuine.

April was thrown into confusion, if she didn't meet her contact she would be in trouble, if she refused her employer she could jeopardies her position, worse still - if her contact saw her in the car with the minister her fate might be finally sealed. April began to shiver with a mixture of confusion and apprehension as Elizabeth came after her father with a letter for him to post.

'What's the matter April?' she asked, seeing the maid's agitation.

A possible solution was beginning to form in April's desperate mind.

'The master has offered me a lift home but I would rather walk - you see Miss, I'm due to meet my boy on the way home and I was too embarrassed to say anything.' Elizabeth laughed out of compassion for the shy housegirl.

'That's all right April, I'll tell him to take you part of the way.' Elizabeth set off to catch up with her father as he was reversing his Mercedes out of the garage.

'Come on April,' she called out, 'he'll drop you off on the way - see you tomorrow.'

'Thank you Miss Elizabeth,' acknowledged April with relief as she opened the passenger door and sat down beside the minister.

'You tell me where to stop April,' he said eyeing the young housemaid. She was certainly very shapely, even attractive, but he knew thoughts of her body were for his fantasies only.

'Yes Sir,' she replied deferentially.

The big Mercedes slowly drove past the guards at the entrance to Carrington Hill then turned left along the wide Jubilee Way. The car drove along the brightly lit road until it began to slow as it approached the waiting figure leaning against the tree. The young African stiffened, he was unsure of the meaning of this unexpected vehicle slowing down, perhaps it contained plain clothes police officers. They were always the worst - beat you first then ask questions. There was no point running; they could legitimately shoot a fleeing suspect. He watched the car intently and breathed a sigh of relief when he saw April sitting in the front passenger seat.

'Thank you Sir,' said April as she got out of the car.

'Goodnight April, see you tomorrow,' he replied hardly bothering to look at the young black man under the tree. The door clunked shut and the powerful car eased steadily away.

'Hello,' said April nervously.

'Come with me,' replied the youth without acknowledging her, 'I have something for you.'

The pair walked towards the alleyway. April paused with uncertainty when she saw the outline of the red and white van partially hidden beneath the bushes.

'It's all right April,' said her escort reassuringly, 'I've something for you in exchange for your excellent work.' April knew she had no option and naively believed he was telling the truth. Perhaps they were going to pay her, or give her a present.

As she passed by the protruding bush, Omo silently stepped out of the shadows and felled her with a cruel chop to the side of her unprotected neck. April had only a split second warning of his presence before she fell stunned to the ground. Two other figures swiftly materialised and turned her on her back. They crossed her arms to stop them getting in the way and swiftly gathering up the prostrate figure, trotted with her to the rear of the van as Omo opened the doors. There was a soft thud as April was thrown in the back. Omo opened a small plastic case he was holding and removed a hypodermic syringe. He examined the phial and clipped it into the needle. He leaned over April, lifted her pattened skirt and deeply injected the contents into her soft rump. The ten milligrams of morphia would work quickly and knock her out for a couple of hours; by then he would have disposed of her. Omo was a man of principles, he accepted that the girl had to be eliminated but she was not a traitor, he would not let her suffer unduly. As he was about to close the doors, April's contact came up to him.

'Man, she was with her boss, the minister - he's gone into town, he's on his own - no security, he might just come back on his own.'

Omo thought rapidly; here was a heaven sent opportunity to take the minister. There would be few occasions in the future when he would be so unguarded. They hadn't rehearsed this though, and he had already used all the morphia brought with them, there wasn't time to get another phial. Could his team manage an unrehearsed and potentially more dangerous kidnapping? If they bungled it there would be massive repercussions from the security forces.

'Are you sure he was on his own, no security with him?' asked Omo.

'Yes, he was on his own, no detective, nothing,' answered the man confidently.

Omo gathered the breathless team around him; they had all heard the exchange and from their looks of determination he knew he could trust these men. Each one was a killer, who had either slit throats, bombed the houses of opponents or firebombed houses while the occupants were asleep. They would fight to the death if cornered; they were the best. It was too late to ask April what the minister was doing; being on his own, he was probably seeing a woman. The minister's extra marital activities were well known to the ANC.

The impassive team listened intently as Omo outlined his idea.

Peter Sachs stopped the Mercedes at the entrance to the ministry compound and showed his pass to the guards. Even though they knew him, they would not dare let him into the restricted area without checking his credentials. Since Peter Sachs had been appointed to his position, lax security had become a thing of the past and word was spreading through the security service and the police that inefficiency was an invitation for serious trouble. Following the recent outbreak of violence at Boibatong, the district senior police officer, Reinhard Stossel, had already undergone the worst verbal thrashing of his life in the minister's office. Even now, the unfortunate individual faced a bleak future. Other senior officers were beginning to take meticulous care with their paperwork now that reports to the minister were frequently commented on in scathing terms and endorsed with red ink before being returned for action.

The barrier was raised and the car swept forward to his personal parking bay next to the ministry entrance. At the door, he tapped the week's security code into the door lock; and without a word to the watchman, signed the duty book. Once inside his office, the minister opened the wall safe behind his desk and removed the soft package wrapped in brown paper. He opened his empty ministerial briefcase but the Colour was too big. He looked round his office and saw that his secretary had left an empty carrier bag beside her desk. He strode into Pamela's office, slipped the Colour neatly into the bright plastic bag then switched the lights off and closed the door to his office.

'Goodnight minister!' came a clipped voice from behind. He spun with alarm having forgotten the building was constantly patrolled throughout the night.

'Hello, and yes, goodnight.' he answered. The uniformed police officer stiffly saluted him and within minutes, Peter Sachs exited the complex.

As he drove back towards the outskirts of Pretoria and home, he began to relax again and patted the carrier bag beside him.

'Oh, what a complex web we dare to weave,' he muttered smugly to himself as he swung the car onto the long rising tree lined drive which would take him back to Carrington Hill.

He was still thinking about his good luck and pending fortune when the Mercedes headlights illuminated the prone figure lying in the road some two hundred yards ahead. He instinctively slowed down to a walking pace as he approached the unmoving form - he peered at the body although he had no intention of stopping.

'Probably another drunk,' he said to himself before his many years of training began to make him think more logically.

'But there's nowhere to drink round here; it must be an accident,' he reminded himself as his thought processes continued attempting to evaluate the possibilities.

'My God, it's April!' he said out loud as he recognised his

maid's dress and simultaneously stopped the car alongside his prone servant.

He quickly looked around but could see no sign of danger. He leaped from his car and went to the figure; it was definitely April and he knelt down beside her. He reasoned that she had been struck by a passing car, why otherwise would she be lying in the road? He again looked around and spoke her name in an attempt to rouse the girl - there was no response but she was still breathing. He felt her pulse and it beat faintly but steadily. His personal car was not equipped with a radio so there was only one thing to do; take her home and call an ambulance. He clumsily gathered April up and carefully took her to the rear passenger door of the Mercedes.

'May I help you?' asked Omo politely from a distance of less than three feet.

Peter Sachs was severely startled at the close proximity of the voice, and nearly dropped the girl. Where on earth did he spring from? he thought, but quickly regained his composure.
'Yes, she's been knocked down, open the door and I'll get her to a doctor.'
'You knocked her down didn't you?' accused the black youth, and now you're trying to get rid of her.' Peter Sachs bristled with indignation at the effrontery of this young black. He was unused to being addressed by anyone in this manner, least of all by a black. He eased April onto the rear seat and slammed the door shut to emphasize his disdain for the youth.

He was about to dismiss this upstart when he froze in his tracks. Peter Sachs, Assistant State Minister for Security, was looking directly into the barrel of an automatic pistol held only inches from his face. When all is said, there is nothing more likely to concentrate one's mind than the threat of imminent death. Peter Sach's body and mind froze. The youth insolently smiled at him then put two fingers to his lips and whistled sharply. In response, the untuned van engine started up and the vehicle slowly appeared from its shadowy hiding place, stopping directly in front of the minister's car. It then reversed slowly up to the armed youth and the rear doors opened. Several young men jumped out and went to the Mercedes where they removed the unconscious housemaid. They turned and , once more, threw her headfirst into the rear of the van. Peter Sachs was bemused by events.

'Look, you're welcome to take her, there's really no need for the gun,' he said with an air of authority creeping back into his voice. He still thought that the youths were intent on saving April from the clutches of a white hit and run motorist.

'Now you as well, get in the van,' hissed Omo still pointing the gun at his head. Peter Sachs felt the onset of panic beginning to rise uncontrollably through his system as the pistol was suddenly and painfully rammed into his ribs to emphasise the order.

'Get in, NOW!' ordered Omo.

Peter Sachs slowly did as he was ordered, his legs going weak as he tried to think logically. The mounting panic was beginning to overtake him and any medication to control his condition was still in his briefcase at home. The van doors were slammed shut and everything went black. Another of the van inmates produced a revolver, cocked it, and held it against the minister's head. Omo walked round to the front of the van and paused, looking into the Mercedes, he saw the carrier bag lying on the front passenger seat. He leant inside and opened the bag. Was this what was so important that the minister would journey out at night without any security? He pulled the Colour partially out of the bag and laughed quietly to himself, the strange flag would make a novel shroud for a VIP body. He jumped into the van and tossed the carrier bag to the floor.

'Let's go, but take it easy,' he said, and the driver eased the van into motion.

They now had to be very careful lest they were stopped by the police. Omo turned to Peter Sachs and showed him the syringe previously used on April.

'Do as you're told, otherwise you get this.' There was no

reply from their shocked prisoner. 'Get ready in case there's trouble,' ordered Omo, his command was answered by the sound of several handguns safety catches being slipped to the 'Fire' position.

The van began to move more quickly once it reached the main city area.

'Where are you taking me, and for God's sake, WHY?' pleaded the minister. The rising urge to strike out, to fight or run was almost overwhelming as the intensifying panic attack caused his heart to pound. Omo turned round and smiled at him in the soft orange glow generated by the passing streetlights.

'Minister, you are a traitor; you are a traitor to your country and its people, and shortly you will be tried for treason.'

'That's ludicrous,' he cried, 'I'm a government minister!' He began sobbing into his hands - the enormity of his plight was just beginning to dawn on him.

'What about the girl, she's injured!' he exclaimed suddenly remembering the motionless form of his maid on the floor.

'No, she's just asleep.' was Omo's indifferent reply.

The van continued to be steadily driven for another five minutes then it was turned off the road into an unlit area. It bumped along the uneven surface of a dirt track then stopped. Omo leant out.

'Have you got her?' queried a voice outside the van.

'Yes,' replied Omo. 'And we've brought the minister to speak up for her.'

Omo laughed, which triggered the others in the van into giggles. Peter Sachs realised they were now in one of the black townships and shuddered with the involuntary chill of pure fear which swept through his body. His mind confusingly raced through the last hour's events and possible outcomes. They would probably only hold him for a few more hours though, they couldn't hold him forever, perhaps they wanted a ransom or to extract some agreement from the government. And anyway, Helena would be waiting at home for him, it wouldn't be very long before she became concerned and reported him missing.

The van jolted forward past the ANC checkpoint and then came to a halt beside a wooden bungalow. The rear doors of the van were opened and the youths jumped out.

'Take the girl into the back and keep an eye on her,' ordered Omo, 'then get him inside.'

'Can we have her?' asked one of the youths. They all knew her ultimate fate was sealed.

'Yes, but keep it quiet,' was his chilling reply; after all she was still drugged and his team had earned their reward.

One of the team pulled April from the van and carried her off towards the rear of the building, the others following like a small pack of hungry jackals.

There were another dozen men standing around the van and Omo nodded towards the minister who was now huddled on the van floor. Several of the men forcefully dragged him from the vehicle and hauled him like a sack of flour into the dimly lit shack. They dumped him on a low metal chair strategically placed in front of a table. His wrists were pulled behind his back and firmly tied with cord; he saw a roll of sticking plaster had been placed on the table and anticipated a strip being torn off and placed over his mouth. He shuddered; if he couldn't speak, he wouldn't be able to reason with these people.

'Please, don't put that over my mouth, I can't breathe through my nose, I'll die,' he pleaded. No one answered.

He sat there for about ten minutes; no one spoke to him in the hushed room. Then the youths from the van began filing back into the room, they silently stood behind the helpless minister to watch the proceedings. Peter Sachs could hear muffled voices in an adjacent room and hoped that, whoever was in there, they would quickly order his release. He helplessly looked about him. The shack was bare apart from a low bunk against the wall and the shabby table and chairs facing him. The room where the

257

voices came from must be the kitchen. He thought the shack would probably be home to a poor black family, he had seen similar shacks when the bulldozers had recently levelled some illegal homes near Johannesburg and he wondered if they all smelt so rancid inside. They probably did, he mused, as he remembered Helena having to tell April to take more frequent baths.

The voices from the kitchen went silent and the door began to open.
'At last!' said the minister optimistically,' now we can get this sorted out.'

He turned to face three elderly, poorly clothed black men as they came into the room. They slowly filed behind the table; the centre figure who wore a crumpled jacket to denote his seniority, nodded and they sat down. Omo was still standing behind the minister; no doubt he would get a severe reprimand from his elders for such a stupid act, thought the minister, and when they realised who he was they would have to let him go.

He wondered whether he would be able to retrace the van's route to this particular part of the township. He might even lead the police team back himself. Yes, that would give him great satisfaction. Peter Sachs stared hard at the three figures fixing their faces in his memory, he would enjoy being present when they were arrested.

A large overweight black lady entered the room and, without looking at anyone, picked the sticking plaster up and put it in the pocket of her pinafore; she then neatly placed a white tablecloth over the table before replacing the sticking plaster back on the table. The minister's eyes were fixed to the roll of plaster, dreading its use on him.

'This court is now sitting,' said the whitehaired man in the centre of the trio.
'Are you Peter Sachs?' asked his colleague.
'Yes,' mumbled the minister. He was surprised - so they did know who he was. 'Look, you've no right to do this to me, just let me go and I'll say nothing, I give you my word.'

His words fell on deaf ears. The chairman looked up and stared coldly into Peter Sachs's face.

'Peter Sachs, you are charged with being a traitor to your country, because of you, millions of innocent people live in poverty and thousands, many thousands, die each year.' He paused to let his words sink in.

'Are you guilty or not guilty?' he asked with feigned deference.

'This is a farce,' protested the minister beginning to lose his dignity, 'you have no right...'

'Correct!' interrupted the man to the left of the chairman, he added, 'Because of you and your wicked policies, we have no rights- but that will all change soon.'

'Guilty or not guilty?' asked the chairman again.

Peter Sachs looked at him and wondered what this man did for a living, he was probably a cleaner or roadworker - and here he was presiding over a state minister, and a white state minister at that. Peter Sachs shook his head in dispair.

'In the absence of a reply from the accused, we will accept a "not guilty" plea,' said the chairman. His colleagues nodded. The chairman stared at the minister without revealing his feelings.

'Nevertheless, I do find you guilty as charged, and is that the finding of you both?' He waited for his fellow judges to reply.

'Agreed,' they chorused.

'Death?' asked the chairman.

'Death.' was their reply.

'This is a farce, you're all mad - let me go!' screamed the minister.

The minister's head was fiercely gripped from behind in an armlock as another of the youths stepped forward and forced a rag into his mouth. Then came the sticking plaster; he desperately tried to shake his head and scream but could do neither. A wide strip was placed over his mouth to prevent him spitting out the gag.

'Take him away,' said the chairman looking coldly at the

minister.

'And the same verdict on the girl?' asked Omo deferentially.

'The same verdict on the girl,' replied the chairman.

The struggling minister was roughly pulled outside and held upright on either side by members of the kidnapping party. He tried to kick out but this merely resulted in a savage blow in his ribs, he snorted through his nostrils for breath and slumped to his knees. Another grinning youth appeared with April, now gang raped and naked, over his shoulder. She was beginning to recover from the morphia and moaned as she drifted in and out of consciousness. Peter Sachs was dragged forward with his legs trailing behind in the township dust.

The gathering group followed Omo in single file along the well worn track and through a gap in a wire fence. Peter Sachs saw they were entering a carpark next to the main highway which led from the township back into Pretoria. During the day the carpark would be full of township residents busily shopping at the daily open market, now it was in near darkness and totally deserted. He was dragged across to the middle of the carpark where a short metal post stuck out of the concrete. His guards forced him down into a sitting position with his back to the post. April was dumped behind him and before he could move, Omo twice wrapped a length of metal hawser round his chest binding him to the post; a loop was thrown round April to prevent her toppling over. Another youth appeared from the bushes lugging a heavy jerry can and Peter Sachs tried in vain to scream out through his gag.

His eyes bulged with terror as he desperately searched back towards the main highway for help - he then realised the execution squad were virtually invisible to passing motorists due to the darkness of the carpark. Even if they were seen, no one would dare help - perhaps someone would go to the police and then it would be at least another half an hour before they investigated. Another figure arrived rolling an old lorry tyre as though it were a hoop; he and several youths lifted it between them, eased it over the top of the post and let it fall heavily on their intended victims' heads. Omo stepped forward and cruelly forced the tyre firmly down, firstly over the minister's head then over April who was beginning to revive from the effects of the injection.

Omo stepped back, looked around the carpark then nodded at the youth with the jerry can. The youth grinned and began splashing the petrol over the bound figures until the can was empty. The two stepped back in anticipation. Peter Sachs struggled to breathe as the stinging fluid began to evaporate into his nostrils, his mind mercifully began to swim from the effects of the asphyxiating fumes.

'In the name of Africa, DIE!' spat Omo as he flicked a match into life and nonchalently tossed it towards the petrol sodden minister and his maid.

For nearly half a minute, the minister's legs kicked desperately at the fiercely consuming flames before twitching to their final stillness. As the relentless flames were fuelled by the melting rubber tyre, Omo was forced back by the heat. He felt a tug at his sleeve and his attention was drawn to the flashing lights of the fire appliance turning into the entrance of the carpark.

'Hell, where did that come from?' he shouted. He was about to join the others now running towards the gap in the fence when he remembered the carrier bag containing the flag. He pulled the material out and tossed the heavy unfurled Colour towards his prized victim's burning body.
'Something to take with you!' he shouted above the roar of the fire and set off to follow the others.

Helena Sachs looked uncertainly at her watch, it was nearly midnight. She shrugged her shoulders; he'd probably fallen asleep with one of his women - serve him right if he got caught. She checked that all the doors and windows were secure but left the front door unbolted so that her husband could let himself in. She read for ten minutes, switched off the bedside light and fell asleep.

261

'Two bodies. One male, one female; and both totally indistinguishable even though they were only burning for a few minutes,' said the senior fireman to the police officer standing nearby. The fire crew had fortuitously been returning from a previous incident when they saw the fire in the carpark and responded.

'And we found this, I'm not sure if it's relevant - it's certainly curious,' said the fireman. He handed the unburnt section of the Colour to the officer.

'Looks rather like a flag; there's a Union Jack in the top corner but it's not a flag I recognise,' replied the policeman.

Early the following morning, Omo triumphantly sat in his office waiting for the congratulatory call from his sector leader. The awaited time passed; ten minutes then twenty - and still no call.

Then at last it came. Omo let the telephone ring a number of times to savour the moment before picking up the receiver. He was relieved to hear the familiar soft velvety voice but immediately realised something was wrong, seriously wrong. Omo was astonished to learn that the first television news bulletin of the minister's death attributed the event to a motor accident. Omo was nearly speechless with incredulity.

'Did you get any photographs?' asked the voice.

'No, we were interrupted by the fire service,' replied Omo defensively.

'Then we can't claim the credit,' was the cool reply.

Omo's world went into a spin of confusion.

'What about the brothers?' he asked. He knew he could easily repeat the action, and this time without the mistakes.

'No, they are to be left alone, their deaths cannot assist our cause, such action would only antagonise the police. We now lie low,' said his leader, 'that is an order.'

The telephone line went dead, Omo sat down

despondantly.

* * * * *

The day before the minister's funeral, Robin had flown Andrew to the small airstrip at Ladysmith. A lounging mechanic demanded fifty rand to drive them the short distance into the town and straight to the bank where Andrew withdrew the diamonds and closed his account. They then visited the cemetery where Samuel and Anneliese were buried together and easily found their grave. The two brothers brushed the headstone clean and pulled out some weeds sprouting from the cracks in the stonework. As they were about to leave, Andrew touched the headstone and closed his eyes.

'Thank you both for everything,' he said quietly but sincerely.

The whole journey from Pretoria to Ladysmith and back had taken only six hours. That evening after dinner, Helena and her two daughters listened in awe as Andrew related the tale of Samuel and the events leading to the recovery of the diamonds. At an appropriate point towards the end of the story, Andrew took a small bulky package from his briefcase and held it out to Helena. She looked at the package for some time before she spoke.

'Are these Samuel's diamonds?' she asked.
'Yes, they now belong to you,' was Andrew's kindly reply.
'Thank you,' she smiled at him, accepting the gift. 'They will give us the security Samuel intended all those years ago, and I sincerely hope publication of the diary brings you great success and reward.'

She raised her hand to Robin who quietly left the room. He returned a few moments later with a soft flat parcel which he handed to Helena.

263

'Please take this,' she said to Andrew as the tears welled up in her eyes.

'I would like you to have the remains of the Colour.'

* * * * * * * *

The reception following the funeral took place in the gardens at Carrington Hill and was restricted to immediate family and selected close ministerial friends. One of the junior ministers who had known Peter Sachs for many years approached Helena and discretely led her to one side.

'My dear, we would like to thank you for your assistance in this sad matter,' he said.

'I understand,' she replied, 'it was the least I could do, but knowing the true circumstances has made it a lot easier.'

Helena still had mixed emotions concerning the announcement of her husband's death. To prevent consternation throughout the country's white population she had reluctantly agreed to the official government account of a burning car accident. Such a report immediately negated any subsequent propaganda claim by the ANC. Whatever the government wanted to do was entirely up to them; she had lost her husband and now just wanted to be left alone with her family.

The junior minister nodded with some embarrassment and shook her by the hand. He hated funerals; and anyway, there was going to be a lot of jockeying for senior positions with the prestigious Sachs' vacancy to be urgently filled. The man wanted to get back to his office in case he was called for. With relief that he could now depart, he headed back to his waiting car and was quickly gone. Helena   watched him go with growing disdain for all matters governmental.

After the official guests had finally departed, Andrew sought out his brother and Elizabeth to say his farewells. He found them talking to Helena who had struggled courageously to maintain her pride and dignity throughout the difficult day. Surprisingly, but perhaps because the official guests had finally departed, she now looked distinctly relaxed and more cheerful as she chatted to her daughters.

'I'm off in a few moments,' said Andrew quietly. Helena looked at him with a sparkle in her eyes.
'You'll come back for the wedding?' she asked mischievously.

Andrew looked in mock astonishment at Robin and Elizabeth and they all burst out laughing.
'We could hardly announce it publicly on the day of the funeral; but I couldn't let you go back to the UK without knowing our good news,' said Helena as she smiled. 'And anyway, it's only natural that as one chapter closes, another opens.'